Praise for

"A Perfect Ten! ... Debut *Star*, a powerful, moving, riveting tale of greed and betrayal, love and self-discovery ... Excellent characterization, great dialogue, and non-stop action make the book almost impossible to put down ... Fast-paced, engaging, witty, and fun to read, *Falling Star* will grab you on the first page and hold you enthralled until the last. I highly recommend this fabulous book!"
- Susan Lantz, *Romance Reviews Today*

"Dishy and fun – in other words, perfect summer fare."
- *Booklist*

"Dempsey has reinvented the glitz novel for a new generation. This is glitz with heart! Clever and glamorous."
- *New York Times* bestselling author Jayne Ann Krentz

"You'll never watch your local TV news program the same way after reading *Falling Star*. Diana Dempsey has poured her experience as a news anchor into a fast-paced novel about television, big business, and the reality of growing old in a youth-obsessed culture. A fun and feisty debut."
- Bestselling author Jane Heller

"(In *To Catch the Moon*) Alicia Maldonado, Deputy D.A. of Monterey County, CA, may have landed the case that could make her career: the murder of golden boy Daniel Gaines, who recently announced his candidacy for governor. Tough and self-assured, Alicia is a likable protagonist who achieved success through grit and determination ... Dempsey's low-on-glamour depiction of the D.A.'s office is on the mark, lending much credibility to this suspenseful novel. The romantic sparring between Alicia and Milo sparkles with wit and adds sensuality to this sizzling, tension-filled mystery."
- *Romantic Times*

"Skillfully plotted and filled with realistic detail ... (*To Catch the Moon*) deftly interweaves romance, murder, and ambition with issues of social status and trust."
- Kristin Ramsdell, *Library Journal*

"Diana Dempsey creates realistic and memorable characters, complete with flaws, that you can really root for; then she puts them into trouble so terrible you can't figure out how they'll ever triumph ... This is an author to watch."

- *Books for a Buck*

"Spicy, sexy, and sultry: (in *Too Close to the Sun*) popular Dempsey has another hit on her hands."

- *Booklist*

"A complex story with several exciting threads, *Too Close to the Sun* is the romance of Gabby and Will, who fall in love almost immediately. Kept apart by their extreme differences, their road is rocky and sometimes seems an impossible journey, but one that comes to a wonderfully satisfying conclusion ... This is a book that will long live in my memory, and it's a story that begs for a sequel, even a series ... *Too Close to the Sun* is an absolute must-buy for everyone, and I highly recommend it."

- Diana Risso, *Romance Reviews Today*

"In each of her books, Dempsey features such strong heroines and pairs them with the perfect match, thus creating fabulous contemporary romances. She has a permanent place on my book shelves!"

- Tracy Marsac, *Romance Junkies*

"How can you not like a character named Happy Pennington, the daughter of a retired cop and the current reigning Ms. America? Well, I liked her! And her sidekicks in crime-solving, fellow beauty queens Shanelle and Trixie, and a hunk named Mario Suave (yes!) and you have a fast-paced, funny, roller coaster ride through Vegas ... I love that Ms. Dempsey nails her locations so you really feel as if you're there. When reading *Ms America and the Offing on Oahu*, I was craving a Mai Tai by the beach. In this second installment of the Beauty Queen Mysteries, I wanted an all-night buffet and a glitzy show ... The Beauty Queen mysteries are on my must-read list, and I can't wait for the next installment."

- Jacqueline Vick, *A Writer's Jumble*

**Available from Diana Dempsey
in print and digital editions**

Falling Star

To Catch the Moon

Too Close to the Sun

Chasing Venus

Ms America and the Offing on Oahu

Ms America and the Villainy in Vegas

Ms America and the Mayhem in Miami

Ms America and the Whoopsie in Winona

MS AMERICA
AND THE
WHOOPSIE IN WINONA

(Beauty Queen Mysteries, No. 4)

Diana Dempsey

BRAMERTON
PRESS

This is a work of fiction. Names, characters, places, and incidents are either the product of the author's imagination or are used fictitiously, and any resemblance to actual persons living or dead, business establishments, events, or locales is entirely coincidental.

Ms America and the Whoopsie in Winona
All Rights Reserved
Copyright © 2013 by Diana Dempsey

This book may not be reproduced in whole or in part, by any means, without permission. Making or distributing electronic copies of this book constitutes copyright infringement and could subject the infringer to criminal and civil liability.

ISBN: 9781494744441

First electronic edition November 2013

Dear Reader,

Back in the deep dark past when I was first imagining a mystery series featuring a beauty-queen sleuth, I thought *Ms America and the Whoopsie in Winona* would be the second in the series, following *Ms America and the Offing on Oahu*. (I never thought twice about setting the first book on Oahu. I loved that idea from the beginning.) Then I began to think that perhaps I should set all the books in glitzy, larger-than-life settings, and hence *Ms America and the Villainy in Vegas* and *Ms America and the Mayhem in Miami* were born.

By then I had visited Winona, Minnesota. I had had a great time. I made my trip one lovely October when the fall colors were, as Happy Pennington would say, "splendiferous." I learned about the Great River Shakespeare Festival, held there every summer, and discovered that the American Queen, the largest riverboat in the world, docks there every fall. Plus, the people I met were so friendly and helpful, and the town itself was so charming, that the notion of setting a beauty-queen mystery in Winona lingered in my mind.

I also loved the title *Ms America and the Whoopsie in Winona*. It's silly. It's funny. It surprises you. Yes. I like to think that all that and more is true of the beauty-queen mysteries themselves.

So now, a few years later, I have the satisfaction of presenting to you *Ms America and the Whoopsie in Winona*. It's especially delightful to me because it's set in the holiday season, which I love, and in addition I believe it has more heart than any of the mysteries so far. And unlike the other books in the series, many of the settings in this outing are real: from Windom Park to the Basilica of St. Stanislaus Kostka to Bub's Brewing Company to the Blue Heron Coffeehouse to Bloedow's Bakery. (If there's a Giant W, I don't know about it.) Not featured in the book but notable all the same is the gracious Colonial Revival Windom Park Bed and Breakfast, where I enjoyed a lovely stay thanks to innkeepers Karen and Craig Groth.

I've also included a special treat (or two) in this book: holiday recipes! Both the fruitcake and the White Christmas Dream

Drop cookies play a role in the story. Enjoy.

Please know that I love to hear from you. Drop me an email at www.dianadempsey.com and be sure to sign up for my mailing list while you're there to hear first about my new releases. Also join me on Facebook (www.facebook.com/dianadempseybooks) and follow me on Twitter (www.twitter.com/diana_dempsey)

Always, all best to you! Keep reading.

Diana Dempsey

CHAPTER ONE

Sadly, many people labor under the misapprehension that a beauty queen's life is nothing but glamour from dawn till dusk. Yet here I stand, Ms. America Happy Pennington, dressed as a sexy Santa in a red velveteen monstrosity, preparing to preside over the opening ceremony for the new Giant W big box store in Winona, Minnesota.

If that doesn't disabuse you of the all-glamour all-the-time fantasy, I don't know what will.

The teenage girl manning the public-address system cranks it once again into life. "Sale on bloat-free suppository laxatives, aisle seven!"

My beauty queen BFF Shanelle Walker sets her hands on her hips. Like our partner in crime Trixie Barnett—the reigning Ms. Congeniality—she's done up as a hot-to-trot elf in an emerald-green minidress complete with capelet and lace-up high-heel boots. I will say the color looks fantastic against Shanelle's cocoa-colored skin. Their hats—green versions of my red Santa cap—perch awkwardly atop both Shanelle's black waves and Trixie's chin-length copper-colored bob.

"I swear," Shanelle says, "if that infernal teenager makes one more announcement, I am going to boot-kick her all the way to the North Pole."

"She is a little over enthusiastic," Trixie agrees. "But this is a big night."

From our vantage point behind a display of inflatable fruitcakes—yes, you read that right—I assess the gathering throng. "Half the town may show up to this thing."

I am exaggerating. I'm told Winona boasts about 27-thousand residents. But I bet a few hundred are already massed on the other side of the cash registers, escaping the frigid temps and ogling the discounted merchandise. They won't be able to get at it until 7 p.m. at least, when the speechifying is concluded and the opening ribbon cut.

Trixie squints her eyes at the crowd. "I don't see your dad, Happy."

"You see the couple who are both wearing two-foot-tall Christmas tree hats?"

"There he is!" Trixie cries. "Wow, does he look happy."

I am forced to admit that even though he's sporting the tackiest headgear this side of Minneapolis, yes, Pop does look happy. And it is largely due to Maggie Lindvig—Winona native, Cleveland transplant, and lady love. I watch multicolored lights blink atop Maggie's longish brunette hair. She may be in her early sixties but she still favors a sex kitten look, with tight clothes and a shimmy in her walk. "Those hats were Maggie's idea. Pop keeps telling me how many fun things she thinks of for them to do."

"She sounds pretty different from your mom," Shanelle observes.

"That must drive your mom batty," Trixie says. "I wish she were here, too."

"Apparently December's a busy month in the used-car business. She claims she can't get away." Ever since my mother took a job as receptionist for Bennie Hana, notorious in the greater Cleveland area for executing a karate chop in his TV commercials about chopping prices, she's become surprisingly slippery. I'm convinced only some of her elusiveness is due to her new 9-to-5 gig. The rest I attribute to her burgeoning social life, which also revolves around one

Bennie Hana.

Again the P.A. system blares. "Santa toilet-seat cover and matching bath rug in aisle three!" the teenager chirps. "Trim the family throne with Old Saint Nick!"

I lay a restraining hand on Shanelle's arm as I turn to Trixie. "I wonder what you'll think of Maggie's sister Ingrid."

"She's one of the people giving a speech, right?"

"I'll be amazed if that woman lets anybody else get hold of the microphone," Shanelle says. Like me, Shanelle arrived yesterday, so she has the lay of the land where Ingrid Svendsen is concerned.

"It sounds like Ingrid had a lot to do with convincing Giant W to put an outpost here in Winona," I say.

"At least to hear her tell it," Shanelle adds.

"She's a big muckety-muck in town," I go on. "Organizes a lot of social events, serves on all the committees—"

"—takes credit for everything," Shanelle adds.

"I get the picture." Trixie nods sagely then brightens. "Well, we should be thanking her because if Ingrid didn't get this brand new Giant W for Winona, we wouldn't be seeing each other again so soon!"

"Truth is, we have Maggie to thank for that, too," I say. "She's the one who suggested to Ingrid that we be part of the opening." Ingrid made sure this is an official Ms. America appearance, organizing it with Atlanta headquarters, but it was Maggie who got the ball rolling. And I know why: she's trying to get on my good side and thinks booking pageant gigs is a way to do it. It's clear all she wants for Christmas is an engagement ring from Pop and she knows that's more likely if I'm on her team.

Problem is I'm not ready to play ball yet, and I may never be.

"I can't wait to look around Winona more," Trixie says. "This town is so cute! Especially with all the Christmas decorations up."

"I'm thinking we can get some of our shopping done

here," I say.

"Nothing like a small-town Christmas," Shanelle says. "I put some bubbly in the fridge so we can kick off our celebrations as soon as we get back to Damsgard."

Trixie's hazel eyes widen. "We're staying at a house that's got its own name? That's like Tara in *Gone With the Wind*!"

I bet Ingrid wouldn't mind being likened to Scarlett O'Hara. "Damsgard isn't *that* big but it is pretty impressive. It's named after some mansion in Norway."

"Lots of folks in these parts are Norwegian," Shanelle says. "Like Ingrid and Maggie. And Ingrid's second husband, who left her the house."

"It's awfully nice of her to put us all up," Trixie says.

"And," I add, "there are so many bedrooms we don't even have to share." Though the second those words leave my lips, I feel a teeny tiny bit glum.

The last time I was a guest in somebody's house was last month in Miami, when we all stayed at Mario Suave's Spanish-style manse. It may not have as many bedrooms as Damsgard but it's pretty splendiferous. I don't have to tell you, dear reader, that some large fraction of the appeal of Mario's home's derives from its owner—pageant emcee and host of *America's Scariest Ghost Stories*—whose hotness, smartness, and all-around scrumptiousness continue to haunt my dreams. And, I will admit, sometimes my awake moments, too.

That would be A-OK if I weren't married to Jason Kilborn, my high-school sweetheart and the father of my 17-year-old daughter Rachel. The self-same husband who just the other day threw me for a loop so big, I'm still spinning in circles.

The public-address system succeeds in distracting me. "Not done putting up your holiday décor?" the teenager inquires. "Then check out our Shotgun Shell Christmas Wreath in aisle nine! Less than thirty bucks when you mail in the ten-dollar rebate!"

"My wreath at home has red twigs and rhinestones," Trixie whispers. "Rhett thinks *that's* tacky."

I'm about to make an uncharitable observation about the Giant W's merchandise when Ingrid bustles up to our trio. She's one of those women who look wispy and ultra feminine but in fact are totally take-charge. She's got platinum blond hair styled in a sleek bob and a svelte build she's showcasing in a red satin dress with jewel detailing. Unlike her sister, she has enough sense not to sport pine-needle headgear.

She homes in on Trixie and extends her hand. "You must be the third beauty queen. I'm Ingrid Svendsen."

"So nice to meet you!" Trixie says. "I'm—"

Ingrid swings her head toward me, brandishing the opening-ceremony schedule. "You're clear on your marching orders? Why aren't you in the sleigh yet?"

"We were just about to—"

"Remember to be quiet while the mayor is speaking. I don't want you drawing attention to yourselves during his speech."

Behind Ingrid, Shanelle shoots me a look. I know what she's thinking. *Ingrid doesn't want us drawing attention to ourselves during her speech.* Not to be immodest but I don't think you should invite beauty queens to an event if you don't want heads to turn. Just saying.

Ingrid resumes her instructions. "And keep quiet when the lights go off for the Christmas tree lighting. Don't ruin the drama of the moment."

"You won't hear a peep out of us," Trixie assures her.

I steel myself before I speak again. "I think only two of us should ride in the sleigh." I watch Ingrid's brow lower. "Shanelle and I did a trial run earlier and I'm not sure it can handle—"

"Nonsense! Three is what we planned." Ingrid spins away.

Our trio has a moment of silence. Then, "She's not the nicest person I've met so far in Minnesota," Trixie observes.

Shanelle harrumphs. "Just you wait till you get to know her better. You ask me, it's no accident she's got two husbands in the grave. If I were married to her I'd probably want to punch out, too."

"I hope for your dad's sake Maggie's nicer than her sister," Trixie says to me.

"She is." That doesn't mean I want her as a member of the family.

Shanelle pokes my arm. "Girl, you really worried about that sleigh? I want to survive this holiday season."

"I never even heard about a sleigh until now," Trixie says.

"They put it in special for the opening ceremony. I'm only a tiny bit worried about it. It's on an elevated track," I explain to Trixie, though by now she can see that for herself. I lead us toward the sleigh, lying in wait at the rear of the store. Here and at the front, just behind the dais, are the two locales where the track is at floor level. It's like an in-store rollercoaster. "It just seemed so herky-jerky when we were in it this morning that I got scared it might not take all our weight."

Trixie eyes the sleigh with suspicion. "Tell me again when I sing my song?" Since Trixie's the only one of us with any voice to speak of, she has the dubious honor of belting out the Giant W holiday song, set to the tune of "Jingle Bells."

"Your music is supposed to start when the sleigh does," I tell her. "When we stop at the dais, jump out and sing. Shanelle and I will be right behind you." I climb into the sleigh. "Come on, let's get into this thing so it doesn't take off without us." Ingrid would really read us the riot act then. I'm halfway in when I hear the P.A. system's latest 411 and freeze in place.

"Smoked chunky kielbasa only four dollars and ninety-nine cents a pound!" the teenager announces. "Aisle thirteen!"

"That's a good price!" I cry. "Especially for smoked chunky."

"You can get it when the festivities are over." Shanelle gives my backside an encouraging push.

We settle ourselves in the sleigh with Trixie in position to jump out first. The Giant W's overhead fluorescents blink to signal that the festivities are about to begin. Trixie takes a few deep breaths. "I'm always nervous before a performance."

Shanelle pats Trixie's leg as I assure her she'll do great. Though that's easy for me to say. I don't even have a speaking part. All I have to do is cut a ribbon.

As the hush of a deep winter's night settles over the Giant W, the cheerful opening notes of "Jingle Bells" blast from the sound system. Before I can get the words "Brace yourself" past my lips, the sleigh takes off.

"Whoa!" Shanelle yelps.

"This thing should have seat belts!" Trixie cries as the sleigh zooms heavenward and we three are slammed back.

Just that suddenly the sleigh jerks to a stop. I catapult forward, barely able to prevent myself from launching. I have a devil of a time keeping my Santa cap on my head, my meta-grip bobby pins, which perform so well on pageant night, stretched to their limit by this monster of a ride.

"Happy!" Trixie cries. I'm sure her panicked vibrato carries to the front of the store. It might have carried all the way to Lake Winona. Ingrid will not be amused.

I manage to return my butt to the bench a nanosecond before the sleigh takes off again. We three queens clutch one another for dear life. I *knew* I was right to be worried about this thing!

Finally the abominable conveyance plummets to floor level and lurches to a stop behind the dais, just past the 30-foot-tall silver Christmas tree that soon will be ceremoniously lit. Trixie doesn't so much jump out of the sleigh as pitch out. Shanelle and I follow on unsteady legs, her elf and my Santa cap seriously awry. Ingrid glares at us but my whiplashed neck and I are past caring.

Seconds later Trixie bursts into the Giant W holiday song:
W, W, bargains every day!
Oh, what fun it is to fill my shopping cart this way, hey!

W, W, discounts every day!
Oh, what fun it is to bring a bargain home today!
Dashing through the aisles,
A coupon in my hand ...

As Trixie masterfully whips through the refrain, Shanelle and I clap to the beat. A photog from the *Winona Post* captures the moment for posterity. I catch my breath and Pop's eye. Like everybody else in the crowd he's bundled in his winter coat. I note that both his and Maggie's Christmas tree hats are now unlit. Ingrid probably made them turn them off so they wouldn't draw attention from her speech. Pop winks at me like he's done a million times before as I stood on one Ohio stage or another competing in some rinky-dink pageant. He's been such a good dad. I just wish he and Mom were still together. Their divorce is this year's lousiest development. Heck, I'd give back my Ms. America title to see them reunited.

Trixie sings the chorus one last time, giving the final phrase "bargain home today" a special flourish. Shanelle and I cheer along with the crowd and then our trio relocates to the back of the dais, right in front of the Christmas tree.

No surprise, Ingrid kicks off the proceedings. "Happy holidays, fellow citizens of Winona!" she brays. "I'm so glad you could join us this evening to celebrate the opening of the Giant W in our fair city! Of course as soon as I heard—"

As Shanelle predicted, Ingrid takes credit for luring Giant W to Winona. There are two men on the dais with her—the mayor and a store executive—but it takes forever for her to cede the mic and retreat to the rear of the dais to stand in front of the sleigh. The suit kicks off with a lame joke about a reindeer in a bar before detailing the Giant W's many charms.

Finally the mayor takes control. "What do you say we light the Christmas tree?" he calls, and as the crowd roars its approval the overhead fluorescents switch off and the Giant W is plunged into darkness. Indeed it is a dramatic moment, and as Ingrid ordained I remain as silent as Santa creeping down a chimney.

I keep expecting the tree's lights to blaze on—I know from this morning's run-through it's decorated with about a thousand strings of multicolored W's—but they never do. In the distance a train's lonely horn pierces the evening quiet. The crowd inside the Giant W begins to shuffle and murmur. Then several feet to my right, where Ingrid is standing, I hear a sharp popping sound.

I gasp. Trixie clutches my arm. "What in the world is that?" she whimpers. I'm afraid I know but I don't dare say it aloud. A few screams rise to the ceiling while I hear a thump, like a heavy sack dropping. Then the sleigh noisily whirrs into life.

"Turn on the lights!" the mayor hollers and none too soon we are once again bathed in their fluorescent glow.

Now it's Shanelle grabbing me. "Where the heck is Ingrid?"

She's not on the dais with us anymore. The mayor and the suit still are, but not her.

Overhead, near the furthest cash registers, the fast-moving sleigh jerks to one of its famous stops. To my astonishment I see that it's not empty. Nor does its cargo remain inside.

Ingrid Svendsen, snazzy red holiday dress and all, pitches headfirst from the sleigh like a duffel bag being tossed onto an airplane's conveyor belt. I thought I heard a gunshot and now I know I did, because there's no mistaking the bloody wound on Ingrid's chest. The crowd shrieks in horror. We all watch in morbid fascination as the hostess of the evening's festivities belly flops onto the linoleum floor of Winona's brand-new Giant W, narrowly missing a register and upending a display of Christmas sweater wine-bottle covers.

On cranks the P.A. system one last time. "Ceremony's over! Clean-up at register five!"

CHAPTER TWO

We beauty queens know life is full of challenges and it is best to meet each one head-on with optimism and good cheer. But I must say that the sight of Ingrid's ladylike corpse, now splayed amid a widening pool of blood, does not produce in me a fierce determination to pinpoint her killer.

It just makes me tired.

Trixie grabs my arm. "Let's secure the crime scene! Make sure nobody leaves the building! Keep everybody away from the body! Hey, you!" she cries and makes a beeline for the *Winona Post* photographer, who's next to Ingrid's prostrate form preparing to snap his first shot. Not if Trixie has anything to say about it.

As the mayor barks orders to corral the fractious crowd, I hear the Giant W executive on his cell phone calling 911. I admit I'm relieved: for this murder at least I don't have to be the grownup taking charge.

I shoulder my way through the pulsing mob at the front of the store to find Pop, who's moved from where he was standing. He finds me before I find him and grabs me in a hug. His face is red and he's breathing hard. "You all right, my beauty?"

"I'm okay, Pop. You don't look too good, though." Which surprises me. My father retired from police work a few years back. He never made it to homicide detective but he saw a murder or two in his time.

"I don't know where Maggie is!" He sounds panicked. I realize he's clutching both Christmas tree hats in his hand. "She was right next to me and then she was gone!"

"She can't have gone—" I start to say when he cranes his neck to look behind me.

"Maggie!" He barrels in her direction and wraps his arms around her. I see she's wearing a stunned expression.

It hits me like a stiletto heel in the gut. Poor Maggie! It was her sister who was murdered. For a moment it takes my breath away, the fragility of life. Minutes ago Ingrid was holding court on the dais. Then in a flash her work on this earth was done. I'm stepping away to grant Maggie some privacy when Shanelle takes my arm.

"You all right?" she asks.

"I cannot believe this is happening again, Shanelle!"

"Believe it, girl. Murder follows you like you got it on a leash."

"I just don't know if I'm up to another one of these. The last one took every brain cell I've got."

"How do you know you're gonna have to solve this one? Winona may not be as big as Vegas or Miami but for all we know it's got a crack police force. After all, look how fast those black-and-whites got here."

Through the store's front windows I see cop cars rolling into the parking lot, sirens wailing and lights flashing. Cops with guns drawn soon stream into the Giant W, bringing with them frigid night air.

"You're right." After all Sheriff Andy Taylor solved every crime that came his way and Mayberry was a lot smaller than Winona. I watch one of the cops stop Trixie from swatting at the photographer with her elf cap.

"We can do something to help out, though." Shanelle pulls me toward a knot of teenagers, the youngest Giant W staff, clutching one another in a teary, trembling huddle. I remember how scared Rachel got when Peppi Lopez Famosa was murdered in Miami, and Rachel wasn't even in the theater when it happened.

The P.A. system teen, a petite redhead, is among the group. "I don't know what to do!" she wails as we join them. "I'm supposed to make announcements but—"

I rub her back. "You've made enough announcements for one day. Let's just sit tight until the cops give us instructions."

A lanky dark-haired boy named Kevin pipes up. "They'll want to talk to me for sure. I just hope they don't take my twenty bucks."

"Why would the cops want your money?" Shanelle asks. "Hey, weren't you working the lights? Why didn't the Christmas tree light up?"

"How do you think I got the twenty bucks?" His tone is snarky. "The note said to keep all the lights off for at least a minute. That I'd get another twenty if I did it right." He looks away and kicks at the floor. "Now I'm thinking maybe I shouldn't have done it."

Shanelle and I exchange a look. And, I confess, this first clue in the murder of Ingrid Svendsen does goose me from an investigative point-of-view. I extend my hand toward Kevin. "Cough it up. The note and the twenty."

Kevin grumbles as he digs in the pocket of his cords even though he predicted this would happen. "I threw out the note. In the garbage can in the break room."

"Take me there." This I want to see, even if it requires digging through trash.

Going to the break room requires us to pass within a few yards of the deceased. As I nod at the officer standing guard, I sneeze. And not one of those dainty, genteel sneezes, either. More like a huge honker.

Kevin guffaws. "You probably contaminated the whole store."

"Put a sock in it, Kevin." Out of desperation I wipe my nose on the sleeve of my Santa minidress and pretend I haven't been feeling a tickle in my throat all day. "How'd you get the note, anyway?"

He's explaining how it was mailed to his house when we arrive at the break room. Kevin gestures to a tall gray garbage bin. "Hope you Dumpster dive in your spare time."

I ignore the sarcasm and kick off the proceedings with a delicate inspection of the top few inches of the garbage. "How long ago did you throw out the note?"

"When I got in. Around noon."

More than six hours ago. Fabulous.

I roll up my already germ-laden sleeves. "You're helping me," I inform Kevin, and before long we are plowing past burrito wrappers, more corn dog sticks than I care to count, and innumerable paper plates bearing half-eaten pizza. "You Giant W workers need a crash course in healthy nutrition," I mumble. "Hey, is this it?" I extract a small white sheet of paper with typewriting on it. Unfortunately it is soaked not only with used coffee grounds but other even less desirable lubricants.

"That's it," Kevin confirms.

While he's off getting a plastic bag to hold it in, I peruse this pathetic piece of evidence. Its typewritten contents are as Kevin described. "I can't believe you did this no questions asked," I tell him as we exit the break room.

"A twenty's a twenty."

Can't argue with that. We're walking up aisle twelve to make our way back to the front of the store when we pass a rack of hanging calendars and what do I see? *Men of NASCAR Pit Crews*, featuring my husband on the cover.

Yes, the cameraman who took the test shots was right. Not only did Jason make the calendar cut: he scored the cover.

He's standing shirtless next to a race car, in the hot sun, showing off the sort of 6-pack abs you'd expect of a cover boy. He's shooting water from a bottle into his mouth but most of it is running down his torso to disappear into his tight, slightly undone jeans. With his longish dark hair, olive-tone skin, and bad-boy demeanor, he looks dangerous, sexy, and hot, hot, hot.

Kevin watches me drool over the calendar. "You look

good, lady, but you're weird."

I put the calendar back. I guess the Giant W's wares aren't all bad. Between this and the discount kielbasa, if I were a local I'd shop here all the time. "That guy on the cover is my husband," I tell Kevin.

"Yeah, right."

We arrive at the front of the store and I'm about to repeat my assertion when I notice a short gray-haired lady standing over Ingrid Svendsen's corpse, so close she must be someone official. She's wearing low-heeled ankle boots, a camel-colored walker coat with a faux fur collar, and a matching brimmed hat. She must've just arrived, as a light dusting of snow still clings to her hat. She lowers her head, clasps her hands, and closes her eyes.

"Is she *praying*?" Kevin sounds incredulous.

"Looks like it. And you know what? It's not a bad idea."

He shrugs and joins his teen coworkers. Shanelle and Trixie join me. "That's the homicide detective," Trixie whispers.

I'm surprised. And pleased, when I think about it. A Miss Marple who's a real-life cop.

"You find the note?" Shanelle wants to know.

I hold up the plastic bag and explain the latest to Trixie. "Whoever killed Ingrid," I whisper, "had to know exactly how the opening ceremony would go down."

Trixie nods, hazel eyes wide. "An inside job."

"That should narrow the field," Shanelle says.

"Maybe," I say. "But there's a schedule, remember?" All three of us have copies. "Any number of people could've gotten their hands on that."

"But the killer had to know stuff that's not on the schedule," Shanelle points out. "For example that Kevin was in charge of the lights."

"They had to know his home address, too," Trixie points out, "to mail him the note and the twenty."

I ponder that truth as I watch the detective work the crime

scene. Now she's examining the sleigh.

"It takes brass to kill somebody in plain sight," Shanelle puts in. "Even though it was so dark nobody could see a thing."

It's similar to what happened in Vegas. In that case, thick pink smoke did the job of pitch darkness. "The surveillance cameras won't be any use at all."

"The ones outside in the parking lot might be," Trixie points out. "They'd show the people who bolted right after the shooting."

"Some people sure as heck did," Shanelle says. "I almost did myself."

I'd lay odds the killer was smart enough not to draw attention to him or herself by making that mistake. Meaning they remained among us until they could leave without attracting notice. "I wonder if the cops will check everybody here for gunshot residue."

"They already started doing that," Trixie reports.

One cop calls out to the homicide detective and my ears perk up. "Did you hear him say Dembek?" I say. "I went to school with a Nadine Dembek! This detective is probably Polish!" Since my last name is Przybyszewski—Pennington is the pageant name my mom came up with—I find that possibility deeply meaningful.

I don't talk about it much—in fact I don't talk about it at all—but lately I've been harboring the fantasy of becoming a homicide detective in my post Ms. America life. I know, I know, I'd have to go to cop school and be a regular cop first, probably for ages, maybe forever, but the idea that I might, *might* eventually trade my tiara, scepter, and sash for a gun, badge, and holster is pretty darn thrilling. So it gives me a boost to see a Polish female like myself achieve that dream.

We three are tested for gunshot residue but it seems an eternity before it's our turn to be interviewed by the good detective. By then she's already spoken with Pop and a shell-shocked Maggie, whose hands she held warmly in her own. I watch my father escort Maggie outside, his arm around her shoulder. She's so lucky to have him. As we're introduced to Detective Rita Dembek, I probe our ethnic connection and discover that indeed it is real.

"Winona has a sizable Polish community," she tells us. "Now you ladies tell me what your roles were in today's ceremony."

We share every detail we can think of. I'm proud to hand over the plastic bag bearing Kevin's note and the twenty.

"So Ingrid Svendsen drove you here to the store in her Mercedes," she confirms. "We'll need to examine that. I'll ask an officer to drive you back to Damsgard."

I'm surprised the detective knows both the name of Ingrid's house and the make of her car. Apparently Trixie is, too. "Was Mrs. Svendsen well-known here in Winona?"

"Oh, yes, dear. One of our most prominent citizens." She glances down at her notebook, filled with spidery writing. Her granny glasses slip down her nose and her hand flutters as she turns to a new page. She bites her lip as she examines her notes.

I watch her. Then, "If you don't mind my asking, how many murders do you have here in Winona?"

"Not many at all. One every two years, I'd say. Very often it's a murder suicide involving a husband and wife. That can't be the case here."

"No," I agree. "Ingrid Svendsen was a widow."

Detective Dembek nods solemnly. "I remember a case years ago when a man named Donald Howard was released early from custody. He was supposed to be in for life for hiring a hit man to shoot his wife but they let him go after twenty years. The day he was sprung, so many people called each other up to share the news that the phone system jammed and you couldn't get a free line."

We three nod in understanding. That wouldn't happen in a big city. It goes to show what big news a homicide is in Winona.

"Did you grow up here in Winona?" I ask.

"Born and raised. On 4th Street over by St. Stan's."

"Did you always want to be a detective?" I feel Shanelle's eyes on me as I pose the question.

"Oh, I've always been a crime buff. Other girls dreamt of their wedding day. I dreamt of putting a man in handcuffs." A blush tinges her cheeks. "You know what I mean. An old spinster like me."

After confirming that we'll be at Damsgard for a few more days, Detective Dembek leaves us to continue her work. I give my nose a mighty blow into the Kleenex Trixie has procured for me. "You go back to the house without me," I say. "I want to watch a while."

"Don't stay too long," Trixie says. "It's already nine o'clock and in case you haven't noticed, you've got a cold."

Unfortunately, I have noticed.

As Trixie goes off to get their coats, Shanelle gives me one of her penetrating looks. "So you got no interest in solving this case, huh?"

I lower my voice. "I'm thinking Detective Dembek could use a little help."

"She seem nervous to you, too?"

"I know I would be. She doesn't get the chance to investigate much homicide and I'm sure she doesn't want to put a foot wrong. And with Ingrid Svendsen so well-known, there'll be lots of scrutiny."

"Which means lots of pressure. Well, one good thing." Shanelle chuckles ruefully. "I bet you'll find lots of suspects. Strikes me Ingrid Svendsen was better at making enemies than she was making friends."

I sigh. "This investigation could get complicated."

Shanelle winks. "Just the way you like it."

CHAPTER THREE

Hours pass before I'm able to wrangle alone time with Detective Dembek. By then it's quite late and only a handful of cops remain on the premises. Never one to be timid, I plunge right in and tell my Polish compadre about my crime-solving history.

She listens carefully then lowers her voice. "That is impressive, my dear. And it is true that I don't get a lot of practice doing homicide. And if you don't practice—"

"I know. You get rusty." Even though no one's nearby, I make my voice as quiet as hers. "But I have been practicing. I'm in tiptop crime-solving shape." My nasal passages might not be performing at peak levels but my brain cells are. And now that I feel I could be useful, I'm as enthusiastic as ever. "I know I would learn so much from watching you work, too," I add, and that's no empty praise.

"I've never been one to turn down help." She closes her notebook. "Though of course there will be information I can't share."

"I understand."

"There is something I can tell you now, though," she adds, and my ears perk up. "We found the murder weapon underneath a display case in aisle fourteen."

Just hearing that makes me shiver. "What was it?"

"A .38 Special. There was a pair of discarded surgical

gloves not far away."

So the killer could keep prints off the gun and residue off his or her hands. That takes forethought. Just like making sure that the lights would be kept off for a long time. Clearly this murder was planned. It was no crime of passion.

We head for the exits, a black-and-white at the ready to ferry me to Damsgard. "There's one last thing I have to mention, Detective. Do you know they announced earlier that Giant W has smoked chunky kielbasa on special for just four dollars ninety-nine cents a pound?"

Behind her granny glasses the detective's blue eyes widen. "That's a fabulous price for smoked chunky."

"You're telling me! But I can't help but feel it's in bad taste to indulge in premium sausage so soon after ... you know ..."

Detective Dembek nods in agreement. "Kielbasa and murder do not go together."

As we say our good nights, I feel I've found a kindred soul.

I don't know what kind of mansion Damsgard is back in Norway but here in Winona it's a Victorian. It's a lovely blue-gray color with white trim and is positively humungous. I pass through the picket fence and scurry up the long, straight brick path. I note it's clear of snow and bet Pop worked off steam by shoveling, like he used to do at our house back in the day.

The house is especially magical because it's decorated for Christmas. And when I say decorated, I mean decorated. There isn't a room that isn't done up for the season. As I forage in my black Hobo for my key, I admire the evergreen wreath on the bright red front door, festooned with gold ribbon, pink silk roses, and beads. Unlike last night when I arrived, though, the white lights strung through the trees in the front yard and across the façade are not illuminated. This night is not for merrymaking.

I've barely stepped into the foyer when Trixie finds me. She's wearing a cream-colored flannel nightgown featuring a leaf and berry pattern and red trim at the neck. "Everybody else is asleep," she whispers. "Do you want some stew?"

I crinkle my nose. "Is it Maggie's from last night?"

"It's not too bad if you drink enough red wine with it. Come on," and she pads in her fluffy slippers down the hardwood corridor to the expansive kitchen at the rear whose bay windows overlook the snow-covered garden, now lit silver by the moon. The kitchen has fancy cream-colored cabinetry and a red, cream, and black mosaic backsplash. Even this room has a Christmas tree: a small one atop the table in the nook. Its only ornaments are angels made from white lace handkerchiefs. I sit down next to it and Trixie brings me a bowl of stew and a glass of wine. You can guess which one I sample first.

"How was everything when you got home?" I whisper.

"Maggie was already in bed. Your dad stayed with her for a while, then he shoveled."

I knew that.

"Some police officers showed up to take away Ingrid's computer and her files. They said they'd be back tomorrow, I guess to look for more clues. Then we had dinner," Trixie concludes. "What you're having plus ice cream. We left some for you."

I'll eat it, too. I may be Ms. America but when I travel I let loose a bit. That'll have to change soon, as in mere months I'll be facing the specter of international pageant competition.

"When the phone rang we let the voicemail pick up." Trixie scrunches her nose. "It was so strange hearing Ingrid's announcement. And it's going to be so hard telling people what happened to her."

"I bet we won't have to tell many people. This news will travel fast."

"I'm dreading the next few days. We have to help Maggie plan the funeral."

"Otherwise it'll all be on her shoulders." I'm pretty sure Maggie is Ingrid's only close relation, since Ingrid was widowed and had no children. There were no other siblings in their family, either. I down the rest of my supper while bringing Trixie up to speed on my conversation with Detective Dembek.

"She's going to be so glad you're here to help her." Trixie sets down two bowls of chocolate chip ice cream. "I had some earlier but I figure on a day like this I have a good excuse to eat two desserts."

"I like the way you think." I glance around the kitchen. "Can you believe Ingrid called this place stuffy?"

"What?" Trixie yelps, then slams her hand over her mouth and gazes toward the ceiling, above which our fellow residents are trying to sleep.

"Yup. She kept saying the house needs updating. I don't agree."

"I don't, either! It's gorgeous as it is."

"Well, those renovations won't happen now." I barely stop myself from licking the bowl clean. I let myself do that only when no one is watching. "You ready to go up? I'm dying to get out of this Santa costume." Oops. Bad choice of words.

Trixie rises from her chair. "I want to hear all about Rachel and Jason and your mom but that'll have to wait."

"I want to hear your news, too. Did Rhett get that job in Savannah?"

Trixie's eyes gleam with pride. "He did. He found out just the other day. And he's taking it."

"How exciting! Congrats to Rhett!" I give her a hug. "You seem really happy about it."

"Well, Rhett's thrilled, the kids will come around, and I'm ready for a change. After getting fired from my job and all."

I carry our dishes to the sink. "I want to hear all about it in the morning."

Trixie giggles. "If you have any news about Mario, you can tell me about that tonight!"

I feel her gaze on my face. "Can I make a confession?"

"Oh, boy. Should I sit back down?"

"It's just that now that I'm out of town and there's been another murder I kind of expect him to show up. You know what I mean? Even though it's crazy." I don't say: *And even though I shouldn't* want *him to show up.*

"It's not crazy. He showed up both other times."

"And I found out in Miami that was no coincidence." Trixie and I stare at each other. "And now I've got kind of a problem with Jason."

Trixie's features contort. "Oh, no. Happy—"

"We can get past it," I add with more confidence than I feel. "You know what? I'll tell you about it in the morning." If I talk about it, I'll get upset. And then I won't be able to sleep. And then I'll get even sicker.

With the promise that she'll hear the details over breakfast, Trixie precedes me up the staircase. Evergreen garlands with big plaid bows are twined around the banister. "The policemen took us to a drugstore on the way here so we could get you Nyquil," she whispers as we hug good night. "I put it in your bathroom."

That's Ms. Congeniality for you.

My bedroom is Christmas-y year-round, with forest-green walls and crimson window treatments and bed linens. It has a fireplace, believe it or not, and a Nativity scene has been arranged on the ivory-colored marble hearth. After admiring my surroundings, I treat my scummy self to a eucalyptus-scented bath. I've just finished applying my moisture recharge night cream when I hear somebody walk past my door, whistling softly. The footfalls sound too light to be Pop's, and I sure hope they don't belong to a spectral Ingrid, but even that possibility doesn't keep me from creeping back into the dark hallway and then down the stairs to investigate.

The treads belonged to Maggie, I realize. I spy her in the elegant dining room, with its rust-colored walls, French doors, and coffered ceiling. Under the half-lit chandelier a fully dressed Maggie is bustling about.

Whistling a happy tune.
Using a tape measure to get the dimensions of the room.
And surveying everything she sees with a jocular air.

Maggie is so preoccupied taking measurements and jotting notes that I watch her for a matter of minutes and she never notices me. Eventually I back silently away and return to my room. Despite the soporific trio of red wine, hot bath, and cherry-flavored Nyquil, it takes this beauty queen quite a while to fall asleep.

I awaken the next morning to an overcast sky, falling snow, and a stuffed-up nose. I wander down to the kitchen to find a full coffeepot and Shanelle over the electric cooktop scrambling eggs and frying bacon. That's about the best morning tableau you can get in my book. Like me, Shanelle is wearing drawstring flannel sleep pants and has her hair pulled back by a headband. I help myself to java and in return for a plate of food submit to an interrogation about my late night at the Giant W. Then I pose a question of my own. "Have you seen Maggie yet this morning?"

Shanelle keeps her voice low. "She's not grieving too much to eat, I'll tell you that."

"Well, to be fair she and Ingrid weren't close. I think this last week is the first time they saw each other in like five years."

Shanelle shakes her head. "That's sad. Anyway, she's out running errands with your father. They said they'd be back soon."

I'm still inhaling my meal—I feed both colds and fevers—when Maggie and Pop blow in through the front door. "—glad I've got a big, strong man like you to carry all these groceries," I hear Maggie say.

"You know me," Pop replies. "Always glad to help."

I sip my coffee. Now that I've been observing Maggie at close range for a few days, I'm starting to understand her hold on my father. It's not just that she's a sex kitten who's also a card-carrying member of the AARP. It's also that just like

Pop, she's big on traditional male / female roles. Sometimes I wonder if she's one of those women who feign helplessness because they think it will make them more appealing to men. And with some men, I bet it does.

Seconds later the two of them join us in the kitchen. Pop hoists the groceries atop the island and gives me a kiss on the head before disappearing to parts unknown.

The Lindvig sisters may have shared DNA but their fashion choices had nothing in common. Where Ingrid always looked like she was dressed for a committee meeting, Maggie never saw a pair of jeans she judged too tight. She also owns quite the collection of snug sweaters featuring ultra-low V necks, one of which she's sporting now.

I rise to give her a hug. "I am so, so sorry about your sister."

She shakes her head. "It's so hard to believe she's gone."

We're all silent. Then, "May I pour you some coffee?" I offer.

"That would be nice." She sighs as she accepts a mug. "I thought it would be good if Lou and I went to the grocery store. There isn't enough food in this house. Of course with all her money my sister never learned to cook."

After an awkward silence I pipe up again. "I hope you'll let me help with the arrangements, Maggie. I know Trixie and Shanelle want to as well."

"That's so thoughtful of you, Happy. It's women's work, don't you think? We should go to the funeral home right away, if you ask me."

"Maybe we should wait for the police to release Ingrid's body," I suggest.

"I don't think so," Maggie says. "Waiting won't make it any easier. Do you think the funeral home is open yet? It must be."

Shanelle raises her brows at me over Maggie's head. As I make for the sink with my plate, I note magazines poking out of the grocery bags. I can't help but read a few of the titles:

Victorian Homes and *House Beautiful*.
 Maggie rises to her feet. "I'll call the funeral home but first I want to look for a few things in Ingrid's desk in the library."
 I take a wild guess. "Like her will?"
 "Do you think it would be in there? That's where I would've kept mine. I'll look for it right now." She abandons her coffee and scoots out of the kitchen at high speed.
 I am a pensive queen as I load the dishwasher. One data point I can ignore. Two, even. But I am getting smacked upside the head by evidence that only hours after her sister went to that big gingerbread Victorian in the sky, Maggie Lindvig is gearing up to assume Ingrid's place here on earth as the mistress of Damsgard.
 I gesture for Shanelle to follow me upstairs. We waylay Trixie for an emergency tête-à-tête in my bedroom. I relay what I observed in the dead of night and Shanelle fills Trixie in on this morning's developments.
 "Maggie is ready to put her sister in the ground," Shanelle concludes. "It wouldn't surprise me if she wanted to schedule the funeral for this afternoon."
 "When I saw Pop after the lights came back on at the Giant W, he was really agitated because he didn't know where Maggie was. Meaning"—I pause for effect—"she was not standing next to him when Ingrid got shot."
 Trixie gasps. Shanelle speaks. "Well, the cops tested her for gunshot residue, right? Like they tested everybody who was still there. If she had some on her, they'd have found it."
 "But remember that the killer wore surgical gloves, then flung them and the gun down aisle fourteen."
 "Do you really think she might've done it?" Shanelle wants to know.
 "Well, she might have. She had motive and she had opportunity."
 "How much do you know about her?" Trixie asks me. "Like why she moved from Winona to Cleveland?"

"She moved decades ago but I don't know why. She owns a nail salon in Rocky River. It's known for Margarita Fridays," which I've always thought was a clever promotion. I'm snarky enough where Maggie's concerned to doubt she came up with it herself. "She has a son named Donovan, who's got to be in his forties, who always struck me as kind of a lump. I think he works part-time in the salon—"

"Doing nails?" Trixie looks aghast.

"More like running the register."

"There's nothing wrong with men doing nails," Shanelle points out. "In my experience they do excellent forearm massages."

"True," Trixie allows.

Shanelle brings us back to Topic A. "Did you catch that remark Maggie made about Ingrid never learning to cook because she had so much money she didn't need to?"

"That's the big difference between those two," I say. "Money. Ingrid lives in this big fancy house and Maggie's in a tiny condo. That she rents." I know she wants to move in with Pop and I'm also well aware that she tried to prod him into buying them a condo in Florida. I wouldn't be surprised if she's got her eye on his pension.

Uh oh. I'm thinking just like my mother.

Trixie pipes up. "And if Maggie is Ingrid's only close relation—"

I nod. "—there's a good chance she'll inherit everything."

Shanelle emits a low whistle. We look around us. In this case everything is a lot.

CHAPTER FOUR

"I know we're supposed to be thinking about the murder," Trixie says, "but I'm dying to know what's going on between you and Jason!"

I take a deep breath. I hate even to say the words because that makes the whole thing more real. "Remember that NASCAR driver Jason flew down to Miami with? He offered Jason a job on his pit crew."

Trixie's hands fly to her face. "Oh my Lord!"

Shanelle eyes me keenly. "That's great and it's not great, right?"

"It's a real feather in Jason's cap, I'll tell you that. Lots of guys finish pit school but almost none of them get jobs on crews. Certainly not right off the bat. And those jobs pay well, too. But here's the thing. It's not in Cleveland."

"I bet it's in Charlotte!" Trixie squeals. "Can you believe it? Just when I'm moving away!"

"Jason and I have never moved anywhere. We've both lived in Cleveland all our lives. And now—" Tears rise to my eyes.

Shanelle rubs my leg. "Girl, you can't stop change."

Trixie hands me a tissue. I blow my nose. Between the tears and the congestion, I'm a snot-ridden mess. After a while I can talk again. "I kind of got used to our being separated while he was in pit school, you know? And of course I've been traveling for Ms. America. But this is different. This isn't a short-term thing. It's—"

"Open-ended," Shanelle supplies.

"I think you'd have to move with him," Trixie says. "You can't let a husband move away from you and expect everything to be A-OK."

Shanelle arches her brows. "Especially not a husband who looks like yours."

"You should see the men of pit-crews calendar," I say. "He did make the cover."

That elicits another round of whoops and hollers. We pledge to visit the Giant W to buy a few copies the second it's not unseemly to return to the scene of the crime for such a self-indulgent purpose.

"So does Jason want to take the job or not?" Shanelle wants to know.

"He says he's still deciding but I think he's already decided."

"Meaning yes," Trixie says.

"He has to let Zach—that's the driver—know next week." I rise to look out the window and see my father shoveling again. I wonder what stress *he's* trying to work off. "It's a wonderful opportunity for Jason, so much more exciting than being a plain-old mechanic. But it means we'd have to sell the house and uproot Rachel and move away from my parents. And I'd have to give up my job, too." I'm the personal assistant to a senior executive at an energy company back in Cleveland and my boss gives me tons of leeway to meet my Ms. America obligations. It would be very hard to match that flexibility anyplace else. I turn around and throw up my hands. "But the bottom line is I can't stand in Jason's way. I'm pursuing my dreams. I have to let him pursue his."

It's so ironic. I'm the one who pushed Jason to go to pit school when I won Ms. America and scored all that prize money. Now it's lit a fire under him, which I've always wanted but never expected. I guess I figured Jason would go to pit school and have a good time there and then we'd return to our normal lives. Now I'm having trouble grappling with Jason the High-Performing Husband. I wonder why. Maybe I've gotten a little too comfortable being the one who gets all the attention.

If that's true, I don't like what it says about me.

Trixie is asking about Rachel's reaction to all this when we're interrupted by a knock on my door. It's Maggie. "I called the funeral home," she reports. "The woman who runs it is waiting for us." She glances at her watch. "We should've gotten there earlier. They've been open for an hour already."

"Did you find the will?" I ask.

"No, but I did find the name of Ingrid's lawyer. I've called her, too."

We three queens promise to be ready in fifteen minutes. My bet is Maggie will be ready in ten. Pop is clearly relieved that Maggie excused him from this excursion. He says if he stays at Damsgard he can let in the cops, who are supposed to come by again today. That is true but I think there's something else going on. Despite his career as a cop, my father has never been good at facing life's harsher realities. Of which death is the harshest. And that's one topic you can't avoid at the funeral home.

I've just decided to pair my black turtleneck with crimson-colored skinny pants featuring a muted brocade print when my cell rings. "Hey, mom," I answer.

"You've got a cold!" she shrieks. "When did you get sick? Probably the minute you got off the plane. I told you they had germs in Minnesota."

My mother is not happy that I agreed to visit the home state of Pop's reviled lady friend. If she got her wish, I'd write off the entire upper Midwest. "I got sick yesterday. But that's not the big news." I lower my voice. "Maggie's sister was murdered during the Giant W opening ceremony."

"Did that Maggie do it?"

I hesitate a beat too long.

"I knew it! I could tell she was bad news from that time she ran up to me in the pickle aisle."

"Mom—"

"Your father always had a fascination with sickos. Just like you're developing, young lady. But in my opinion getting all lovey-dovey with one is taking it too far."

"We don't know that Maggie did it."

"How many other suspects do you have?" When I can't name a single one, she continues. "I gotta go. Bennie talked some woman into buying a Pontiac Grand Am with ninety thousand miles. Can you believe that? He could sell a nun a ticket to paradise. I'll talk to you later. By the way, Rachel is fine but she still doesn't want to fill out any college applications."

That's another source of tension in my life. I can't go into it now because I'm already in enough of a state.

Fifteen minutes later I find myself in front of the Lang Funeral Home. It is an unremarkable two-story redbrick building but the mortician herself is a surprise from tip to tail. That is, unless you've met a Goth mortician before.

Galena Lang, whom I'd guess to be in her mid-fifties, greets us wearing a midi-length black knit dress with a lace-up front, a brown corset belt, and Victorian ankle boots. Her eye shadow and nail varnish are charcoal gray, her skin is ivory, and her long blond hair is accented by indigo streaks.

"So sorry for your loss," she tells Maggie in a cigarette voice as she ushers us into her dimly lit office. We settle onto plump sofas upholstered with subdued plaid fabric. Boxes of Kleenex can be found on every horizontal surface. Framed hand-embroidered sayings about death hang on the walls. *A man's dying is more the survivors' affair than his own – Thomas Mann. And they die an equal death: the idler and the man of mighty deeds – Homer.* I would have to agree with both those sentiments.

We accept hazelnut-flavored coffee and Galena settles in with a Black Cherry soda. "What a unique name you have,"

Trixie says. "Your parents must be creative people."

"Not hardly. They named my brother Joe. Me they named after the township we lived in, about two hundred miles west of here."

"If you don't mind my asking," Shanelle says, "how did you get into this line of work?" Shanelle's been hinting she might be interested in a change of career. From beauty queen to funeral director would be a leap but she does have the application of pancake makeup down pat.

"It was my husband's family business," Galena tells us. "He's gone now, too."

Somehow we've managed to circle back to the topic of Death. "Do you have any idea what you'd like for your sister?" Galena asks Maggie.

"I was thinking something simple," Maggie replies.

"My most popular option is the two thousand dollar special. That includes a wake, with the deceased in a nice casket of your choosing. After that we switch to a cardboard box for cremation or burial."

"I'm not sure we need a wake," Maggie says. "Or a fancy casket. We Lindvigs have always had simple tastes. How much would it be if we start with a cardboard box?"

Galena scribbles on a pad of paper and produces a lower price.

"Does that include embalming?" Maggie wants to know. "Because I don't think we need embalming. That would slow things down, too, right?"

"There's always cremation," Galena offers. "Would you consider that?"

"That depends. How much does it cost and how soon can you do it?"

Shanelle, Trixie, and I exchange a look. When Maggie said she wanted "simple," I guess what she really meant was "cheap" and "fast." Maybe she didn't want my father to come to the funeral home because she didn't want him to witness her so blatantly trying to hasten her sister's sendoff.

Galena produces a few more prices but Maggie remains dissatisfied. "Any way we could get it lower?"

Before Maggie inquires about the Dumpster option, I pipe up. I'm not Ingrid Svendsen's biggest fan but somehow I feel the need to prop up her side. "Wouldn't a wake be customary for a prominent citizen like your sister, Maggie?"

Maggie ponders that. "We are the daughters of a judge."

Shanelle picks up the thread. "Probably lots of folks will want to pay their respects."

"I don't think that many will," Maggie says. "My sister wasn't easy to get along with. Plus I don't want this to take forever. Waiting won't make it any easier," she repeats in what is rapidly becoming her catch line of the day.

"Perhaps we might have a few moments alone," I suggest to Galena.

She rises. "I got a pending. I'll go check on it."

As is typical for me, I plunge right in. "You understand you won't be paying out of your own pocket for Ingrid's funeral, right, Maggie? Her estate will cover the costs."

Maggie blinks at me. "But I'm her only living relative. So her estate is coming to me. So basically it *is* me who's going to pay for it."

It's hard to know how to respond to that. Nevertheless Trixie takes a stab at it. "I know for me, I'd feel better in the long run if I gave my sister a proper sendoff."

"Well, maybe, but I don't think my sister would do that for me. Besides, Ingrid always had it so easy. She always got whatever she wanted. Husbands, houses, you name it. I had to work outside the home but she never had to. So now things will even out a little bit. That seems fair, doesn't it?"

Galena knocks on the door and pokes her head inside the office. "My pending's hanging by a thread so I'd like to wrap things up here. You made any decisions?"

Maggie rises to her feet. "Maybe you can answer one last question for me. When do they usually read the will? Before or after the funeral?"

"After. Your sister is being autopsied today so I expect to take delivery tonight."

I close my eyes. Galena makes Ingrid sound like a SubZero.

"Then I think we should skip the wake and do the funeral the day after tomorrow," Maggie ordains. "In the morning. And read the will in the afternoon. After all, waiting won't make it any easier."

CHAPTER FIVE

"We don't usually do this in the middle of the day," Trixie reminds me.

We're back at Damsgard and I'm pulling the cork out of a bottle of sauvignon blanc. "It's five o'clock somewhere." I ogle our takeout lunch. It's a Minnesota specialty: turkey, mushroom, and wild rice soup, served with a toasted slice of baguette smothered in melted gruyère cheese. Comfort food if ever I've seen it. And boy, do I need both that *and* the nectar of the gods. For one thing, even though I've medicated myself with every cold remedy in the book, my congestion is worse. For another, Maggie's irreverent display at the funeral home only added to my fear that she might've been the one to put Ingrid on the noon express to heaven's door.

"Let's be fancy and eat in the dining room," Shanelle suggests. "I especially like the decorations in there."

Not only is Shanelle crazy for snow globes—there's a collection atop the credenza—but little Santas line the narrow wainscot cap.

We serve our meal on the Lenox *Holiday* pattern china and settle around the mahogany dining table. Beneath the glittering chandelier Trixie raises her crystal wineglass in a toast. "To Ingrid Svendsen. May she rest in peace."

"And may Happy figure out why she's resting so soon," Shanelle mutters.

"I need more suspects. I can't focus entirely on Maggie." I sip from my wineglass. "And for that I need to know more about Ingrid's life."

"Maybe you can get Maggie to open up about her," Trixie says.

I taste my soup, which proves to be delectable. "I have to get Pop to open up about Maggie, too. That'll be tricky if he senses I'm suspicious of her."

"Just how serious are those two?" Trixie wants to know.

"Maggie's angling for a proposal." I set down my spoon. I can't eat while I discuss this deeply disturbing topic. "Last weekend when Rachel went to Maggie's salon, Maggie said flat out she was hoping to find a diamond ring from Pop under the Christmas tree."

"That's how my friend Roseanne got engaged," Trixie says.

"Christmas and Valentine's Day," Shanelle says, "the two most popular times for a man to propose."

"Throw in New Year's Eve and you've got the trifecta." My proposal came not on a holiday but when the home pregnancy test came up positive.

"We could talk to the neighbors about both Lindvig sisters," Shanelle suggests. "Winona might be small enough that everybody knows everybody's business."

"That's a great idea," I say. "We could also search the house for clues." The cops did that while we were at the funeral home. I need to call Detective Dembek to ask if they found anything.

"We should be searching the house right now, when Maggie isn't here," Trixie whispers. "Because I don't think she'd take kindly to it."

"We best eat up then," Shanelle says, and our spoons increase their speed between bowl and mouth.

We're slurping in silence when the doorbell rings. I can't help it. My heart leaps because my first thought is: this could be Mario!

I know. That's not good for a woman who's married to Jason. But if you knew Mario the way I know Mario, I bet you'd have the same reaction.

It's not Mario. In fact it's not a man at all. It's a slim, attractive blond I'd guess to be in her late sixties. Actually, she sort of resembles Ingrid. She's wearing a snazzy nipped-waist parka in gunmetal gray with what I believe to be genuine shearling around the hood and cuffs. Beside her trousered legs stands a trendy brown-leather spinner and matching satchel.

"I came the instant I heard!" she cries and pushes forcefully past me into the foyer, hauling her luggage inside with her. She pivots to face me again. "And you are?" she demands.

Usually it's the newcomer who has to identify herself but apparently this well-turned-out female isn't shy. "I'm Happy Pennington and these are my friends Shanelle Walker and Trixie Barnett."

She eyes us for a moment then throws back her head and theatrically swings out her left arm. " 'To me, fair friend, you can never be old, for as you were when first your eye I eyed, such seems your beauty still!' "

"Shakespeare?" I guess.

"Of course 'tis the bard! Sonnet 104. About the passage and ravages of time. Which you three have yet to suffer." She gives me a penetrating onceover. "How did *you* come to know Ingrid? I never heard her mention you."

"I'm a family friend," I lie. "Shanelle, Trixie, and I came to Winona to participate in the Giant W opening ceremony. I'm sorry but I didn't catch your name?"

She looks shocked that I have to ask. "I'm Priscilla Pembroke! Surely you've heard of me."

I'm too polite to reply that I have not. "I gather you don't live in Winona?"

"I live in Manhattan." She says it as if living anywhere else would be preposterous. "You would have had to know Ingrid only for a minute or two to hear her speak of me. We were as close as two friends can be. And now"—Priscilla staggers then lays her palm against her forehead—"she's gone! 'Death, a necessary end, will come when it will come!' " She lowers her head and gives me an expectant look. "Julius Caesar, of course. Act two, scene two, page two."

"So ... you're an actress?" Shanelle guesses.

She hurls a glare like a hate bomb in Shanelle's direction. "I am an ac-TOR! I will not be limited to female roles. I can play anything: man, woman, or beast." She grabs the handle of her spinner. "I'll show myself to my room."

I race to bar her from proceeding upstairs. "Priscilla, you'll have to wait for Ingrid's sister to get back before you do that."

Her nostrils flare. "You cannot seriously mean to keep me from a home I know as well as my own."

"It's not up to me. Maggie is Ingrid's closest relative and you'll have to speak to her."

It's only after Shanelle and Trixie flank me in a show of solidarity that Priscilla backs down. "I'll prove to all of you how intimately I know Ingrid," she huffs. "In fact, even though she swore me to secrecy, I will tell you where her shrine is."

"She has a shrine?" Trixie says.

"To the goddess Freyja!" This time Priscilla throws out both arms. "The name means lady. She is one of the pre-eminent goddesses of the Norse pantheon. A high-ranking member of the tribe of deities known as the Vanir."

Trixie's features twist in confusion. "Why would Ingrid have a shrine to this Freyja?"

"Because she was a worshipper! Like so many women drawn to Freyja's wisdom and her pursuit of passionate fulfillment in life. I believe no heathen goddess is so loved, and so misunderstood, as Freyja. She is incredibly complex." Priscilla eyes us dubiously. "Too complex for many to understand."

I watch Trixie's eyes widen with every word Priscilla

utters. Pantheon. Tribe. Vanir. Heathen.

"Are you a worshipper, too?" Shanelle wants to know.

Priscilla lowers her voice. "I have been known to participate in the honor rituals. They're celebrated every Friday the 13th."

That's coming around again in just a few days. "All right," I say. "Show us Ingrid's shrine." This I've got to see.

With a triumphant spin, Priscilla makes a beeline for the library. Either she's a fantastic actress or she really does know her way around Damsgard. This is yet another spectacular room with gorgeous floor-to-ceiling bookshelves and a formidable antique desk with elaborate carvings. The Christmas tree in the corner is bedecked with red ornaments and ribbons; Santas perch on the steps of the rolling bookshelf ladder; and holiday stockings dangle from the fireplace mantel.

"I don't see a shrine in here," Shanelle says.

Priscilla raises a silencing hand in our direction. She can't seem to tear her eyes from the oil painting that hangs above the mantel. It features brightly colored sailboats tearing around on what looks like a stormy sea. I'm no art expert but I'd describe it as impressionistic.

Finally she abandons the painting and walks to the bookshelves in the corner by the Christmas tree. I don't see what she does but presto!—the shelves swing back to reveal a secret room.

We three queens gasp. "It's just like in the movies!" Trixie cries.

Priscilla flings us an exultant look. "I told you I knew my way around Damsgard." She flounces into the secret room and you can bet we immediately follow.

It's a small windowless room and, yes, there is a shrine inside. Well, more of an altar really, draped in crimson and forest green fabric that crashes to the oriental carpet. On top of it are arrayed several tall gold vases holding stalks of wheat. I also note sprigs of dill and small sculptures of animals. A cat, a bird, and—

"What's this?" I hold up a gray stone sculpture that looks like a fat, hairy pig with a prominent snout.

"That's a boar." Priscilla takes it from my hand and returns it to the altar. "Occasionally Freyja rides a boar. Sometimes a falcon."

Shanelle guffaws. "I thought you were going to say she sometimes turns into one."

Priscilla narrows her eyes. "Freyja has been known to shape shift. It is her choice whether to fly, ride an animal, or be carried in a chariot drawn by felines."

I guess that's where the cats come in. "What's this?" I hold up a palm-sized uneven chunk of translucent golden stone.

Priscilla removes that, too, from my hand. "Freyja is associated with amber. As legend goes, she received a fantastic necklace of amber by sleeping with four dwarves on four succeeding nights."

Wow. I guess that's how Freyja found that "passionate fulfillment" that Priscilla referred to. Personally, if I went in for that sort of thing, I would prefer taller men. But to each her own.

"Amber has been meaningful to many over the centuries," Priscilla tells us. "It has been found in Egyptian tombs and was even used as currency among the Assyrians and the Phoenicians." Priscilla gazes at each of us in turn. "It is sometimes called 'the jewel whose power cannot be resisted.'"

I shiver, hearing that. All this is freaking me out. It's so far removed from my own experience. And never would I have guessed that anything "heathen" would come within a million miles of Ingrid Svendsen.

Then again, this just proves Ingrid had secrets. It was no doubt one of those that got her killed.

"Why was Ingrid into all this?" Shanelle wants to know.

Priscilla edges closer. "You're so narrow-minded you can't think of a reason? Perhaps she was not bound by Western tradition, as you seem to be. Perhaps the Icelandic sagas resounded in her heart. Perhaps she espoused the heathen values of warriorship and understood the value of bold action."

"You said she swore you to secrecy," I say. "So Ingrid was making a point of keeping all this to herself?"

"Wouldn't you have done the same thing?" Priscilla demands. "In a town where eyes snoop and tongues wag?"

I hope they do wag. In fact I'm hoping I can make Priscilla's tongue wag. I don't know what to make of this nervy Manhattanite but if she knows Ingrid half as intimately as she says she does, she'll be a font of information. "Perhaps you'd like to join us for a glass of wine and some soup," I suggest. I make a point of leading Priscilla out of the secret room. I have a suspicious enough mind that I'm worried she might try to trap us in there given half a chance. "I'm sure by the time we're done with lunch Maggie will be back from her errands."

"That would be delightful—" she's starting to say when again the doorbell rings.

I march into the foyer and throw the door open, castigating myself for once again hoping to find Mario Suave on the stoop. No such luck. While this latest arrival is indeed a man, and a man roughly Mario's age, too, it is not Mario. With his beard, longish dark hair and tweed jacket, he's a professor-type who's just sexy enough that some students would fall in love with him.

He holds out his hand. "I'm Peter Svendsen." He waits a beat, then, "Erik Svendsen's son."

"Ingrid's ... stepson?"

He nods. I step back to usher him in out of the cold. As he stomps the snow off his shoes, behind me I hear clattering noises. Then the kitchen door at the side of the house bangs. Maggie and Pop must've come back in that way for some reason.

It's only when I'm introducing Peter to Trixie and Shanelle that I realize Priscilla is no longer among us. Her luggage is gone, too. Nor is there any sign of Pop or Maggie having returned.

    I race to the kitchen. The side door is ajar. I pull it open even though I already know what I will see in the freshly fallen snow. Footprints. And the tracks left by a trendy leather spinner.

CHAPTER SIX

Trixie has trailed me into the kitchen. "First we can't get rid of Priscilla and then she disappears! Where did she go?"

"The tracks lead to the street." I give my nose a hearty blow. "I presume she came by car."

Trixie throws out her arms. "How weird is that?"

I'm mystified, too. And freakish behavior by an out-of-towner who claims to be the BFF of the murder victim certainly raises a host of questions in my mind.

I want to know more about Priscilla Pembroke. Though I don't know how I'll ever find her again.

First things first. We rejoin Shanelle and Peter Svendsen in the living room.

This is an amazingly beautiful space, too, with the same rust-colored walls and coffered ceilings as the dining room plus stunning white built-in cabinetry and plush velvet-upholstered seating arrangements. Poinsettias and garlands abound. And the Christmas tree in this room is the grandest of all. Since it's a real tree, it gives off a marvelous pine scent. A gazillion glittering ornaments hang from its branches, also adorned by green mesh ribbon flecked with gold.

"We're all so sorry about your stepmother," I tell Peter after we offer him a glass of wine. It turns out he's already heard through the grapevine that Ingrid invited all of us to stay as guests here in his childhood home.

"Thank you." He clasps his hands between his knees. "I will admit to you that we weren't close. Still, it's a shocking thing."

"I imagine you've talked to the police."

"I didn't have much to tell them. The truth is that since my father died I've had as little as possible to do with Ingrid."

Peter seems in the mood to dish the dirt. I'll take him up on it. "It sounds like you disapproved of the marriage."

"My sister and I both did. Nora moved to Chicago and got married years ago so she's less involved than I am. But she knows the gossip just like everybody else does."

This is getting good. I lean forward. "What gossip is that?"

"Ingrid Svendsen did to my father what she did to her first husband. She homed in on a well-to-do older man and insinuated herself into his life. Granted, my father was divorced."

"Her first husband wasn't?" Trixie interjects.

"Far from it. He was a well-known doctor with a wife and young kids. He was at least fifteen years older than Ingrid. But did she let any of that stop her?"

I watch Peter Svendsen get het up. Clearly he's no fan of stepmommy dearest.

"Ingrid might have put on a good show," he goes on, "but she was nothing but a scheming opportunist. Nora and I went ballistic when my father got it into his head to marry her."

"You must've tried to talk him out of it," Shanelle says.

"I tried, Nora tried. We couldn't reason with him at all."

I have to wonder if the Svendsen heirs were more worried about their inheritance than their father's happiness. "Was Ingrid a good wife to your father?" I ask.

Peter grudgingly admits she was. "Except for how much money she spent. Too much was never enough. And I'd be damned if I'd let her get her claws into Damsgard."

My ears perk up. "What do you mean?"

"She led you to believe she owned the place, right?" He

snorts. "She did that all the time. It drove me crazy."

"She *didn't* own it?" Shanelle says.

"No way! That's one concession Nora and I wrung out of Dad. He stipulated in his will that Ingrid could live here until she died but that's it. The house was never in her name. Never. And now that she's gone Damsgard and everything in it will come to me."

Whoa! I fall back against the sofa cushions. Shanelle, Trixie, and I look at each other and I can see they're as astonished as I am. This is a major news flash.

For Maggie, it'll be gargantuan.

That is, if it's true. Peter Svendsen has a vested interest here. He may not be speaking the whole truth and nothing but.

"In fact, that's why I'm here," he goes on. "I haven't been in the house for four years, since my dad died. I couldn't bring myself to watch Ingrid play lady of the manor. Now I don't have to anymore." He stands up. "I'd like to look around."

Man, it's a full-time job keeping people from wandering in off the street and wanting to traipse through the house. I don't feel I can stop Peter Svendsen, though, the way I stopped Priscilla Pembroke. After all, I'm only here at the behest of someone who's no longer among the living. I'll just keep an eye on him. Make sure he doesn't lift anything.

Peter, Trixie, and I have wandered into the library—where the secret-door bookshelf is back in place—when I get it into my head to ask if he ever met Priscilla Pembroke. "She said she was one of Ingrid's best friends," I say.

"That's not much of a recommendation in my book." He runs a loving hand across the antique desk. I wonder if he ever sat there and did homework as a boy.

"Priscilla is an actress," Trixie adds. "She's very theatrical."

Peter groans. "God save me from actresses."

"It sounds like there's a story there," I guess.

"An epic tale. Don't ask."

Before Peter takes his leave, he wants to know how long

we'll be staying in Winona. At this point that's a good question.

"Another few days," I reply vaguely. "I hope that won't be a problem for you."

Peter pulls open the front door and cold air rushes inside. It's already pitch dark out and we three queens haven't even finished lunch. "None of this will happen fast," he says and I know he's referring to the day he longs for, when Damsgard will be his.

I have to wonder if he took action to hurry that day along.

So far this investigation is easy as pie. I plop my butt in the house and wait for potential suspects to come to me.

Speaking of which, we've rewarmed our soup and replenished our wine when Maggie breezes in through the front door, Pop right behind her. They're both loaded with shopping bags. Bolts of fabric protrude from one of them.

"Been busy?" I inquire.

Neither of them stops to chat. "I don't know what I'd do without your father," Maggie tells me on her way to the stairs. "He's going to take me to Minneapolis tomorrow. I'm so terrible with directions I don't think I could even find it on my own."

Judging from Pop's expression he's less than thrilled with that ambitious excursion, a two-and-a-half-hour drive each way. But I won't come to his rescue because I could use the time to give Damsgard a thorough search. "By the way, Maggie," I call, "did you ever hear your sister mention a Priscilla Pembroke?"

"I never heard that name," Maggie says before disappearing upstairs.

"She hasn't given herself over to grief yet," Shanelle remarks after Maggie and Pop disappear upstairs.

"I don't know if she's cried even one tear over her sister," Trixie says. "It makes me feel bad for Ingrid."

"Me, too." I lower my voice. "But remember. Not a word about the secret room or what Peter Svendsen said about him inheriting Damsgard." Right now I'd prefer to be the one with the inside info. Plus I'd like to see how Maggie behaves while she believes she's in line for a windfall from her dead sibling. Which she may well be.

"Agreed," Shanelle and Trixie whisper.

I dispatch the rest of my soup. "I'm going to go talk to Pop." I wonder if he's upset, because when I go to find him he is once again shoveling.

I join him on the sidewalk. He always shovels not only the driveway and the walkways around the house but the sidewalk, too. And he doesn't dump the snow on other people's lawns, either. What I know about shoveling etiquette I learned at his knee. "I'll get another shovel and help," I tell him.

"No, you're all dressed up."

"I am not. This is normal for me." Granted, the heels of my boots are four inches and the only coat I brought with me on this trip is a plum-colored Melton wool with impeccable seaming. But it's a knockoff! And besides, this is standard wintertime garb for Ms. America Happy Pennington.

I find another shovel in the garage and get to work. "It's nice how peaceful and quiet it is here in Winona," I say after a while.

He grunts.

"And I like how the houses are in a square around the park," I add a minute later. "It's how I imagine houses in London."

Silence.

"We'll have to go read the plaque about the statue tomorrow in the light," I say.

He stands his shovel upright in a pile of snow. "Out with it already. Say what's on your mind."

I abandon the small talk. "Fine. Have you noticed that Maggie isn't exactly mired in grief?"

"Everybody grieves in their own way. You know that."

"All she's done since her sister died is plan how she's going to redecorate Damsgard. At the funeral home she couldn't wait to get Ingrid buried so everybody could move on to the reading of the will."

He flushes, and not from the exertion of shoveling. "As I recall, young lady, *you* were plenty darn eager to get *your* check after you won Ms. America."

"That's different! I won that prize money fair and square." My fellow contestants might quibble with that assessment but that's my story and I'm sticking to it.

"And maybe Maggie has all this coming to *her* fair and square." He gestures to take in Damsgard and its expansive lot. "Maggie always had it a lot tougher than her sister. Why do you think she left Winona in the first place? Her father may have been a judge but he didn't leave her any money to speak of. She had to work for a living."

"Wasn't that true for Ingrid, too?"

He leans closer. "Ingrid *married* money. Twice."

That's what Peter Svendsen said.

"Maggie wasn't so lucky," he goes on. "Donovan's father wouldn't marry her. Heck, he was such a deadbeat he wouldn't even support his son. And Maggie didn't have any skills. All she could do was nails. And since she didn't want the snobs around here to see how far she'd fallen, she left."

I ponder that. I do have to give Maggie credit for uprooting herself—which I am having trouble doing—and for starting a business that flourishes to this day. I step closer to my father. My breath puffs in the frigid night air. "I admire you for defending Maggie, Pop, really I do. But you know as well as I do that this doesn't all add up."

He looks away.

Even though I tossed my shovel, I plow forward. "So where *was* Maggie, exactly, when Ingrid got shot?"

He shakes his head and says nothing. He won't meet my gaze.

"You were upset that she wasn't right next to you when the lights came back on."

"That's because I was afraid something happened to her!"

"So where was she? How did she explain it?"

"She did not kill her sister!"

"Are you saying she hasn't told you where she was? If she is innocent I do not understand why she can't just say where the heck she was when her sister got shot."

He points his finger at me. "You better not be thinking what I think you're thinking, young lady." He grabs his shovel and stomps up the driveway. Then he delivers the sort of line I hear from Rachel. "I'm not going to talk about this anymore."

"You can't pretend this isn't bothering you, too," I call after him, but his pace does not slow.

I finish the shoveling. There's no doubt that shoveling is an excellent activity when a person is trying to think things through. At least for us Przybyszewskis.

CHAPTER SEVEN

It's a few hours later, while we three queens are sitting around in our jammies watching the big-screen TV and waiting for my new pore-refining white clay masque to work its magic on our complexions, that once again the doorbell rings.

I spring to my feet. "I can't believe it!" For this must be Mario. Not only is the third time the charm but clearly the gods are toying with me by making sure the sexiest man alive heaves into view while I am makeup-free, wearing droopy cotton, and engaged in an unsightly beauty regimen.

"I'll get it," Trixie offers.

I leap up the stairs to the landing, prepared to dash inside my room to render myself presentable, when I hear Trixie loose a shriek of excitement.

"Mrs. P!"

It's my mother!

I pound back down the stairs. "What in the world are *you* doing here?"

She throws out her arms. "You think I don't know how to get on a plane?"

I have to say, she looks good. Since she started working outside the home, she dabs on makeup every day, styles her light red hair in a large pouf, and experiments with fashionable clothing. I am impressed to see her decked out in a classic black wool car coat with a trendy funnel-neck collar.

Trixie releases her and I give my mom a hug. "Since when do you fly to another state on a moment's notice?"

"Since my daughter comes down with a cold that could kill her." She hugs Shanelle. "And I will have you know that if those crazy planes let a person bring homemade chicken soup on board, I would have that with me. Close that door so we don't all catch our death." She peers at us quizzically. "What the heck do you three have on your faces?"

"Let me take your coat, Mrs. Przybyszewski," Shanelle says while Trixie shuts the front door and starts babbling about the masque.

"You might want to try it, too, Mrs. P. It feels kind of tingly but that's because it makes your skin look younger by accelerating cell turnover. Happy says the clay is mined from the Iberian Mountains, one of the purest clay resorts in the world."

My mother waves a dismissive hand. "I don't need that crap. My skin is already radiant and as soft as a baby's bottom. At least that's what that Bennie tells me. Oh look, Happy! There's your father."

"Hazel!" Pop could not look more astonished if it were Ingrid who just materialized in the foyer. And in contrast to my mom's coiffed hairdo and zingy zebra-stripe top, he's at quite a disadvantage appearance-wise with his uncombed hair and bedraggled striped pajamas.

"I know it's a shock to see me," my mom says. "It's a shock I could get off work." She turns to me. " 'Indispensable,' that's what Bennie says I am now. And he doesn't just mean in the office. Anyhow, I said to Bennie: Bennie, when my daughter needs me, what else can I do but go to her?"

My mom is laying on the Bennie thing a little thick but she's never been known for subtlety. And now that I see a certain gleam in her eye, I'm 100 percent sure I know why she showed up in Winona.

She got wind from Rachel that Maggie is trying to finagle

a marriage proposal from Pop. And the original Mrs. Lou Przybyszewski wants to do what she can to head off that abomination. My burgeoning congestion is just a convenient excuse.

Sort of makes me wonder if she pulled some trick to get me sick. Like rub my coffee mug with used Kleenex she collected at bingo. I love my mom but I'm on to her.

Maggie sashays into the foyer wearing a low-cut black negligee and leopard-print marabou slippers with 3-inch heels. My mother walks forward to grasp her hands. "Condolences on your loss. I've already lit a candle for your sister and I plan to say a novena." My mother is positively purring. This is quite the performance, I'm sure for my father's benefit. No one would ever guess she believes she's talking to a sister killer. "If there's anything I can do, please let me know."

Maggie blinks at my mother. "I can't get over that you're here in Winona."

"It's a surprise to me, too," Pop says. He seems a trifle wary. I don't blame him.

"I'm hoping you can find a little room for me somewhere in this big house," my mother says. "Of course I *could* stay at a hotel—"

Maggie's eyes light up but I head her off. "Of course you'll stay here, Mom. There's a lovely bedroom on this floor with an en suite bath. I'll go make sure the bed has clean sheets."

"How about some cocoa?" Trixie offers, and an hour later we all retire to our rooms with full bellies and the kitchen smelling of chocolate.

I'm more relaxed than I've been all day but I text Jason anyway. These days, what with his job offer, our interactions are often a tad strained.

I'm slammed, sweetie, he texts back. *Made any decisions I should know about?*

Darn. That's all he wants to talk about these days. *Not yet. But you should know there's been another murder.*

My cell rings. It's Jason. "What the heck happened?" he wants to know and I give him the download. "You don't seriously think Maggie did it, do you?" he asks.

"She doesn't seem the type but you never know. She had motive big time. And she went AWOL right when Ingrid got shot."

Jason looses a low whistle. "Your dad sure knows how to pick 'em."

I know he's not referring just to Maggie. "What's Rachel been up to?"

"Cramming for a physics test tomorrow."

"Another one?"

"It's an AP class, babe."

The only insight Jason and I have into advanced-placement classes is through our Einstein daughter. "By the way I saw the calendar. You look amazing, Jason."

He chuckles. "Kimberly told me it's selling so fast they had to print more copies."

"That's fantastic! But who's Kimberly?"

"The photographer. You've heard me mention her before."

"Really?"

"Sure you have. She's the one who predicted I'd land on the cover."

"Oh, you're right, you did tell me it was the photographer who said that." Somehow it never occurred to me the photographer was a woman.

"Anyway, I really am slammed. How about we talk tomorrow? And remember I have to give my decision to Zach next week."

"I know. I love you."

"Love you, too, babe," and then he's gone.

The next morning my cell wakens me when it's still dark and I would much rather remain comatose. But this call I have to take. It's from Sebastian Cantwell: Ms. America pageant owner, besmirched tycoon, and, I soon learn, Giant W stockholder.

"The shares are down seven percent in two days, Ohio." His British accent gets even more pronounced when he's mad. Sometimes I can barely make head or tails of what he's saying. "Apparently investors take a dim view of a murder happening on the store premises."

"I think we'd all rather the murder hadn't happened, sir. But I am investigating. I think it'll help that the homicide detective is cooperating with me." Not that I've spoken with Detective Dembek since the night of the murder. My bad.

"Wrap this thing up ASAP. I want those shares to recover. Then you can do something else for me."

"Do you need a favor?" I try to be obliging to the man who wrote me a check for a quarter of a million dollars.

"You can testify on my behalf. My trial's coming up fast."

Sebastian Cantwell has been charged with creating false losses in the pageant to avoid taxes. It never sounded all that bad to me but Mario assures me it's a felony. And since on the QT Mario helped the feds with the investigation, he's sure Mr. Cantwell is guilty. I'm more inclined to give my pageant owner the benefit of the doubt, though I admit I always prefer to be on Mario's side.

"I'm happy to testify but I doubt I would be of any help," I say.

"You'd do great, Ohio." The call disconnects. Sebastian Cantwell is never one for prolonged goodbyes.

I'm in the kitchen making coffee when Pop and Maggie come in through the side door bearing a wide flat white box that emits an extremely tantalizing aroma.

"Donuts," Pop says.

"From Bloedow's." Maggie pronounces it BLAY-doughs. "They were voted best donuts in Minnesota last year."

"Yum." I select a long frosted one that's got to be a thousand calories. Guess I'll be doing a long run today, snow or no snow.

"That's one of their bestsellers," Pop says. "The maple

long john."

One bite makes me think it was made in heaven, not Winona.

"They still fry them in lard," Maggie assures me, "like they did ninety years ago."

Make that an extra long run.

Trixie and Shanelle join us in short order. Shanelle goes for a traditional glazed and Trixie a chocolate-cake donut. "I'm getting a head start on my holiday weight gain this year," she mumbles, her mouth half full.

When my mother appears, she's already made up and dressed in navy slacks and a cute blue paisley blouse with turned-up cuffs.

"I hope you slept well in the maid's room," Maggie says.

My mother produces a beatific smile as she selects her usual jelly donut. "I always sleep like a baby, don't I, Lou? Nothing on *my* conscience."

Meow. "So what's on the docket for everybody today?" I ask.

"Well, the funeral's not till tomorrow," Trixie murmurs, and Maggie spins toward my father. "I think they should read the will here at the house."

I get a brainstorm. "Excellent idea! How about in the library?"

From behind Maggie, Shanelle winks at me. She knows about the secret room right off the library so she can guess what I'm up to.

"That should work," Maggie agrees. "I'll call the lawyer."

Since I'm on a roll, I keep going. "You two are thinking of driving to Minneapolis today, right?" As I say that, I realize that with my mom here it will be difficult to search the house. I know from experience that I can't count on her to keep her mouth shut.

"Can she do that?" my mom asks me, gesturing toward Maggie. "The cops will let her leave town?"

Maggie frowns at my mother. "Why wouldn't they?" She

turns to my father. "What have you been saying, Lou?"

Interesting. Maybe Pop *has* been pestering her to explain her whereabouts when Ingrid was gunned down.

Before Pop can answer Maggie bursts into tears. "I had nothing to do with Ingrid getting shot!"

"So where were you when it happened?" I ask. As soon as the words pop out of my mouth, I realize they sound pretty accusatory. Still, I do want that question answered.

Maggie keeps sobbing. "I can't believe you're asking me that! What do you have against me? I got you this opportunity here in Winona, didn't I?"

She makes it sound like she lined me up at Carnegie Hall. "It's a perfectly reasonable question. One you should have no trouble answering."

She keeps crying for a while, and I note with interest that Pop doesn't try to comfort her. Eventually, since I don't let her off the hook, she comes out with it. "Fine! You're so desperate to know? I wanted one of those inflatable fruitcakes."

"Why didn't you just say so?" Pop hollers.

My mother throws out her arms. "What in tarnation is an inflatable fruitcake?"

"Hey, hold on a minute." Pop frowns at Maggie. "Are you saying you *stole* it? While we were all standing there in the dark?"

She starts crying harder and I start wondering if her tears are a ploy to make us back off. Finally, "They were expensive!" she wails. "I don't have the kind of money the rest of you people have."

Boy, will my mom make hay with this! Suspected sister killer *and* tchotchke thief. I see the triumphant glint in my mom's eye. "What in the world would anybody want with an inflatable fruitcake?" she wants to know.

Maggie struggles to explain. "It's so you can put fruitcake on the holiday table but nobody has to eat it. Because nobody ever wants to eat fruitcake."

Pop and I meet each other's eyes. That is so not true.

"People only eat it to be polite," Maggie insists. "Everybody knows that."

Pop shuffles his feet. "Well, truth be told, Hazel here has been known to bake a darn good fruitcake."

My mother bows her head in a false show of modesty. I know her heart is soaring.

I chime in. "In fact, Mom's fruitcake is so good that we have neighbors call us in early December just to make sure their names are still on her gift list."

"I don't believe it." Maggie sets her jaw. "There's no such thing as good fruitcake. You're both making this up."

"There's only one way to prove it." My mother produces such a sweet smile I nearly go into insulin shock. "How about you and I have a fruitcake bake-off?"

CHAPTER EIGHT

"Now *that's* the way to get the season started!" Pop bellows. "Hazel's fruitcake!"

Maggie throws out her arms. "Seriously? You expect me to bake a fruitcake? Well, fine. I'll do it. But not until after the funeral. Some of us are in mourning."

Only a honker of a sneeze keeps me from disputing that assertion.

The doorbell rings. "I'll get it," I offer, and without thinking twice I run to the front door in my ancient PJs with my hair in a pile on top of my head and my nose red from non-stop blowing and half of a maple long john donut in one hand and a snot-filled Kleenex in the other and who is standing there but Mario Suave.

"Happy," he says, "just the woman I've been looking for," and he cracks that trademark dimple-flashing smile that appears on his *America's Scariest Ghost Stories* posters and you know what? It doesn't matter that I look like hell on wheels.

He looks fantastic, of course, his skin tanned from L.A. sun and his dark hair perfectly imperfect and his musky cologne breaking through my congestion to assail my nostrils. He's dressed in sleek black trousers and a camel-colored overcoat that must have cashmere in it because it feels so darn soft. I know how soft it is because I'm hugging him. I'm hugging him for a little too long, I realize.

I back away and tell a lie. "I can't believe you came to Winona!"

He winks at me. "Didn't I tell you there are ghosts in Minnesota?"

I hear commotion behind me. Everyone is coming into the foyer from the kitchen. Delighted shouts and cries are ringing out.

Mario lowers his voice. "Ghosts ... and angels."

I get a few minutes to collect myself as Mario is greeted and hugged and backslapped and escorted to the kitchen for coffee and a Bloedow's donut. We have a moment of solemnity when he offers Maggie his condolences. She seems so undone by his celebrity that she can't speak, no matter the topic. All she can do is stare.

"Maybe you can share some local knowledge with me," Mario suggests to her at one point. I can tell he's trying to cheer her up, which goes to show how considerate he is. "That's always a great way to improve the show."

She clears her throat. "So you'll be working on your show here in Winona?"

"Why else would I be here?" He gives me a sly wink and nobody says a word. Mario may have had a good cover in Vegas and Miami but we all know why he really came to Winona: Mom knows, and Trixie and Shanelle and me and even Pop.

If Jason knew Mario had shown up here, he'd know why, too.

"I've got a shoot this afternoon," Mario goes on, "on Cummings Street on the west side of town. It's said to be haunted by a very lively spirit." He shivers dramatically and we all chuckle.

"How is Mariela?" Trixie wants to know. "Mariela is Mario's 16-year-old daughter, who lives in Miami," she adds for Maggie's benefit.

"She's just fine. Shopping constantly and trying to make

me believe it's for Christmas gifts."

"How did her audition go?" Shanelle asks. We all know Mario pulled a string or two so his drop-dead-gorgeous daughter could try out for a new teen TV drama.

"She got a callback but then she flubbed her lines." He meets my gaze. "She didn't practice enough. Just like for the pageant."

Mariela was a shoo-in to win Teen Princess of the Everglades but then in the finale not only tripped over her evening gown but delivered a catastrophic answer to the final question. She placed fifth and was not happy about it.

"It could've just been nerves," Trixie suggests, charitable as ever.

"Nerves aren't her problem." Mario finishes his coffee. "Failing to prepare is."

Pop pipes up. "And how is Consuela doing?" He's much higher on Mariela's mother than we three queens are.

Mario chuckles and shakes his head. "Prepare yourselves, ladies! She's talking about entering Ms. Florida."

"But she has to be married to compete!" Trixie cries.

The Ms. America pageant of which I am the proud title-holder is the nation's foremost pageant for married women.

"I think she's got that part well in hand," Mario replies.

I detect chagrin in his voice. "Do you mean, with Hector?" I'm referring to the married man with whom Consuela was catting around as recently as last month. Maybe she finally succeeded in prodding him to leave his wife.

Mario shakes his head. I'll have to get that story later.

I take a deep breath. This is potentially big news, on a few levels. For one thing, Consuela getting married presumably means she'll stop making a play for Mario. I shouldn't care but I do.

From a pageant point-of-view, this is potentially alarming. Consuela is a total bombshell. If she becomes a contestant—and is smart enough to do one of her amazing pole-dancing routines as her talent—she could well win her state. Meaning

I'd encounter her again at the national competition, where I will crown my successor.

I know I'm getting way ahead of myself but my stomach drops when I imagine the horror of Consuela Machado winning the crown and succeeding me as Ms. America. How in the world could I relinquish my beloved tiara to her? And be forced to smile the entire time as if I were thrilled to do so?

I can't let myself think about that. It's too appalling a scenario. With everything else going on in my life, I'm frazzled enough.

Mario takes his leave vowing to return in an hour to go running with me. He claims he could use the exercise. The man is as well muscled as a Ford Mustang.

"Normally I wouldn't approve of you running around in these temperatures with a head cold," my mother tells me. "But I'm for anything to get you closer to that Mario. You're healthy. You'd get over the flu."

After Pop and Maggie leave for their day trip to Minneapolis, I place a call to Detective Dembek to inquire if the department found anything of interest at Damsgard. She tells me they're still combing through Ingrid's computer and desk files.

"We'll return Mrs. Svendsen's Mercedes later today," she says. "And I let her sister know that we released the body to the funeral home last night."

So the burial won't be delayed, nor the reading of the will. Maggie will be pleased on that count. "Anything good from the surveillance cameras outside the Giant W?" I ask.

"We've identified almost all the people who ran outside right after the shot was fired. Naturally we're talking to them. We haven't turned up anything of value yet. Nor were there any fingerprints on the note sent to that boy Kevin."

That's no surprise. "Maybe the shots taken by the *Winona Post* photographer would be useful." I remember Trixie swatting at the man with her elf cap when he attempted to photograph Ingrid's bleeding corpse. "He was taking pictures of the crowd before the ceremony began."

"Yes, analyzing those photos is another way to confirm that we did GSR tests on everyone who was present."

I'm now enough of an aficionado that I know GSR stands for "gunshot residue."

"I've also begun to talk with some committee friends of Mrs. Svendsen," Detective Dembek goes on. "Unfortunately neither Mayor Chambers nor Mr. Fitch from the Giant W have been able to shed any light on the matter."

I've already concluded that neither of them could be guilty. They were in enough proximity to Ingrid to have shot her but the killer disposed of the gun and surgical gloves in aisle fourteen while the lights were still out. I was standing behind both the mayor and the suit so I know they were on the dais the entire time. I suppose they could have handed off the gun and gloves to an accomplice but that would've been hard to pull off.

Even though Detective Dembek thinks her homicide investigation skills are rusty, I'd say she's doing a fine job. I bring her up to speed on the visits from Priscilla Pembroke and Peter Svendsen and explain why I'm suspicious of them both. Finally, even though I'm conflicted about it, and even though my father would go ballistic if he knew, I share my concerns about Maggie. "She doesn't really seem like the type and I know it's shocking even to consider that she might have killed her own sister—"

"Murderers are so often next of kin."

I have heard that sad fact. "She might say something revealing during tomorrow's reading of the will. Maybe you should be there." I know I'll be in attendance, at least in a manner of speaking. I'll be eavesdropping from the secret room. I can't wait.

We chat for a bit longer then end the call. Trixie waylays me as I'm about to dress for my run. "I found a great place to take your mom to get her out of the house," she whispers. We duck into my room for a confab. "The Polish Cultural Institute and Museum."

"They have one of those here?"

"Can you believe it? Detective Dembek said there's a large Polish community in Winona and there must be. Anyway, with all the exhibits and the gift shop I can keep her there for hours. But they close at 3."

"So I've got to get cracking with the search as soon as Mario and I are done with the run." If I were a lesser beauty queen, I'd skip the run. But given the calories I've been ingesting, I have to exercise. I want to maximize lots of things in my life but not my blimp potential.

"What are you wearing to go running?" Trixie wants to know.

I show off my triple-waistband black capris—which streamline the hips and minimize the booty—and my lightweight hot pink performance jacket.

"I love that shirring on the front," Trixie purrs. "Very feminine. What about to hold back your hair?"

I produce my plum-colored chunky-knit headband with the rear button detail.

"I want one!" she cries, the best reaction you can get from a fellow fashionista.

Mario returns to Damsgard perfectly outfitted for a cold-weather run in a flash all-black outfit. He cocks his head at the statue holding pride of place in Windom Park, across the street from Damsgard. "Let's stretch there," he suggests.

Our running shoes crunch on the icy snow sparkling in the December sunshine as we approach the fountain—of course shut down for winter—over which the statue presides. She is We-No-Nah, the Dakota Indian girl for whom the town is named. She's depicted shielding her eyes as she gazes into the distance, pelicans and turtles at her feet.

Mario reads from the plaque. " 'Legend tells of her love for a simple hunter instead of the warrior chosen by her father. Rather than marry a man she didn't love, We-No-Nah climbed to the top of a bluff overlooking the river, proclaimed her true love and jumped to her death.' "

He falls silent. I feel his eyes on my face. Finally he speaks again. "Most of us don't have to go to such extraordinary lengths for love."

This is a little heavy for me. The L word has no place in any conversation I have with Mario, even if we're talking about a headstrong Indian girl who died centuries ago.

I make my voice light. "Those pelicans fell down on the job. They should've caught her before she hit the ground." I jog in place a few times. "Come on, let's go," I say, and off I tear. Mario follows, as I knew he would.

One of these days he and I are going to have to talk about what the heck we're doing. That'll be a serious discussion. But I'm far from ready to have it.

CHAPTER NINE

"Who's that on your porch?" Mario wants to know when we finish our circuit and come to a panting stop in Windom Park.

I double over, my hands on my thighs, and squint in the direction of Damsgard. Indeed there is a woman on the porch. I know immediately who she is. I recognize her chic gray parka with real shearling at the collar and cuffs. "That's Priscilla Pembroke! She's come back." I pull Mario behind the gazebo so Priscilla won't see us and explain who she is. "She's looking for something," I add.

"No doubt about it."

We watch as she bends over and feels around the base of the topiary. We've already seen her lift the holiday welcome mat and peer underneath.

I grab Mario's arm. "She must be looking for a key! She wants to break into the house." Boy, was I right to peg Priscilla as nervy. I wonder what she's after? Obviously she came back for something. It's safe to say this behavior doesn't remove her from my suspects list. I gesture for Mario to follow me and we make our way toward the house.

Priscilla sees us as we mount the steps to the porch. "Hello!" She makes a good show of appearing delighted that we've returned, which I doubt is true. She gives Mario an approving once-over. "Who's your handsome friend?" she asks me.

"This is Mario Suave, the host of *America's Scariest Ghost Stories*. Mario, Priscilla Pembroke."

"I *knew* I'd seen you before!" Priscilla bats her lashes coquettishly. "I'm an actor, you know." She throws out her right arm in a gesture I'm quickly getting familiar with. " 'The crown and comfort of my life, your favor, I do give lost; for I do feel it gone, but know not how it went!' " She regards Mario with the same expectant look she gave me a few times yesterday.

"Shakespeare?" he guesses.

"Hermione in *The Winter's Tale*. A role I love. Such a majestic character, isn't she? So dignified. Possessing such serenity in the face of such rage and insults. I played her here in Winona, you know. At the Shakespeare festival."

"I'm sure you were marvelous," Mario says, and Priscilla beams. "Do you find many opportunities to act here in Winona?"

"Oh, I don't live *here*. I live in Manhattan. I flew in yesterday for poor Ingrid's funeral."

"I'm amazed you heard so quickly about her death," I say.

"Oh"—Priscilla's gaze flutters about—"I have friends here. From my festival days." She steps aside so I can unlock the front door to the house.

I make no move to do so. "I have to say I'm surprised to see you. You left so suddenly yesterday."

"Oh"—more fluttering—"I had a call I just had to deal with. You know how it goes. There is something I'd love to chat about with you, though." She steps closer to the front door.

I glance at my sport watch as if I'm terribly busy. "Now isn't the best time. How about I call you later? Why don't you give me your cell number?"

Again she glances at the door. Clearly I'm thwarting her. It's sort of enjoyable. She plasters on a fake smile and leans forward confidentially. "You know tomorrow is Friday the

13th."

"I believe it is."

She lowers her voice. "And the honor rituals are always on Friday the 13th." She glances at Mario as if reluctant to elaborate in his earshot.

I arch my brows and say nothing.

She's forced to go on. "I propose that we hold an honor ritual tomorrow. No offense to *you*," she winks at Mario, "but just for us girls. I'm sure you'd find it quite worthwhile, Happy."

"It does sound interesting." That's no lie. "But tomorrow is Ingrid's funeral. I'm not sure it's appropriate—"

"Oh, the timing couldn't be more perfect. Not only is Freyja the goddess of sexual pleasure, eroticism and desire"— she flicks a glance in Mario's direction—"she is also known for selecting the heroic dead and transporting them to the realm of the gods."

This Freyja sounds like quite a piece of work. "Well, then why don't you give me your cell number," I repeat, because I really do want a way to track Priscilla down if need be. "That way I can call you later to set it up."

Her eyes brighten and she claps her hands. "Splendid! I'll bring everything we need. You won't have to worry about a thing." She gives me her number then blows a kiss our way as she walks down the stairs. " 'Parting is such sweet sorrow that I shall say good night till it be morrow!' "

Even *I* know that one. "*Romeo and Juliet*," I mutter as Mario and I enter the house. As we head to the kitchen for water, I tell him more about my initial encounter with this mysterious thespian from the Big Apple, who by the way isn't exhibiting much grief over her supposed best friend's demise.

"Why did you agree to this honor ritual thing?" he wants to know.

"It will give me a chance to observe her." We sit at the table in the nook and I jot down Priscilla's number so I don't forget it. "Maybe I can let her think she's on her own in the house for a while when actually I'm watching her. Then I might be able to find out what she's after."

"I don't like it. Remember, you know nothing about this woman. She might be dangerous."

"She's certainly up to something." I swig my water. "But don't worry. There'll be lots of people in the house."

"That won't help if she's got a gun. And I don't like that she didn't want me to be here."

"She knows you could take her down." I flex my biceps. "She should know I could, too. Even though I'm sick with a cold."

He doesn't smile. "You've been lucky so far, Happy. But some day your luck will run out."

"I've got my trusty pepper spray." Jason wanted me to get a gun and that was my compromise. It even helped me fend off a crocodile.

Shanelle joins us, wearing jeans and a berry-colored pointelle-knit sweater with batwing sleeves. She gestures to her watch.

"I know. The search." I rise to my feet. "But get a load of this, Shanelle. We just caught Priscilla Pembroke ferreting around on the porch trying to find the key to the front door."

Shanelle's eyes fly open. "We best change the locks! So even if she does get her hands on some spare key or other, she still won't get inside."

"That's a good idea. I'm sure Pop'll help." Nothing makes my father feel more useful than a list of Honey Do's.

Mario downs the last of his water. "I have to get going myself. Jennifer will kill me if I'm late for the shoot."

I've met his producer Jennifer Maddox. By now, with all of Mario's sudden trips around the country following me, she's probably not my biggest booster.

"And I *am* going to be here tomorrow night," he adds. "Whether Priscilla Pembroke wants me to or not."

That's certainly good news from my point-of-view. And even better, I bet Mario will be packing heat. Unbeknownst to almost everybody, including Shanelle, Mario does some work for the F.B.I., most of it having to do with the entertainment industry. He confided that secret job to me while we were on Oahu. I am very gratified he trusted me with it.

"I'll call you after the shoot," he says as I let him out the front door. "Wish me luck with the ghosts and goblins."

It's amazing, I think as I push the door closed. Mario has been around only a few hours but already it feels totally normal to have him here.

And I'm already anticipating the sadness of having him gone.

Worrisome.

Shanelle comes out to the foyer. "We got to talk about that, girl."

"Not now. Now we search." The cops have combed the entire house but nevertheless I view this as a useful exercise.

"Don't think you can put me off forever," Shanelle warns.

I ignore her. "So where do we start?"

"I don't even know what we're looking for."

"Anything weird. Anything bizarre. Anything that doesn't add up."

She points at the front door through which Mario just exited. "That right there doesn't add up."

"Not now! I promise we'll talk about Mario later." I set my hands on my hips. "The cops still have Ingrid's desk files and computer. I say we start in her bedroom."

We take the stairs two at a time but are paralyzed at the threshold to Ingrid's bedroom. It is glorious, like everything else at Damsgard, decorated from floor to ceiling in the palest of yellows. Filmy fabric drapes the windows and shades the four-poster bed, covered with a white matelassé spread and half a dozen sumptuous pillows. Spectacular orchids perch atop both graceful white dressers. And the Christmas tree beside the fireplace is adorned with yellow balls and beads and ribbons. The whole room has a golden glow.

"Snooping in here," I whisper to Shanelle, "feels like more

of an intrusion than snooping anywhere else in this house."

"That's because this is Ingrid's most private place," she whispers back. "But do you want to figure out who murdered her or not?"

"You start with that dresser and I'll start with this one."

There's no way around it: much as I try, I can't stop feeling darn ballsy pawing through Ingrid's undergarments and nightgowns and scarves and jewelry. "She had some nice pieces," I whisper across the room to Shanelle, holding up a floral brooch with aqua-colored enamel petals and pavé crystals on the keenly worked brass stem.

"That looks like Oscar de la Renta to me," Shanelle whispers. "Why are we whispering?"

"I don't know. Reverence for Ingrid's spirit, I suppose. I'm moving on to the closet." And it's there, in the inner zipped pocket of a worn black tote in pebbled leather, that at last I find an item that seems weird to me.

Shanelle pads over to join me. "What's that?"

"It's the receipt from a body shop." I flatten the crumpled slip of paper against the top of the nearest dresser. "What's bizarre is that it's in Minneapolis. Why would she go to a body shop a two-hour drive away?"

Shanelle shrugs. "Maybe that's her favorite one. If I had a fancy car like hers I'd probably go to a special body shop myself."

"True." My cell beeps with a text. "Shoot, this is Trixie already. She's warning us that she and my mom are on their way back."

"Let's make a quick pass through the third floor," Shanelle suggests. "There could be some really good stuff up there."

A rarely used third floor indeed would make a prime hiding place.

Shanelle and I race up the much less impressive staircase to the third level, which covers a small fraction of the footprint of the house. Here there are three rooms in a state of disrepair. The walls look like they were painted decades ago and the hardwood floors haven't been varnished in ages. The rooms are relatively clean, though, and store items like suitcases and an ancient sewing machine and stacks of boxes filled with who knows what. Actually we don't know what's in the third room, because it's locked.

I try twisting the doorknob one more time.

"It's not going to open this time, either," Shanelle tells me, "no matter how much we want to get in there."

I hear a commotion below, then the sound of my mother's voice. "I'll be back," I warn the stubborn doorknob in my best Arnold Schwarzenegger voice.

We find Trixie and my mom in the kitchen unpacking groceries. "How was the Polish museum?" I inquire.

"Very informative." Trixie sets several bags of dried fruit on the granite counter, alongside light and dark brown sugar. "It had lots of documents and parish records and old newspapers."

"Handcrafted items, too," my mother says, "like embroideries. And cherished family heirlooms." She glares at me to signal that in her judgment I don't cherish our Przybyszewski heirlooms to the extent I should.

"It's in a building that used to be the headquarters of a lumber company," Trixie goes on. "Apparently that was a good business here until about a hundred years ago."

"Then kaput!" My mother twists open a bottle of brandy and gives it a good sniff. Even though it looks like the cheap stuff, it appears to pass muster. "Where's that Bundt pan we bought?" she asks Trixie.

"Don't you and Maggie have to bake your fruitcakes at the same time?" I ask.

"Why?" my mother demands. "The two fruitcakes have to be tasted at the same time but nobody said they have to be baked at the same time."

"You like to make yours early?" Shanelle asks.

"Never you mind the details." My mother looks away then relents. "Let's just say I like mine to steep."

I glance at the brandy. I'm getting the picture.

CHAPTER TEN

We three queens leave my mother alone in the kitchen and huddle in the dining room as I bring Trixie up to speed on our search. We're debating whether we should try to break into the locked room while my mother's occupied with her baking when the doorbell rings. This time it's Peter Svendsen.

We relieve him of his black wool coat. Again he's wearing cords, which today he's paired with a cable-knit sweater. As I close the front door I note that the sun is already low in the sky and snowflakes have begun to fall. Night is not far off.

He passes on our offer of coffee. "I can't stay. But I wanted to ask about the house tour on Saturday. I'm hoping you'll go ahead with it despite the circumstances."

Peter tells us that Damsgard always participates in Winona's holiday tour of Victorian homes, all specially decorated for Christmas.

"Traditionally it's a candlelight tour from 4 to 7. A number of homes are open to the public but Damsgard is always the showstopper," he assures us.

"The house is so beautifully decorated," Trixie says. "It would be a shame if people didn't get to enjoy it the way we have."

"I see no reason not to go ahead with it," I say. To me it sounds like a good opportunity to meet more locals, which could be useful. "Maybe we could put up a photo of Ingrid and have visitors sign a guest book with their memories."

Peter looks less than thrilled with that idea but is too gracious to pooh pooh it. "One other thing. By any chance have you run across the plans for Ingrid's renovation?"

Shanelle and I glance at each other. In fact we did come upon them when we were scouring Ingrid's bedroom. They were rolled up on top of an overstuffed chair next to the hearth, as if she'd been studying them while enjoying a fire. "I think I *may* have seen them," I say.

"I'd like to take them with me, if you don't mind," Peter says.

Since I can't think of a reason to say no, I run upstairs and bring them back down.

Peter can't resist rolling them open then and there. Within seconds he begins shaking his head as if he can't believe what he's seeing. "So the rumors were right!"

"Rumors?" Shanelle repeats.

Peter sets his jaw as his dark eyes scan the architectural drawings. "I heard what she was planning but now to see it with my own eyes—" He rolls the plans back up, his movements jerky and fast.

"Are the renovations more extensive than you imagined?" I guess.

"It's absurd what she was planning," Peter spits. "As if Damsgard could be improved in any way. And as if *she* had the right to make any changes at all, let alone changes on this scale."

"Did you discuss it with her?" Trixie wants to know.

"Talking to that woman was like talking to a wall. She was going to do what she was going to do." He lowers his voice. "Unless I took legal action."

"I'm no lawyer but I'd guess you could make a good case," I say. "Especially if she wasn't really the owner of the house." I'm still not sure that's true but now is not the time to challenge Peter on that point.

"Ingrid was nothing more than a tenant," Peter snaps, "a glorified tenant." He turns away and bites his lip as if attempting to gain control of his emotions. Then, "Sorry. I shouldn't be getting into this with you. I better go." He grabs his coat and out he goes, slamming the front door shut behind him.

"Boy, he and his stepmother did not get along," Shanelle observes.

"I'm surprised Ingrid would make renovations to a house she didn't own," Trixie says. "Maybe she was in denial."

"Or maybe she figured she'd be in the house for the rest of her life," I say, "and so she wanted the house the way she wanted it."

"And maybe she had deeper pockets than Peter," Shanelle suggests. "So his threat of legal action didn't faze her."

Trixie shakes her head. "That makes me sad, family members saying they're going to sue one another."

"What makes me even sadder is family members killing one another," I mutter.

"Do you mean Peter?" Shanelle wants to know. "Or Maggie?"

"They're both on my list," I whisper. We're still in the foyer but I glance toward the kitchen. My mother's hearing is fantastic when she wants it to be. "And when I look at it from Peter's point-of-view, he had a strong motive to want Ingrid dead. She was only in her late sixties. She could have stayed in this house for decades. And maybe she would've gotten away with making those big renovations she wanted."

"Then he would have had to watch this house get changed," Trixie breathes, "and he thinks it's perfect the way it is." She looks around. "I have to say I agree with him."

We're silent. My phone beeps with a text. It's Mario. *Can I come over?*

As if I would ever say no. *Sure! How did your shoot go? I'll be right over.*

"Mario's on his way." I make for the stairs. "I have to

shower something fierce." I'm still wearing the clothes I went running in.

I decide that the evening's outfit will be my slim-cut charcoal gray heathered-cotton dress, which features an elegant bateau neckline and shirred side seams. I pair it with black opaque tights and my trendy new suede booties with faux snake-embossed trim. No one will be surprised to see the boots sport 4-inch heels. After I medicate myself with yet another round of cold remedies, I apply a light makeup and leave my hair loose. I've been ready only a minute or two when Mario arrives. He brushes past me to halt in the foyer. Somehow he doesn't seem his usual calm self.

I take his soft camel-colored overcoat. "You okay?"

He smiles but it's a wan effort. "It was kind of a"—he hesitates as if he's trying to find the right word—"surprising afternoon."

"I'm excited to hear about it." I lead him toward the kitchen. He may be upset but he still looks dreamy in jeans, a plaid shirt, and a lightweight navy sweater with a quarter-zip and mock turtleneck. "Trixie's making Bocce Balls," I tell him. "Have you ever had one?"

"Whatever it is, I'll try it."

He must've had some afternoon. We amble into the kitchen to watch Trixie pour amaretto and OJ over ice then top the concoctions with maraschino cherries. Trixie's changed, too, into a sporty knit dress with three-quarter sleeves and color-blocked stripes in dark blues and grays. My mom fusses with the knobs on the oven then joins us.

"Whatever you're baking smells delicious," Mario tells her.

"Maybe you can judge the fruitcake bakeoff," she replies coyly.

"I'll tell you about that later," I say to his questioning look then suggest we all repair to the living room. "First I want to hear about your shoot."

Shanelle joins us looking adorable in tight black jeans and

an ivory floral chiffon top with a smocked bodice, bloused elbow sleeves, and a billowy peplum hem. We settle on the velvet sofas and spend a few minutes admiring all the garlands and poinsettias and especially the tree, its fairy lights and ornaments glittering.

"So the shoot was at a house on Cummings Street," Mario begins. "Over the years quite a few people have claimed the place is haunted."

"No offense to you but who believes that crap?" my mother wants to know.

"Mom—"

"No, it's okay, Happy. I'm not insulted. Your view is shared by many people," Mario assures my mom.

She preens but I cringe. Sometimes I'd prefer my mother keep her opinions to herself, particularly those regarding my marriage to Jason and her romantic aspirations for me where Mario is concerned.

"I do believe in ghosts," Trixie says. "And I want to know what kind of spirit haunts that house."

"One that likes to make a racket." Mario gulps his drink. "A couple of students from the university lived there for a while but eventually couldn't take it anymore. They said it was total pandemonium. Banging on the air ducts and crashing noises from the furnace room down in the basement—"

He falls silent. A log tumbles in the fireplace, sending sparks shooting up the chimney like winter fireflies.

"You"—Shanelle clears her throat—"*you* didn't hear anything, did you?"

It takes him a few seconds to respond. Then, "Not only did I hear things"—his dark eyes gaze into mine—"I saw them."

CHAPTER ELEVEN

Trixie squeals, Shanelle gasps, and my mother slaps her thigh. "What kind of cockamamie story is this?"

"Let Mario tell it!" I cry. Even though the fire is blazing, I will admit that I feel a chill. "What exactly happened, Mario?"

He swallows. Then, "We heard sounds like china breaking. Even though I'm positive my crew and I were alone in the house."

"Where were the sounds coming from?" Trixie asks.

"The basement."

Everyone who's ever watched a horror movie knows that's the worst possible place for inexplicable sounds to be coming from. "I hope you didn't go down there to investigate."

"I had to. It was unbelievably cold." He gives me a meaningful look.

I guess what he's getting at. "You mean … deathly cold?"

"Like a tomb?" Trixie whispers.

"Cold like Minnesota!" my mother yowls. "Have you people forgotten we're in Minnesota? And it's the middle of December?"

My mother's outburst kills the eerie mood, at least briefly. "Those sounds must've come from an audiotape playing somewhere," Shanelle says. "Somebody must've been playing a trick on you."

"That's certainly what I would think. But then"—Mario

hesitates—"then we *saw* something we couldn't explain. It was in one of the bedrooms."

"What was it?" I'm almost afraid to ask.

"A shadow on the wall." Mario gazes into the distance as if he's remembering the spectral form. "The shadow of a man."

"And it didn't come from you or your crew?" Trixie breathes.

"It couldn't have. None of us were in that room. We were in the hallway outside, looking in. Believe it or not we were able to catch the shadow on tape. That is, until—"

We wait. I for one am breathless.

"Until it disappeared under the closet door," he finishes.

"You mean," I say, "it slithered underneath?"

He nods. "Pretty much."

Shanelle frowns. "Slithering is not good."

I shiver. I might have to sleep with my mom tonight. "I bet you opened that closet door." Mario is so brave!

"I tried to. It was locked. I couldn't get it open."

Shanelle and I glance at each other. I can't help but think about that locked room right here at Damsgard. I'll wait until morning light to try to get in there. I return my eyes to Mario. He seems truly shaken. "Is this the first time anything like this has happened on one of your shoots?"

"This is a first," he confirms.

He and I have never discussed it but I've always had the idea that even though Mario hosts *America's Scariest Ghost Stories*, he is himself a skeptic where the supernatural is concerned. Somehow carrying an FBI badge and believing in ghosts don't go together in my mind.

"Well," my mother chortles, "you'll get your best ratings ever with that show!"

"I'll tell you one thing." Mario manages a chuckle. "When Jennifer showed the suits back in L.A. our tape from today's shoot, they stopped giving me flak about coming out here to Minnesota."

"They'll want you to shoot here all week," my mother predicts.

If that happens I'll send those ghosts on Cummings Street a thank-you card.

We're recovering from the ghost story by debating where to go for dinner when Ingrid's land line rings. "I'll get it," I offer. It is my turn. Shanelle and Trixie have been fielding almost all the incoming calls. "Hello?"

The caller immediately piques my interest. "That you, Mrs. Svendsen?" He booms so loudly I have to hold the phone away from my ear. "I got something you'll want to hear about Galena Lang."

I may be doped up with cold meds but I immediately grasp that this is more intriguing than your typical phone call. "I'm so sorry but I've got a head cold and I didn't quite catch what you said?"

"You can't hear me? I'll talk louder."

As if that were possible.

"It's Hubble," he hollers. "And I got some confidential info on Galena Lang. Just like you wanted."

Now I grant you, if I were a totally upfront beauty queen who didn't have a secret investigative agenda, I would confess to this Hubble person that I am not Ingrid Svendsen. In fact, I'd probably go so far as to inform him that Mrs. Svendsen can no longer be found at Damsgard but is holed up at the Lang Funeral Home on Frontenac Street and not in a position to take phone calls, either. Instead I say: "That's good news. What can you tell me?"

Then he gets cagey. "Not over the phone. Plus I'm owed my payment."

"Your payment. Right. How much do I owe you?"

"Three hundred dollars. Just like we talked about."

"That sounds right," I lie.

"Cash. Like last time."

"Yes, of course." I try to think fast, not always my strong suit. "Will this be the last payment I'll be making?"

He roars with laughter. "I doubt it! You'll want me to dig more when you get a load of this."

I am now dying to hear this dirt on Galena the Goth Mortician. "Where do you suggest we meet?"

"How about where we met last time?"

Darn! "Maybe you could jog my memory. I just can't bring things to mind the way I used to."

"At the lake, remember? By the boat landing."

"Right, right."

"How's about nine tonight? Shouldn't be too many people out there at that hour."

"Nine tonight is good." Then it dawns on me there's another problem with this scheme. "You know, since my congestion is so bad—"

"It is bad," he says. "You really sound different."

"It's very bad," I assert, "and it might get even worse if I'm out in the cold. So I wonder if I might send my niece to meet you. She'll have the cash."

"I suppose that's okay. How much does she know about all this?"

"You can share all the details with her," I assure him. "She's one of my closest confidantes."

"What's her name?"

My mind cranks. "Trudy. Trudy Barnett. Lovely redhead. You'll like her."

"I'll see her then." Click.

Now I have to get Trixie—sorry, Trudy—on board.

Everyone is chatting about dinner when I return to the living room. I sit down next to Trixie. "You want me to figure out who murdered Ingrid, right? I have a way you can help."

"If it doesn't involve haunted houses, I'm in," she tells me. Like every beauty queen worth her sash, Trixie is game for anything.

"No haunted houses," I tell her. "But it does involve a late-night clandestine meeting by the lake where you'll trade cash for information."

"What?" Trixie screeches.

I hasten to explain. "I'd do it myself but he'd recognize my voice. He mistook me for Ingrid on the phone because he thinks she has a cold and sounds different. And we can't have Shanelle do it because she doesn't look like she could be Ingrid's niece."

"I'm not pale enough," Shanelle says.

"And Mario can't do it," I go on, "because Hubble might recognize him from TV."

"I could do it!" my mother cries. "You could've said you'd send Ingrid's friend instead of her niece. You never give me enough credit." My mother glares at me. "But I don't mind too much because what I want is dinner." She rises to her feet. "I'm taking the fruitcake out of the oven. Then I want to go eat."

"Yes, let's," Shanelle says. "I missed lunch and I'm starving."

I missed lunch, too—quite the rarity for me—so I'm also ravenous. "Let's swing past the lake so we can scope out the location then go get dinner. Plus I have to go to the ATM." Three hundred smackers is a lot to dole out for what might be useless information but maybe I can expense it to the pageant. Mr. Cantwell has said more than once that my sleuthing is excellent P.R. for the organization.

Trixie gripes about my changing her name to Trudy but, as I expected, she understands that I blurted it out in the heat of the moment. In short order she courageously accepts her mission. Mario, Shanelle, and I will keep an eye on her from a hidden vantage point, which all of us find reassuring. While we grab a hasty meal at a café popular with students from Winona State, we explain to Mario what little we know about Galena Lang.

"Maybe she and Ingrid had an ancient feud," Trixie says.

I can tell Trixie's getting into her role. "The only time anybody hires a P.I.," I say, "which I'm pretty sure is what this guy Hubble is, is when they need to check somebody out."

"Who would need to check out the local mortician?" Shanelle wants to know. "I mean, even if you want to use her services you don't need to know whether she bounces checks or is secretly married."

"If they were feuding," Trixie says, "it's weird that Galena was Ingrid's mortician."

"Who knew?" I say. "I got the idea Maggie picked Lang Funeral Home because it's the most established place in town. Anyway, Trixie, remember to find out what Ingrid told Hubble about why she wanted Galena Lang investigated."

"If she told him anything," Mario says.

"I want to get a load of this Galena Lang." My mother swipes her lips with a napkin. "I hope she has the good sense not to put Goth makeup on the newly deceased."

We drop my mom back at Damsgard so she can begin "steeping" her fruitcake. I note Pop's rental car is once again in the driveway. So Maggie and Pop are back from their Minneapolis day trip. Let's hope the love triangle doesn't erupt into another homicide in the next hour.

We three queens plus Mario return to Lake Winona driving two cars: our rental plus Ingrid's silver Mercedes. To make sure that Hubble doesn't see us, we park on a residential side street a few blocks from the boat landing. I'm sure the lake is a lovely recreational area on a warm day but now when it's pitch dark out, barely twenty degrees, and deserted, it's a little spooky.

We boldly bundled Trixie into Ingrid's warmest coat so she wouldn't freeze. It's a delicious garment: a mid-thigh black puffer with a cinched silhouette and fur trim on the hood.

"I feel positively toasty in this," she says as we gather curbside to review her instructions.

"It's styling, too," Shanelle observes.

"I agree. And that's good because being well-dressed always gives me confidence," Trixie says.

Spoken like a true beauty queen.

"We'll be watching you from the rental car just up the

street from the boat landing," Mario assures her. "Don't worry about a thing."

"I won't. In fact I'm kind of excited!" Her hazel eyes shine.

Trixie gets in the Mercedes and drives off. We wait a few minutes then take a different route to park in our prearranged spot. Mario cuts the engine. We see the Mercedes parked ahead, and Trixie waiting by the boat landing, her breath fogging in the frigid air.

"I'm kind of excited, too," I murmur. "This is like a stakeout."

A few minutes pass before a nondescript Japanese sedan parks behind the Mercedes. A huskily built man in a parka and wool cap emerges and greets Trixie at the boat landing. We watch her hand over the wad of cash stashed in her pocket. Hubble doesn't bother to count the bills.

"He must think Ingrid's good for it," I whisper.

Hubble and Trixie engage in an animated conversation. Every once in a while Hubble glances around as if to make sure no one is observing the tête-à-tête. I always freeze in place when he does that. At one point Trixie's mouth gapes as if she just heard something shocking.

"I am dying to know what he just told her," Shanelle says.

Then Hubble pulls out his wallet and hands Trixie something.

"Good," Mario mutters. "I think she just got his business card."

That was part of her mission, too. We want to be able to contact Hubble again.

Finally the two amble back to their cars and shake hands before parting. We don't budge until both have driven off, then return to Damsgard via a circuitous route.

We find Trixie in her bedroom as prearranged, since it's probably best at this point to keep everything on the QT. Read: keep my mother out of it. Trixie's skin is still pink from the cold and her hazel eyes still shine with excitement.

"What did you find out?" I whisper.

Trixie takes a deep breath. "Mr. Hubble said he thinks Galena might be doing something illegal."

CHAPTER TWELVE

"*Might* be doing something illegal?" I hope I didn't shell out three hundred smackers for "might" be. "What's the illegal thing he thinks Galena's doing? And how is he going to prove it?"

"He doesn't know what the illegal thing is," Trixie says. "Or how he'd prove it."

I shake my head, visualizing my money swirling down a drain.

"Hear me out," Trixie says. "Mr. Hubble told me he found out that Galena nearly filed for bankruptcy back in the fall then all of a sudden she had enough money to go on a trip to England to attend some Goth festival."

"I wonder if she went for Whitby Goth Weekend." Now that he hasn't seen a ghost in a while, Mario's typical self-possession has returned. "I saw something on TV about that. It's gotten to be a pretty big deal. Thousands of people go, from all over the world. Not just Goths, either. Steampunks, metallers, bikers, whatever."

"Anyway," Trixie goes on, "if she's almost bankrupt, how did Galena get the money to go to Europe? Mr. Hubble says he's close to finding out more, if Ingrid is interested. I told him she'd let him know."

"Hubble's information isn't good enough to justify another payment," I say. "Plus he seems too loud and boisterous to be a real P.I."

"He is one all the same," Trixie says. "He used to be a policeman but he told me he can make better money this way."

He sure can. Thanks to me, he's three hundred dollars richer. "What did he tell you about why Ingrid hired him?"

"All he would say was that Ingrid told him Galena was trouble. That's the word he said she used. 'Trouble.' "

"When did she hire him?" Shanelle wants to know.

"About a month and a half ago," Trixie reports.

"So obviously there was bad blood between Galena and Ingrid but we still don't know the source of it," I say. "It had to have been pretty serious if Ingrid went to the trouble and expense to hire a P.I." Now that I've seen his business card, I know for sure that Hubble is a private investigator.

"Why didn't Ingrid just have Mr. Hubble come here to Damsgard for their meetings?" Trixie says. "She lives alone. No one would have been the wiser."

"Maybe she didn't want him to see how rich she is," Shanelle says. "She probably figured his fee would go up if he knew."

That's not a problem I've ever had.

Trixie grimaces. "I felt bad when Mr. Hubble told me he hoped Ingrid felt better soon. I knew that wasn't going to happen."

We're all silent as we ponder Ingrid's sad fate. Then I pipe up again. "Hiring Hubble to investigate Galena Lang is another thing Ingrid was keeping secret. There's a pretty long list now."

"True," Shanelle says. "Secret number two: that she worshipped the heathen goddess Freyja. Number three: that she didn't own Damsgard."

"Really?" Mario says.

"That's what Ingrid's stepson Peter Svendsen claims," I say. "We don't know it for a fact yet. We'll find out tomorrow when the will is read." I am really looking forward to that. I have high hopes that it will be a revealing moment.

As we say our good nights, I realize I soon may be adding

Galena's name to my suspects list. She might have had a motive for murder. Clearly there was recent conflict between her and Ingrid if Ingrid hired Hubble to investigate Galena just six weeks ago.

I walk Mario downstairs to the front door. I won't see him again until late tomorrow because he has shoots lined up all day. I wonder if Winona's ghosts have gotten the memo.

He steps outside. "It's hard to believe this house is missing any Christmas decorations but you know what I can't find? Mistletoe." He winks at me as he heads down the snowy path to the sidewalk. "And believe me, I've looked."

That gets me shivering again. But this time there's no ghost in sight.

It's only after I'm ready for bed that I remember to text Priscilla Pembroke about conducting one of the Friday-the-13th rituals for Freyja tomorrow evening here at Damsgard. She replies instantly that she would be honored to preside and will bring all the necessary accouterments.

Then another idea occurs to me. *Will you be coming to Damsgard earlier in the day for the reading of Ingrid's will?*

Perhaps, she replies. *The dear always did say she would leave me something.*

I'm slipping downstairs to get a glass of water when I hear voices coming from the room Pop and Maggie are sharing. Since Maggie is among my suspects, the tone is agitated, and I am shameless, I tiptoe close to their door to eavesdrop.

"Why shouldn't I have asked her?" Maggie demands. "She's my sister!"

Low muttering sounds, which must come from my father.

"She had more than she knew what to do with," Maggie asserts. "And Donovan and I are the only family she had left. She was a skinflint, is what she was."

My father must've moved closer to the door because now I hear him clearly. "She had a point, that after all these years of working you should have something to retire on."

"Easy for you to say! You have a pension from the police

department. You don't get one of those when you run your own business. Plus you know I never got any help from Donovan's father." Silence, then in a superior tone: "And after tomorrow when I finally get what I deserve, maybe it'll be *me* who doesn't want to get married, not *you*."

I wait a bit longer but that's the end of that conversation. I'd say the two of them retired for the night in less than perfect harmony. That's fine with me.

I hasten to complete my water run. And even though as I return upstairs the Nyquil is beginning to take effect, I am not too addled to grasp the meaning of what I just overheard. To wit: Maggie asked Ingrid for money to help her retire; Ingrid said no; Maggie was seriously irked but she's over it now because she believes that tomorrow, after the reading of Ingrid's will, she'll get her long overdue payday.

Seems to me Ingrid's death came at a pretty convenient time for Maggie. And there's good news in all of this for me: in mere hours Maggie may be so rich she'll no longer have a financial incentive to marry Pop.

Something else may be working in my favor. I perceive the two of them have been out of sync ever since Maggie admitted she stole an inflatable fruitcake from the Giant W. That sort of thing wouldn't sit well with Pop. It doesn't sit well with me, either. And I still think her crime spree may have extended beyond theft to murder.

The next morning I rise to an early alarm. I don't want to miss the chance for a few minutes alone with Pop and I know the best time to catch him is first thing over coffee. Indeed I come upon him alone in the kitchen in his pajamas and robe, sniffing Mom's fruitcake. He's unwrapped some of the cellophane and is holding it up to his nose. He looks enraptured, and having eaten Mom's fruitcake I understand why. I wish she were awake to witness this display.

I pad into the kitchen in my jammies and slippers. "Morning, Pop." I give him a nuzzle. "I'll make the coffee. Maggie still asleep?"

He looks sheepish as he rewraps the fruitcake. "If she doesn't have to get to the salon, she's not an early riser."

I busy myself with the coffeepot. "What did you two do yesterday in Minneapolis?"

He settles at the table in the nook. "I don't want to tell you because you're going to think what you thought before. That she doesn't care what happened to her sister."

I spoon ground coffee into the filter. Maggie probably wanted to go shopping for home décor items. And yes, that would be my assessment.

"That's a lot of hooey," he adds.

"I couldn't help but overhear you two last night," I lie. "Talking about Ingrid refusing to give Maggie money so she could retire."

His face flushes. "That's none of your business."

I pour water into the coffeepot. "When did they have that conversation?"

"I'm pleading the fifth."

Meaning: either the night before Ingrid was shot or the morning of the very day.

"Ingrid should've had more sympathy for Maggie," Pop goes on. "For Donovan, too. Ingrid never understood how hard it was for Maggie to raise Donovan all on her own. She didn't understand anything about being a mother."

I turn on the coffeepot then pivot to face my father. "Those sound like Maggie's words, Pop. Not yours."

He juts his chin. "It's true all the same."

"I know it can't have been easy being Ingrid's sister. I only knew her for a day but it was obvious that she could be hard to get along with. But Maggie's attitude still bothers me."

"You know what bothers me? How you look when you're around Mario."

"We're not talking about Mario."

"Maybe we should be. You're a married woman, my girl."

"I haven't done anything wrong."

"Maybe not yet. But you've thought about it. And that's a

sin."

Technically I don't think it is but I'm not up on the nuances. I turn back around to watch the coffee percolate. It gives me something to do as I debate whether or not to confide in my father.

Even if Pop's advice is sometimes a bit conservative for my taste, it's still pretty solid. And I could use some wisdom. So I plunge ahead. "You're right, Pop. There is something going on between Mario and me. And it's not going away." I see I've got his full attention. "I'm going to tell you something but I need you to keep it to yourself."

"You don't want me to tell your mother."

"She'd go ballistic if she heard this." My father is silent as I explain about Jason's job offer. I pour us each a mug of java and join him at the table. The white lace angels on the Christmas tree listen to my predicament with impassive faces. "So the bottom line is Jason is trying to decide if he wants to take the job and I'm trying to decide if I'll move with him to Charlotte if he does."

My father looks stunned. "You mean you might not? A wife's place is beside her husband."

"Problem is that even though it's ridiculous at my age, it scares me to move away from Cleveland. I've lived there all my life. You're there, and Mom's there, and all my friends except for Trixie and Shanelle. Plus my job is great and they give me so much flexibility. It is true that after Rachel graduates she won't be in Cleveland anymore. She'll be who knows where." I have to collect myself after I say that so I don't start bawling. "I mean, I love all the travel I do for Ms. America but I like being home, too. And home has always been only one place for me."

"What does Mario have to do with all this?" my father wants to know. "Because he's got nothing to do with Cleveland."

"He's just so darn handsome and sexy and successful and exciting! He's sort of unreal. And he's like the road not taken,

Pop. Mario is all the boys I never dated and all the opportunities I never had because I got pregnant and got married at age seventeen."

"And because of that you've got a wonderful daughter and a wonderful husband."

"And I love both of them with all my heart. But all of a sudden my daughter is grown up and about to leave home and my husband isn't the only man I have feelings for."

There. I said it. And even though it makes me a terrible wife, I can't help wanting to know what might happen with Mario. I don't want to give him up. I'm far enough gone that I don't even want to give up the fantasy of Mario.

"Mario has feelings for you, too, my beauty. I can see it." My father's eyes moisten. "Of course, how can he help himself?"

Now there's no way I can stop the tears. "Oh, Pop! I'm just so confused."

CHAPTER THIRTEEN

My father bundles me in a hug. It's such a release just to have a good cry. Especially without makeup on so there's no cosmetic repair I'll have to do afterward.

Eventually I cry myself out. I blow my nose and wipe my eyes and down more coffee and even though I'm as deeply conflicted as ever, I do feel better. "I don't want you to make any rash decisions either, Pop."

"You mean where Maggie's concerned." He looks out the window at the rear garden, where weak sunlight is revealing a fresh layer of snow. "She is pretty traditional so I suppose it shouldn't surprise me that she's so fixed on getting married."

"Even if *she* is, *you* don't have to be."

"I know that, my beauty." He rubs my leg. "Your old pop didn't live all these years without learning a thing or two."

Something occurred to me first thing this morning. "You know, Pop, Maggie might find out this afternoon that she'll inherit Damsgard. If that happens, won't she want to move here to Winona? It's where she grew up, it's a lovely community, this house is gorgeous—"

"And she has a business in Cleveland. And a son there, too."

"But if she had the money to retire from her business, she would. And Donovan would probably go where she goes." Since he lives with her now and "works" at her salon. "And she would want you to move with her, I know she would." Pop would be tempted, too, especially if Rachel, Jason, and I all move. Pop's condo doesn't compare to Damsgard. And moving to Winona would be a fresh start for him, which might look pretty darn attractive.

That would leave Mom with no family in Cleveland. Though I suppose after their divorce, Pop doesn't really qualify as "family" for her anymore.

My father shakes his head. "Don't do what your mother does. Don't get ahead of yourself."

I do make that mistake. I take a deep breath and try to tamp down my anxiety. "And of course there's the whole other thing. I really am worried that Maggie—"

He raises a hand to forestall me. "I don't want to hear another word about that. Maggie might not be grieving like you want her to but she had nothing to do with what happened to her sister. Are we clear on that?"

"Fine. Okay." Not that this erases Maggie from my suspects list.

"You want a piece of advice from your old pop? Do what I do when I need to talk something out. Go talk to a priest."

My skepticism must show on my face.

He goes on. "I know your mother always says priests have no business counseling people about marriage because they've never been married themselves. But sometimes they know more than you think they do." He points to the ceiling. "Because they're getting inspiration from the man upstairs."

"I'll think about it." Unlike my parents I'm a lapsed Catholic, but it's true that I always find comfort when I step inside a church.

A short while later as I'm donning the same charcoal-gray dress I wore the prior night—it's the only funeral-appropriate outfit I brought here to Winona—I get a call from Detective Dembek.

"Good morning, dear," she says. "I thought you might be interested in seeing the photos the *Winona Post* photographer took at the Giant W opening."

"Oh, I am! Is there anybody in the photos that your department didn't test for gunshot residue?"

"A few people. There are still some we can't identify, both in the photos and in the surveillance video from outside the store."

We agree to meet before Ingrid's service. I finish dressing and make for the Lutheran church, which turns out to be a lovely, simple structure of beige stone with exceptionally gorgeous stained-glass windows.

"Winona is the stained-glass capital of the country, you know." Detective Dembek is wearing the same camel-colored walker coat she sported at the crime scene. She escorts me through snow flurries to her black-and-white, parked a few blocks away so we're not seen together by anyone arriving early for the funeral. We both judge it better that no one know we're in cahoots. "As a matter of fact," she goes on, "stained glass is how the Svendsen family made their money. Some years ago the son Peter took over the business from his father."

I didn't know that. We settle in the rear of the police car and the detective turns on her tablet to access the file with the photos. There are quite a few of them. I pay careful attention to the shots of the crowd, all taken before Ingrid was gunned down. On one shot I catch my breath. "So Galena Lang was there." She's partially hidden behind a hefty male but I spy her.

"Yes. From Lang Funeral Home."

Lots of people attended the opening so Galena's presence might not mean anything. But it gives her opportunity. And it's possible she had motive, too. I return my eyes to the photos. One face I seek but don't find is that of Peter Svendsen.

"I know you're suspicious of him," Detective Dembek says, "and I am, too, even though I have no evidence he was at the opening."

"Where does he say he was?"

"At a Lamaze class with his wife. Which checks out, though he arrived nearly half an hour late."

"What time was the class?"

"Six p.m."

That's interesting. That's the same time as the Giant W opening. So Peter's so-called alibi has a big fat hole in it.

The detective and I stare at each other. I know she's thinking the same thing I am. "I've been examining his finances," she goes on, "and he's seriously upside down on his home. He and his wife own a large property up on Garvin Heights Road."

"That would only make him want Damsgard more."

"And it doesn't mean much that he's not in these photos. The killer might well have taken care to avoid the camera."

That would've been smart. I digest this information about Peter Svendsen and swipe to the next photo. It's another crowd shot and who do I see but—

"Priscilla Pembroke!" I'd recognize that nipped-waist parka with genuine shearling trim anywhere. "Look how she's got her hood up even though she's indoors. I bet she's trying to hide her face. She told me flat out that she didn't fly in from New York until the day after Ingrid was murdered. But that's a lie. Not only was Priscilla in town, she was at the opening."

Detective Dembek pushes her granny glasses up her nose and squints at the photo. "With her hood up it's hard to see her face. But she looks vaguely familiar to me."

"She's an actress. Maybe you've seen her in something. She also looks a lot like Ingrid. That could be what you're picking up on."

"Possibly."

"There's another thing. I think Priscilla was trying to break into Damsgard when she thought nobody was home." I share the clues that led me to that conclusion. "Priscilla is supposed to come over to Damsgard tonight," I go on, disclosing Ingrid's history as a Freyja worshipper and the honor ritual we're holding in honor of the heathen goddess.

Then I divulge that Ingrid hired a P.I. to investigate Galena Lang, who according to him suddenly seems to have lots more money at her disposal.

Detective Dembek jots notes in her spidery hand. "So many surprising things going on in people's lives. That was certainly true for Ingrid Svendsen. We're reviewing her financial transactions now but so far nothing stands out there."

I watch the detective. She looks unperturbed but I doubt she feels that way. "You must be under a lot of pressure to solve this murder. I feel some urgency, too, but nobody's breathing down my neck."

"Our chief understands these things take time." The detective pats my knee. "You're helping, dear, and I appreciate that." She glances out the window. "I would say the last mourners are arriving."

The church's parking lot must be full because in the next block people are emerging from parked cars with the doleful clothing and expressions that signal they're about to attend a funeral. Detective Dembek and I say our goodbyes and I exit the black-and-white to make for the church. En route I find myself following Peter Svendsen and a heavily pregnant blonde I presume to be his wife. I'd say with a baby on the way, this is a particularly bad time to be upside down on his home. But it's interesting that despite Peter's open disdain for his stepmother, nevertheless he wants to pay his respects. Then again, it could just be for show.

I arrive at the church to find it so packed that it's standing room only. There's one person I see no sign of and she supposedly flew in from New York for this very event. I go so far as to walk up one aisle and down another but nowhere do I see Priscilla Pembroke. It is possible she's late.

I'm back outside the church, snowflakes dusting the shoulders of my coat, when the hearse arrives, driven by Galena. She looks her usual Goth self. Maggie and Pop walk solemnly behind the casket, carried by pallbearers. Her head bent, Maggie clings to my father's arm. He and I exchange a nod. Regardless how fraught her relationship with her sister, I know Maggie must be feeling terrible sorrow today. She had one sibling in the world and that sibling is gone.

The service begins. Still no Priscilla.

Twenty minutes later my cell buzzes with a text. It's Shanelle.

If you don't need to be there come back.

I skedaddle. When I arrive back at Damsgard I see immediately why Shanelle summoned me. Together we survey the shards of glass on the porch floor from the newly broken dining room window.

"I'm glad some of us stayed home," Shanelle says.

"What happened?"

"I was in my room and all of a sudden I heard glass breaking. Trixie and I raced downstairs screaming at the top of our lungs. We must've scared off whoever it was."

"This is the window I'd break if I was trying to get in." The double-hung window is easily accessible from the porch and has a traditional sash lock. The would-be burglar simply broke the upper part of the window then reached inside to twist open the lock. Were it not for the screaming, one lift later they would've been able to clamber inside and go about their nefarious business. In a big city this house would have an alarm system with every window wired but that's not the case here. "It's too bad there are so many footprints in the snow," I say. "We can't tell which ones the perp left."

"At first I thought it must be Priscilla but she was at the service, right?"

"Au contraire. Which is pretty shocking given what she told us." We enter the house. Now with the broken window it's almost the same temperature inside as outside. "I don't know what to think about Priscilla. But the truth is that anybody could've done this. There are people who read obituaries so they can burgle the homes of the deceased during the funeral services."

"That pretty much defines scum of the earth in my book."

I can't disagree. "Where are mom and Trixie, by the way?"

"They went to the grocery store to buy walleye for dinner."

That's a Minnesota specialty I'm looking forward to trying. And I bet tonight's repast will be delicious. My mom will trot out every culinary trick she knows to show off in front of Maggie.

I stand in the foyer and text Detective Dembek with details of the break-in. She responds that she'll dispatch an officer right away to dust for prints, though neither of us expects any to be found.

Shanelle hugs herself. "That is one chill wind blowing in here. We need to replace that window ASAP."

"I'll call that hardware store we passed to see if they can recommend somebody to take care of it."

They do me one better. They declare they'll send over one of their own people free of charge. "Been selling to Damsgard all my life," the proprietor informs me. "It's the least I can do for the family, especially with this tragedy."

Unfortunately I can pry no useful gossip out of the man when he appears an hour later, shortly after the Winona P.D. officer departed without useful prints. But once he's done with the window, I ask if he'll do me another favor and unlock a room upstairs.

Minutes later he takes his leave and I cajole Shanelle into accompanying me to the third floor. It may be the middle of the day but Mario's ghost story from last night is still reverberating in my mind. As we set foot onto the shadowy third-floor landing, we see that the hardware man left the door to the previously locked room slightly ajar. I push it open cautiously, Shanelle right behind me.

We stand on the threshold and gasp in unison.

"I can't believe it," Shanelle whispers.

I can't, either. Because what this room holds is a prison cell.

CHAPTER FOURTEEN

Floor-to-ceiling bars create a cell that takes up about half the room. Inside are a toilet, sink, cot, and small wooden desk and chair.

Shanelle and I approach the cell. We could go inside, because the door is open, but neither of us does. We stand outside the bars and stare. We may not have found a ghost in this room but I'd say we've come upon something equally spooky.

"I'll be the one to ask the obvious question," I say into our stunned silence. "Why does Damsgard have a prison cell?"

"I can't answer that, girl," Shanelle murmurs. "But it gives me the creeps."

"The cot looks slept in." The drab sheets are mussed and the thin blue blanket is pulled back. There's an indentation on the pillow as if a head rested there.

"I wonder how long this has been here," Shanelle says. "Like, was it here when Peter and his sister were growing up? Is this where they sent the kids for time outs? If so it might explain why Peter's kind of tightly wound."

I shudder to think. "Or did it go in afterwards? I don't know how we find out. That'd be sort of an awkward topic to bring up in conversation. 'Hey, Peter, when did your folks put in the prison cell?'"

Shanelle gets into the faux jocularity. " 'You planning to

keep it when you move in or maybe you think it's time to take it out?'"

" 'And what about a permit? Is that required or not?' "

We chuckle but it's hard to feel jolly when you're staring at those bars. We leave the room behind us and return downstairs.

I feel rejuvenated once we step into the cheery kitchen. I pour us mugs of coffee. "I say we leave the third floor off the Christmas tour. What do you think?"

"I think you best get Detective Dembek on the horn." Shanelle pours cream into her coffee. "That cell is too weird for words. She needs to know about it. And if she hasn't questioned Peter Svendsen already, she can probe him about that thing."

"Your wish is my command."

Detective Dembek professes astonishment about the cell and assures me she'll bring it up when she next speaks to Peter.

Maggie and my father return and in short order retire to their room. Both are so spent, I don't even bother to tell them about the attempted break-in. My mom and Trixie come back to Damsgard with enough groceries to feed a battalion. We fix a lunch of soup and sandwiches, some of which I carry upstairs for Maggie and Pop. I spend time doing research online on my suspects, not that it proves very valuable. I do find a bio of Peter Svendsen but the only thing I learn is that he spent a year in England during college. I also discover that Priscilla Pembroke does have quite the list of acting credits. Most of them are theater roles but there are a few parts in TV and movies, too. The role of Hermione in Winona's production of *The Winter's Tale* doesn't show up but maybe "ac-TORS" like Priscilla keep their regional theatrical work to themselves.

Then a different question plagues me. What does one wear to eavesdrop on the reading of a will? I select my slim light gray trousers—which have a terrific drape—and pair them with a knit top with a faux wrap front in a leopard-spot print enlivened by a red background. I look so pulled together it's a shame no one will see me.

Half an hour before everyone is scheduled to arrive, I get into position. Fortunately I earlier confirmed the location of the switch that swings back the bookshelves that reveal the secret room, because it's none too easy to find. Trixie joins me—partly to keep me company and partly because she loves the secret room—and Shanelle moves the shelves back into place, leaving only the narrowest of gaps.

"Let's do a test," she says. "Can you hear me from here? Here?"

Happily, we can.

"You've got to report on everything that happens in every other room," I say.

"I know. I'm your eyes and ears. Good luck."

The secret room is exciting in lots of ways but it's windowless, pitch dark because we can't turn the standing lamp on, and not particularly comfortable. We both put our cell phones on silent mode and I entertain myself by using the flashlight app to shine a thin beam of light around the room.

"I wish there were chairs in here," Trixie whispers a few minutes later. She looks cute in jeans and a white peasant blouse with black trim outlining the keyhole neckline.

"You and me both." We're sitting on the floor leaning back against the wall. Only an oriental carpet cushions our bony butts from the hardwood beneath. Apart from the shrine to Freyja, the lone other furnishing is a bookshelf. It's not snazzy like the gorgeous carved built-ins in the library but all the volumes are the serious-looking leather-bound kind.

I examine the offerings. "I suppose we could read until people show up."

Trixie joins me. "I don't think I'm going to find a romance novel here."

"No chance of that." I select *Robinson Crusoe*, which has been on my To Read list forever, and give my nose a thorough blow so I can get through the reading of Ingrid's will with clear nasal passages. I'm fighting my way through the part of the book where Robinson thinks about how "the calamities of life were shared among the upper and lower part of mankind"—which is so true—when I hear sounds of life in the library.

Trixie's head jerks up from *Tess of the D'Urbervilles*.

I raise a warning finger to my lips and she nods in understanding. We both shut down our flashlight apps. Now we must be as silent as beauty queens waiting to hear who won the tiara. Seconds later, in the library, a woman speaks.

"Now it won't matter that your pension could support all three of us."

Maggie, I whisper to Trixie, my ears pricking up. I don't like what Maggie's saying but I darn well want to hear it.

"After today," she trills, "*I'll* have enough money for Donovan and me to live in high style."

"Good for you," Pop says. "Glad you're not counting your chickens."

They lapse into silence. A few minutes later someone else enters the library. "I'm Peter Svendsen," I hear, "and this is Walter Chapman."

Interesting that Peter's here. Is it possible he's mentioned in Ingrid's will? More likely he wants to stake his claim to Damsgard every chance he can. And who's this Walter Chapman he brought with him? Apparently Maggie wants to know that, too.

"I'm the lawyer for the Svendsen family," a gravelly male voice says. "I had the honor of representing Erik for many years."

"Erik is Ingrid's second husband," I whisper to Trixie, "who left her Damsgard." At least *sort* of left her Damsgard.

"But you're not my sister's lawyer," Maggie says.

"No," Walter says. "Now I represent Peter and Nora's side of the family."

Trixie makes a small sound. I bet she's thinking what I'm thinking. It's not always a good thing when a family has "sides."

As the quartet in the library sit down and muse aloud about

when Ingrid's lawyer Anita Shea will show up, I start to worry that I made a mistake by not alerting Maggie to Peter's claim that Damsgard will go to him after Ingrid's death. I can't fault myself for not wanting to bother her about something that may not be true but that wasn't really why I did it. I wanted to see how she'd react if she found out that the riches she's begun to count on didn't fall in her lap.

Anita Shea arrives and introductions are made all around. We learn that Anita is not just Ingrid's lawyer but also the executor of her will. "Shall we begin?" Anita says, and I swear that even from the secret room I can feel the tension in the library mount.

"Where's Priscilla?" Trixie whispers.

Here, too, she's a no show. Apparently if "dear Ingrid" left Priscilla anything, it wasn't enough to warrant her appearance at the reading of the will.

A throat clears and then Anita begins to read. " 'I, Ingrid Jane Lindvig Harris Svendsen, of the city of Winona, county of Winona, and state of Minnesota, being of full age and sound mind and memory, do make, publish and declare this to be my last Will and Testament.' "

It's a solemn moment. You can almost feel Ingrid peering down on the proceedings from on high.

For a while Anita reads boring legalese about debts being paid from the estate but then matters liven up. " 'The distribution of my household goods and tangible personal property is outlined in my letter of instruction.' I'll read that in a moment," Anita says as an aside. Then, " 'I hereby give, devise and bequeath the sum of ten thousand dollars to my sister Margaret Louise Lindvig of Rocky River, Ohio. I direct that the rest, residue and remainder of my property be given to—' " and Anita reads the name of an animal shelter in Minneapolis. Then there's more legal-sounding stuff that basically says that if any beneficiaries object to the probate of the will, they will be cut out entirely.

Silence falls. That's it? That seems awfully simple for the

will of a wealthy woman like Ingrid Svendsen.

"Shall I read the letter of instruction?" Anita asks.

"Excuse me," Maggie says, "I'm a little confused," and I will admit that I am, too. "I didn't hear my son Donovan mentioned."

"No, he does not figure in the will," Anita says. "Nor in the letter of instruction."

"He's Ingrid's nephew. Her only nephew."

Anita Shea has nothing to say to that.

"Okay." With obvious reluctance, Maggie moves on. "What about that ten thousand dollar thing? There's more cash than that coming to me, right?"

"I'm afraid not," and Anita reiterates the business about the animal shelter.

Maggie's voice takes on a note of hysteria. "Are you telling me that Ingrid left her money to an *animal shelter*?"

There seems no getting around that. Actually it improves my opinion of Ingrid that she left some fraction of her estate to a worthwhile charity.

"You are mentioned in the letter of instruction," Anita hastens to say. "Why don't I read that," and once again she regales us with legalese. Then it gets juicy again. " 'All jewelry and clothing in my possession at the time of my death are to be given to my sister Margaret Louise. If she does not desire any item, she may sell it and the proceeds will devolve to her.' " Anita reads that with enthusiasm but somehow I don't think Maggie will be appeased.

I am proved right.

"Her jewelry and her clothing, fine," Maggie says. "But what about the Mercedes?"

Anita hesitates, then, "That's going to the animal shelter."

"What? That's ridiculous!" Maggie sputters.

I wish I were a spider on the library wall so I could see this with my own eyes. But I can easily visualize the scene: Pop patting Maggie's hand to try to calm her down and Peter Svendsen watching in smug silence as Ingrid's sister embarrasses herself.

"Well, what about this house?" my father asks. "I haven't heard a peep about Damsgard."

"Ah, yes, Damsgard," Peter says, in what I must say is a slimy superior tone. "Let's talk about that, shall we, Walter?"

More throat clearing, followed by Walter Chapman's gruff voice. "You and I have discussed the disposition of Damsgard, Anita, which is why Peter and I are here this afternoon. Shall I continue or would you like to proceed?"

Apparently Anita defers to Walter, which is what I'd do, too, if I knew what was coming next.

Finally comes the big finish. With what sounds like gusto, Walter reiterates what Peter told us the other day, though in more convoluted legal terms. Despite all the lawyerly mumbo jumbo, the bottom line comes through loud and clear: Damsgard goes to Peter Svendsen.

CHAPTER FIFTEEN

Maggie can't believe it. She is so undone that all she can say is one word. "What? What?"

I feel sorry for her. Trixie must, too. She clutches my hand and together we huddle in the secret room and shake our heads in sympathy. You, dear reader, know I am not Maggie Lindvig's biggest fan. I even think it's possible she's a murderer. Nevertheless, at this moment I am pained for her. I can imagine how hard it would be to discover that a windfall that could change your whole life, and your son's whole life, is not going to come your way.

Finally Maggie is able to expand her vocabulary. "There's got to be a way to do something about this! This can't be what my sister wanted."

I hear Pop's low tone. "Remember what the will said, Maggie. If you contest the probate, you don't get anything at all."

Anita pipes up. "I should mention that you're the beneficiary of your sister's insurance policy as well, Ms. Lindvig. It's separate from the estate so I didn't—"

"How much is it?" Maggie wants to know.

"Five thousand dollars."

I gather Maggie is not impressed because I don't hear another peep out of her. I also feel a tickle in my nose. I pinch my nostrils. *Not now*, I order myself.

"My son Donovan and I are my sister's only blood relatives," Maggie insists.

"No one's disputing that," Anita says.

"Then by rights this house should come to me. My sister's money should, too. You can't give your money to an animal shelter if there's need in your own family."

"It doesn't work that way," Walter pipes up to say.

"Who asked you?" Maggie says.

"None of this is relevant," Peter says. "The bottom line is that my grandfather built Damsgard. It's been in the Svendsen family for generations. Clearly it should stay in the Svendsen family."

"But my sister *was* a Svendsen!" Maggie says.

"Only for four years," Peter snaps. "And my father was more than generous to her. As a matter of fact—"

I miss what is said next—or should I say, yelled next—because now I'm pinching my nose and holding my breath and rocking back and forth desperately trying not to—

"A-*choo*!"

Trixie clutches my arm. I am aware that all argument in the library has ceased. Then—

"A-*choo*!"

I can't help myself. My sinuses are rebelling something fierce.

"A-*choo*!"

The secret entry to our hideaway flies open. Peter stands at the threshold, backlit by the light in the library. I guess the secret room is no secret to him. "What the devil are you two doing in here?"

Trixie holds up *Tess of the D'Urbervilles*. "Reading?"

Trixie and I scramble to our feet, which is not easy to do in high-heeled booties. Behind Peter I see my father, shaking his head. It's not only his lady friend who's embarrassing herself this afternoon. It's his daughter, too.

"Get out," Peter orders.

There's nothing to do but obey. By now Shanelle and my

mom have joined us in the library. Peter strides into the secret room and surveys the shrine to Freyja. "What is this?"

"We've been told it's a shrine," I say.

"I always knew my stepmother was a lunatic. This only proves it." Peter exits the secret room and closes it up. "I want all of you out of Damsgard tonight."

"No!" Maggie shrieks. "I won't go! And stop saying mean things about my sister!" She bursts into tears.

"Emotions are running high," I say, "so let's all please take a moment and calm down." I hand Maggie a tissue from the stash I've been carrying around with me the last few days. "Peter, I apologize for eavesdropping."

"There's no excuse for it. But everything in this house has been crazy since the day Ingrid got her hooks into my father."

"Well, that's ancient history. And it has nothing to do with any of us anyway."

He looks away. I watch a muscle twitch in his jaw.

"And I don't mean to impose," I go on, "but we are your stepmother's guests and she did invite us to stay until Sunday." He begins to protest but I keep going. "Please let us stay until then." I add the *please* even though I'm not sure it's up to him. I don't want to become a squatter but I don't see why I should flee in the dead of night, either.

He shakes his head. "I don't know why I should."

"Because it's the right thing to do."

He jabs his finger at my face. "If so much as a spoon disappears from this house, you'll have me to answer to." He stomps out of the library, Walter Chapman at his heels. The front door slams with such force I'm surprised the newly replaced window doesn't break all over again.

Maggie swipes her tears then approaches brunette, business-suited Anita. "I want to fight this. I want a copy of that paper that says this house belongs to that jerk. I don't believe it."

"I'll get you a copy," Anita promises, though she doesn't look pleased with this turn of events.

"I also think I should get more of my sister's money," Maggie goes on. "Family is family."

Anita lowers her voice. "Ms. Lindvig, it's not appropriate to go into all the particulars but be aware there is not that much money in your sister's estate."

Maggie looks as surprised by that revelation as I am. "There isn't?"

"Erik Svendsen did not leave your sister as much money as she might have hoped. It was a source of some frustration to her."

I wonder if Erik's kids got to him about that, too. They didn't want their father's second wife to inherit the family home or much of the family money.

Anita has to repeat the same thing a few times before Maggie looks even the slightest bit convinced. She pretty much deflates after Anita leaves.

Trixie grabs her in a hug. "Look at it this way, Maggie. Damsgard has some weird things about it. It's not all good."

"The secret room might be weird," Maggie says, "but it doesn't ruin the whole house!"

"She doesn't mean the secret room," my mother says. "She means that prison cell on the third floor."

"Say what?" my father bellows.

Shanelle is offering to escort them upstairs to see it when Maggie bursts into a fresh round of tears. "I can't talk about this anymore!" She points her finger at my father. "And don't you dare say I told you so!" Away she sprints.

"I won't say it," Pop mutters. "I won't say a thing."

"Maybe now would be a good time to have tea," Trixie suggests. "Or cocoa like I made the other night." She succeeds in ushering my parents out of the library.

"Any chance Damsgard doesn't go to Peter?" Shanelle asks me.

"I don't think so. It sounds like Anita and Walter talked about it earlier and that's why Walter and Peter were at the reading of the will. If the claim were bogus, Anita would say something, wouldn't she? As executor of Ingrid's will, she's obligated to protect Ingrid's interests."

"Poor Maggie." Shanelle lowers her voice. "But it's only poor Maggie if she didn't kill her sister. Just goes to show a body needs to do her research beforehand."

I shake my head. Maggie does strike me as the kind to act now and think later. What a tragic irony if she killed her sister hoping to claim her fortune when there was no fortune to be claimed.

"Maggie gets only ten thousand dollars in cash," I tell Shanelle. "Plus five thousand from an insurance policy."

"That's hardly chump change, girl."

"It is if you were expecting millions."

In the few hours until dinner, I create a spreadsheet and input all the information I have on my suspects, every detail, no matter how small. The person about whom I know the least is Galena Lang. I have to remedy that tomorrow. I'm about to go downstairs for dinner when I get a text from Mario.

I'm running late but I'll be there for the goddess ritual.

No problem. Any ghosts today?

None. Whew ...

I have to smile. You'd think the host of *America's Scariest Ghost Stories* would love to run across actual phantoms but I guess not.

We sit around the mahogany dining table and raise a glass to Ingrid. Maggie is beyond subdued; she seems drained. And my father—who's doing his best to buck her up—looks exhausted as well.

But despite all that, everyone at the table has seconds of my mother's walleye, which is crunchy on the outside, flaky on the inside, and fantastic all around. Not only that, my mom looks like she stepped off the set of a cooking show, with her red hair styled and her face made up. I note my father sending furtive glances in her direction.

"This walleye is fantastic, Mrs. P," Trixie says.

"It's the best I ever had," Maggie admits.

"And you grew up in Minnesota!" my mother crows. "Well, it was simple as could be. Cracker crust, lemony tartar sauce, what could be easier?"

"And you made your garlic mashed potatoes, too, Hazel," Pop mumbles, his mouth full, and for once my mother doesn't reprimand him.

Maggie and Pop retire right after dinner. They look so thrashed I have no doubt we'll see no sign of them again till morning. Trixie, Shanelle and I help my mom clean up. "What are we going to do tonight?" my mother wants to know.

I'm about to encourage her to spend the evening in front of the TV in her room when Trixie pipes up. "Oh, Mrs. P, you're going to love it! We're having a ritual for a heathen goddess in the secret room!"

That of course requires explanation. "If you want to participate, you have to keep your opinions to yourself," I instruct my mother. "And you must follow my lead."

"I'll do everything you say," she vows. "And I'll be so quiet you won't even know I'm there."

And Pop is the third Earl of Spence.

Mario arrives in the nick of time, dressed in chestnut-colored cords and a spread-collar sport shirt in brown tonal stripes. "Sorry I'm late. After all yesterday's excitement Jennifer and I are having trouble making anything good out of today's shoot."

"Not a single bump in the night?"

"There are supposedly headless Dakota Indian children who roam the Historical Society downtown but they didn't show up for us. Nor did the janitor who reportedly haunts the YMCA."

"If I were you, I'd be relieved." I usher him to the second floor. "Well, I found out a few interesting things today. Namely that Priscilla lied when she said she came to Winona the day after Ingrid was shot. In fact we have picture proof she was at the Giant W opening." I lead him to my room. "For now I think you should stay up here out of sight, at least until we're all in the secret room." The doorbell rings. "That must be Priscilla," I say, and I'm about to spin away when Mario grabs my arm.

"Happy, be careful. And remember what we discussed." He gives me a serious look, the kind he produces when he's warning his viewers they're about to witness paranormal activity they might find disturbing. "Keep Priscilla in the library and the secret room. I'll come downstairs as soon as I'm sure you're in there. Scream if even the slightest thing goes wrong. I'll hear you."

He doesn't say *I'll come running* but I know he will.

I like that.

Priscilla arrives looking fashionable in a slim black nubby skirt, mustard-colored cashmere sweater, and necklace of amber beads in honor of the goddess. She's clearly displeased to discover that yet another female has taken up residence at Damsgard. "Delightful to meet you," she lies to my mother. Then to me: "How fortunate that you found room for one more."

"Isn't it though? Let me take this," and I relieve her of her black carryall. I lead our quintet to the library, where once again Priscilla pauses in front of the impressionistic painting of sailboats on a choppy sea. "You really seem to like that oil," I say.

"It's terribly special, can't you see?" Her tone says: You're an ignoramus if you can't. "Just look at the asymmetrical balance, how recession into space is created by carefully measured intervals? How the artist made such wonderful use of pure, prismatic color? And how he crafted a microstructure of small strokes to create movement and depth as the eye moves about the canvas?"

"Whatever," my mother says. "I like paintings of people. Boats I could take or leave."

"It is nice and colorful, though," Trixie says.

Priscilla sighs as if our bourgeois company is sure to make for a painfully long evening.

"What did you bring with you?" I ask as I allow her to open the secret room. I want Priscilla to feel as if she's directing our activities, though in truth I have an agenda of my own. Earlier I also decided that I would wait before peppering her with questions about when she arrived in Winona and why she skipped Ingrid's funeral.

We enter the secret room and Priscilla unpacks her carryall. "I brought several things to honor the goddess, all of her favorite treats. Raspberry wine, strawberries, and caramel chocolate truffles."

"I'm liking this Freyja better every minute," Shanelle says.

When Trixie and my mom disappear to find wineglasses, Priscilla issues her instructions. "Once they come back everyone in the house must remain in this room. We can't have people randomly walking around. They might take the goddess by surprise."

You'd think it would be harder than that to surprise a goddess but I'll go with it. "Fine. Shall I light the candles?"

"Go ahead. And we must have complete darkness," Priscilla insists, "throughout the entire house."

"You're sure the goddess won't get lost?"

Priscilla narrows her eyes at me.

"Okay," I say, "I'll make sure all the lights are off," and I make the rounds, giving Mario a silent thumb's up when I pass through my room.

Soon we're ready to proceed. The wine, berries, and chocolates are arrayed on the shrine beside the lit candles. My mother, Shanelle, Trixie, Priscilla, and I stand in a half circle, our faces illuminated by tiny flickering flames.

"The only thing that could make this more exciting," Trixie whispers, "is if it were a full moon."

"Silence!" Priscilla bellows. "Let us begin."

CHAPTER SIXTEEN

"Goddess Freyja," Priscilla intones, "in the circle of your moon do we now hail thee." She bows her head. "Beautiful one, thrice burned and thrice reborn. From the deepest night awaken thy knowledge. Wisest of women, teacher of witchcraft—"

"Witchcraft!" my mother hollers. "I'm Catholic! How am I supposed to explain this in confession?"

"Be silent!" Priscilla cries. "Are you so foolish that you think the goddess has no magical powers? Particularly"—and for some reason she turns to me—"over love and lust. Are you willing to be honest about your desires and your primal nature?"

Not really, I'm thinking, especially since Mario is probably well within earshot in the library by now, but Priscilla plunges on.

"If you are, Freyja is the goddess to call upon. She is the one to help you express yourself fully."

That's what I've been trying to *stop* myself from doing.

Trixie pipes up. "I've been reading about Freyja. She's got a lot in common with you, Happy."

Great.

"You were telling me Freyja is known as 'The Fair One'," Shanelle says.

"Exactly," Trixie says. "And she has one child, a

daughter, just like you, Happy. She's adventurous, too, not the type to sit around the house. Of course that's true of all three of us."

"All four now," my mother puts in, "since I got a job outside the home."

Priscilla claps her hands. "Enough! Are you women even capable of being quiet?"

"I'll shut up if we can have the wine and chocolate," my mother says.

"We did miss dessert," Trixie points out.

"I have an idea," I say. "How about you recite more of the ritual, Priscilla, and then we'll all close our eyes and think about how we could bring Freyja into our lives. After that we'll have the wine and chocolate."

Maybe it's the glow from the candlelight but I believe I detect a gleam in Priscilla's eyes. "Excellent suggestion," she says. Then, in a portentous tone, she resumes the ceremony. "As I was the night before your beginnings, I am the light that will shine for you at the end."

"Geez Louise," my mother mumbles.

I knock her in the arm. As I predicted, she isn't trying too hard to keep her vow of silence.

"I wait as a seed within the earth," Priscilla goes on, "as the egg within the womb, as the spirit within the body. Let us close our eyes and ponder Freyja's wisdom."

As Priscilla's voice trails off, I obediently close my eyes. I'm not doing much pondering, though. I'm mostly straining to hear what's going on around me. We are all five of us so quiet that I swear I can make out every breath we take. Then somehow I perceive something else. Movement. The faintest whisper of air on my skin as someone creeps away from our group.

Priscilla! I made sure I was next to her and I know she's the one who moved.

I let her get all the way to the threshold of the library. I am not the least surprised when our cheeky visitor from the

East starts shutting the bookshelf entry to the secret room. That is exactly what I expected her to do! This is why she wanted everybody in the house in the secret room, and all of Damsgard plunged into darkness. She was just waiting for her opportunity to lock us all in there so she could have free rein to do whatever the heck she's been angling to do. I scamper toward the bookshelf wall and apply the tiniest bit of resistance to keep it from clicking shut without alerting Priscilla that I'm on to her.

"What!" my mother yowls behind me. "Are we locked in here? Help!"

"Shh!" I hiss. "We're not locked in. Put a sock in it."

Only with Trixie and Shanelle's help am I able to get my mom to hush up. Then, when she's been reduced to muttering, I cautiously push open the bookshelf wall, just a smidge, barely enough to peer into the dim library, which now is illuminated only by the moonlight streaming through the paned windows.

And what do I see? Priscilla standing on a chair she hauled over from the dining room, lifting the painting of the sailboats away from the wall above the mantel.

I push open the bookshelf wall just as Mario switches on a table lamp. Priscilla freezes in place, the painting in her arms.

"So *that's* what you're after!" I cry.

"Put the painting back," Mario says in a warning tone.

"Or what?" Priscilla demands. The woman is a case study in impudence. Instead of rehanging the oil she stands it on the carpet beside the fireplace and carefully steps down from the chair. She brushes her skirt and straightens. "It's rightfully mine and I'm taking it with me and there's nothing you can do about it," she declares, and again she takes it in her arms and makes a move to exit the library.

Mario blocks her way. "You're not going anywhere, Priscilla."

"I'll call Detective Dembek," I say.

"Don't you dare!" Again Priscilla sets down the painting. She throws a nasty glance at Mario. "I should've known you'd be here." Then to me: "Don't fool yourself that you're anything like Freyja. The goddess would never need a man to defend her."

That stings. "You can insult me all you like but the fact is that you're a thief. I know it was you who tried to break into Damsgard earlier today."

"You know nothing of the kind."

"Ever since you came to Winona you've been using every trick in the book to insinuate yourself into this house. And now we all know why. You want that painting."

She steps closer to me. "I have far more right to be at Damsgard than you do."

"Because of your supposed friendship with Ingrid?"

She raises her chin. "There is nothing supposed about it."

"Then why didn't you go to her funeral?"

"Because I'm not bound by convention like the rest of you. I had a private ceremony for the dear soul to pay her tribute."

"If that was all you wanted to do, you could've done it in New York. Why did you bother flying all the way out to Minnesota?"

Priscilla ignores me and throws out her right arm.

"Here we go again," I say. "What's it going to be this time? *Macbeth*?"

Yes, as it happens.

" 'Give sorrow words!' " Priscilla cries. " 'The grief that does not speak knits up the o'er wrought heart and bids it break.' "

"What's up with this broad?" my mother wants to know. "And why is she so all fired up to have that painting?"

"I have an even better question," I say. "How can she claim it's rightfully hers?"

"Because Ingrid was going to give it to me." Priscilla juts her chin defiantly. "She told me so a million times."

Shanelle pipes up. "Her will was read today and your name never came up."

"As if that means anything," Priscilla sniffs.

"Apparently you're not bound by the convention of wills, either," I say.

"I say we wrap this thing up and have the wine and chocolate," my mother says.

"In a minute," I say. "I have another question for Priscilla. When did you arrive in Winona?"

This time I get the idea she's weighing her words. Then, "I already told you. The day after poor Ingrid slipped the surly bonds of earth."

"How did you find out so fast that she had died?"

"Not that it's any of your business but one of her neighbors told me. I maintain a great number of connections in Winona. I called the airline the second I heard."

"Well, then, you must be psychic. Because I have photographic proof that you were in Winona the night that Ingrid died."

She looks away. This time she's not so quick with a comeback.

"And not only were you in Winona," I go on, "you were at the opening of the Giant W."

"That's preposterous! You're confusing me with someone else." She brushes her blond hair back from her face. "Not that many women can boast my bone structure."

I step closer to Priscilla. "Why are you lying about when you came into town?"

"I'm leaving," she sniffs. "I didn't come here to answer pointless questions." She pushes past Mario.

"I'll make sure she doesn't lift anything on the way out," Shanelle says, and follows in Priscilla's tracks.

"Can't we have her arrested?" Trixie wants to know. "She tried to steal that painting. And I bet trying to lock people in secret rooms is a crime, too."

"If it's not, it should be," my mother says.

"Attempted robbery is a felony," Mario says. "But I think we're better served by Priscilla Pembroke being on the loose."

"I agree," I say. "I want to see what she does next. Plus I

have her cell phone number so I bet Detective Dembek would be able to track her down that way." I bend down to examine the painting at closer range. "What is so special about this, I wonder?"

"Beats me," my mother says. "Look how uneven the paint is. It's thick in some places and thin in others. That Priscilla must like it that way but if you ask me she's got a screw loose."

I squint at the signature on the painting. "The artist's name is Erskine."

Mario already has his cell phone out. "It doesn't ring a bell. I'll look it up."

"I've had enough of an art lesson for one day," my mother declares. "I'm going to crack open the raspberry wine."

"I'll get some ice for it, Mrs. P," Trixie offers.

"There's a Claude Erskine who's a painter," Mario says a few minutes later.

I look over his shoulder at his phone's screen. "His other paintings are the same style as this one. It must be him."

"Listen to this," Mario says, and he begins to read. " 'Last year Erskine's works sold at auction for a total of sixty million dollars, according to auction tracker Artnet. At Erskine's gallery in New York, the waiting list for one of his works, which can sell for upwards of a million dollars, is dozens of names long.' "

"Wow." I eye the oil with new appreciation as Trixie hands me a glass of raspberry wine. Talk about a study in contrasts. "So this painting is worth a lot. And Priscilla is savvy enough to know that."

"Priscilla sounded like a professor when she was describing it," Trixie says. "How does an actress know so much about art?"

"That I can't answer." Mario also accepts a glass. "But if she understood the value of this painting, she had a motive for murder. People have killed for less."

"To me, it doesn't add up." Shanelle passes around the

chocolate caramels, which feature a sprinkling of sea salt. "Why not just steal it? Why commit murder?"

"That's easy," my mother pronounces as finally we indulge in dessert. "She hated Ingrid."

CHAPTER SEVENTEEN

"She couldn't have hated her!" Trixie cries. "They were best friends!"

"We don't know that for a fact," I point out. "That's what Priscilla told us but she told us lots of things that are turning out not to be true."

"And maybe they were best friends," my mother says. "Friends kill each other. Look at that straight-A student down in West Virginia. Her two best friends killed her and buried her body in the woods and kept quiet about it for six months. Don't look at me like that," she says to me. "I like to keep up with that true crime."

"Well," I say, "I have wondered how those two could've gotten so close when Ingrid lived here in Winona and Priscilla is in Manhattan."

"We're close," Shanelle says, "and we've never lived in the same place."

Mario pipes up. "People can form strong bonds very quickly. Usually when they share some intense experience."

Like Trixie, Shanelle and I did on Oahu. We were all three competing in Ms. America only to have one contestant murdered on pageant night and another—yours truly—suspected of the crime. That qualifies as intense in my book.

"My point is this," my mother says. "Why would one woman kill another? She hates her because she has something the other one wants. A guy, usually."

"Or lots of money," Shanelle says.

"So the motive is jealousy," Trixie breathes.

We end the evening mulling murder, as happens so often for me these days.

The next morning, a bright December Saturday, I continue my investigation by showing up unannounced at the Garvin Heights home of Peter Svendsen and his pregnant wife. I'm not so rude as to appear empty-handed. I'm bearing a lovely bouquet of stargazer lilies accented with laurel and eucalyptus.

I gather Peter and his wife are planning a big family because they live in a huge two-story brick house that boasts a three-car garage and expansive acreage. It's a very different setting than Windom Park, with its century-old Victorians and mature trees. Here the occasional house dots the rolling hills, some more glitzy than others. I'm sure in the autumn the leaves are breathtaking but this time of year the main color you see is white, from all the snow. As I ring the doorbell and shiver in the wind, I remember Detective Dembek telling me that Peter is seriously upside down on the property. Inheriting Damsgard would certainly help with that situation.

He looks less than thrilled to find me on his stoop.

"I want to apologize again for my behavior yesterday," I lie. My real reason for the visit is that I like to stop by my suspects' homes if possible. Almost always it proves illuminating.

Peter relieves me of the bouquet. Since I don't immediately turn to go, he's forced to invite me inside so I don't turn into an ice sculpture. "My wife and I are just about to leave for a Lamaze class," he informs me.

I restrain myself from asking if he'll be late to this class like he was late to the last one. Instead I burble with excitement. "How thrilling! First baby?" I step into the high-ceilinged foyer and ascertain that the house is short on color, furnishings, and holiday décor, none of which can be said about Peter's childhood home. I meander into the adjacent living room, where family photos—many old-time black and whites—decorate an otherwise blank wall.

"First of many, we hope." He calls upstairs. "We should be going, Barbara!"

That's a broad hint that I should absent myself but I decide to be willfully obtuse and ignore it. I'm too interested in the photos and this first chance I've had to put faces to names. I point to a close-up of a movie star-handsome older man with a thick mane of white hair. "This must be your dad." I don't say it but even later in life he and Ingrid must have made a remarkably attractive couple. "I don't see any photos of your mom."

"That's because there aren't any." Then again upstairs: "Barbara, we'll be late!"

"You don't have any photos of your mother?"

He grabs a coat from the hall closet and shrugs it on. "When you have a mother who up and leaves, you don't want to be reminded of her every day of the week."

I can understand that. "Well, in the long run your father found happiness again. I hope your mom did, too."

"I don't go out of my way to see her so I wouldn't know." He loops a scarf around his neck. "Barbara!"

This time he gets a response. "All right, already, I'm coming! Boy, are you trying to make up for last time or what?" She sounds snarky, or maybe she's just hormonal, which I certainly would be at her stage of pregnancy. She halts on the stairs when she spies me in her living room. She's a cheerleader-type blonde in a cute plum-colored activewear outfit. Poor thing looks ready to pop. "I didn't realize we had a guest," she says.

I walk forward with my hand outstretched. "I'm Happy Pennington. I apologize for barging in. I'm staying at Damsgard at the moment. Congratulations on the baby."

She nods as if she's heard my name before. Probably with invective attached.

"We really do have to go," Peter says.

"I'll get out of your hair," I say. "I just wanted to assure you that we'll do a good job with the Christmas tour this afternoon. I'm excited to meet more of the locals."

It seems Peter couldn't care less. He ushers me outside without further ado. I'm marooned on the stoop for what seems like forever fumbling in the recesses of my Hobo for the keys to the rental car when I hear the agitated voices of husband and wife soar to the heavens. Of course my ears prick up.

"Why did you have to say I was trying to make up for last time?" Peter says.

"I didn't know anybody was here! Besides, who cares?"

"I care. I don't want her to know anything about us. She's snoopy."

He's got that right. In fact I'm snooping right now.

"You're paranoid," Barbara says. "You're just worried she'll find out your dirty little secret."

I clutch my Hobo. This is getting good!

"Hardly," Peter snorts. "Besides, you know I had a problem with the bagman. I couldn't just ignore it."

I frown. What the heck is a bagman? I have no idea but it sounds sinister.

"I don't want to hear about any of that!" Barbara shrieks. "I don't like it!"

"I told you before and I'll tell you again. I'll stop when the baby comes."

"I'll believe that when I see it."

Darn! Their voices are fading. They're probably on their way to the garage. Even though I still haven't got my hands on my keys I sprint to the rental I left parked on the street so Peter doesn't realize I was eavesdropping yet again. He would think that's all I do and he wouldn't be far off. I'm in the car when I see their gold Volvo SUV back down their driveway and screech onto the road. They're jawing so much I'm not sure they even notice me.

Wow, was I right to come here! That was darn

informative. Peter is certainly sensitive about being late to Tuesday's Lamaze class. Maybe that's because he was busy shooting his stepmother while he was supposed to be helping his wife practice focused breathing techniques. And what was all that about his "dirty little secret" and the "bagman"? I consult my cell phone on the latter and learn that a bagman is somebody who collects and transports dirty money, like for the Mafia.

This puts a whole new spin on things. Could it be that Peter is mixed up with the Mob? Might that have played a role in Ingrid's death? Maybe this explains the prison cell on Damsgard's third floor: it could be to incarcerate people who refuse to pay up.

It's news to me that the Mob operates in Minnesota. Who would think that? This seems like such a wholesome state. Then again, maybe Mafiosi like the Upper Midwest because Canada is just to the north and hence available for spiriting contraband in and out of the country.

Since I'm eager to share these bombshell revelations, I give Detective Dembek a call. Unfortunately I reach only her voicemail so am forced to leave a message.

I'm en route to meet my mother at the Basilica of Saint Stanislaus Kostka, more popularly known as Saint Stan's, when my cell rings with a call from Jason. "I just got off the phone with Zach," he tells me. "He must think I'm holding out for more money because he upped his offer by five grand."

"Wow. He really wants you, Jason."

"This is a good opportunity for us, Happy."

I detect a different tone in his voice. It's a new degree of seriousness or something. I stop at a red light and hold my breath.

"I've made my decision," he says. "I want to take the job."

I let out the breath. "You're sure?"

"I'm sure. This isn't going to come around again. It's now or never."

"You're worried you'll regret it if you pass it up."

"There's no reason to pass it up."

I hear the warning. He's letting me know he will not be pleased if I continue to balk. "Did you tell Zach you've decided?"

"No. You and I need to talk about it first. I figure that tomorrow when you get home—"

Uh oh. "I may not get home tomorrow, Jason. I still haven't solved this murder."

Silence. Jason no longer objects to my sleuthing—he's come to understand how important it is to me—but that doesn't mean he takes kindly to it impinging on our lives. Finally he speaks up. "Well, you still have to make a decision. I told Zach I'd call him Monday with my answer."

"Okay. I am thinking about it." I cringe because that's not entirely true. What I'm mostly doing is shoving this to the back of my mind where I put things I don't want to think about. How mature of me. I see the white domes of Saint Stan's rising in the distance and think of my father's advice. *Do what I do when I need to talk something out. Go talk to a priest.*

"Let me warn you about something else," Jason says. "Rachel and I may go out tomorrow and get the tree."

"Without me?" I screech.

"You're not here, Happy. And from the sound of it you don't know when you will be. And it's only ten days till Christmas."

"Eleven."

He sighs. "I love you, sweetie."

"I love you, too, Jason."

Then the call is over. Minutes later I arrive at Saint Stan's. It's a spectacular redbrick edifice with one huge white dome and several smaller ones. It even has round stained-glass windows that remind me of the famous rose window on the façade of Notre Dame in Paris. Not that I've ever seen that for real but I hope to someday.

I'm pretty freaked out by the reality of Jason's decision

but a few moments standing in that hushed nave calm my nerves. I look for my mother among the scattered worshippers and find her near the front, her preferred location, praying so fervently she doesn't even see me until I kneel down next to her.

"Isn't this a gorgeous church?" I whisper. We slide back onto the pew.

"Romanesque style," she informs me. "Did you see out front on that plaque it's the oldest Catholic parish in Winona?"

"Yes. Since 1871."

"That's even before my time." We both have a chuckle. "A couple years ago they made it a minor basilica."

"How do you know so much?"

"That lady and I got to talking." My mother cocks her chin at a Slavic-looking female about her age praying the rosary in the pew ahead of us. "It was built by Polish immigrants, I'll have you know. They donated nickels and dimes back when they made only a dollar a day."

"Impressive."

My mother hits me in the arm. "Those are your people." Then she resumes the kneeling position. "I got to get back to it."

"Are you saying a novena for Ingrid?"

She frowns. "You're right. I said I'd do that. That's next."

"So what *have* you been praying for?"

Her face assumes a cagey expression. "Maybe I have a special intention."

"Like what?"

"None of your beeswax, young lady."

I bet it has something to do with love and lust. Needless to say my mother wouldn't appeal to Freyja for help in those areas. As Pop would say, she'd go straight to the man upstairs.

I watch her pray, a maternal impediment to any plan to sell my house and relocate five hundred miles south to Charlotte. It would be hard enough if she and Pop were still married. But with them divorced and Mom living alone while Pop gallivants around with Maggie Lindvig? How could I do that to her? Or am I using her as a convenient excuse to avoid doing something I don't want to do anyway?

I could ask her to move with us. She might be game. Then again she's got her new job and her budding romance with car salesman extraordinaire Bennie Hana. I can't tell if she's really interested in Bennie or just using him to make Pop jealous. I know it's mean of me but I hope it's the latter.

I need to go to confession something fierce.

I enter the confessional and kneel. The priest slides open the screen over the grille that separates us and I mouth the familiar words. "Bless me, Father, for I have sinned. It's been, oh, I don't even know how long since my last confession."

"That's all right," he murmurs, "I'm glad you're here now." He sounds paternal and understanding.

I run through my litany of transgressions. He listens and nods and assigns me several prayers to recite for my penance. He's about to give me the final blessing but I interrupt him. "Before I go, do you mind if I bring up something that's bothering me?"

"I'll help if I can."

I give him the full download: Jason, Mario, Jason's new job in Charlotte, my deeply conflicted feelings. I hope there aren't too many other sinners in line for confession because it takes quite a while. Finally I run out of things to say.

The priest sighs. Then, "Maybe you and your husband could take a break. Like Rachel and Ross did on *Friends*."

I must admit, that is not what I was expecting. "Really? The Church would be okay with that?" Then I think of a hitch. "I don't think Rachel and Ross were married when they took a break, Father."

"Oh, you're right. Too bad." Then he chuckles. "By the way, I was joking. Trying to lighten the moment. Something told me you have a sense of humor."

I laugh weakly. "Wow. You really threw me."

"Got your hopes up, didn't I? Sorry. No, I'd be in trouble if I gave advice like that. Here's what I really think," and he explains the Catholic view of marriage, which I already knew: that it is a gift from God and a lifelong union that allows no other.

"So the bottom line is, make it work," I conclude.

"To quote Tim Gunn from *Project Runway*."

"You're good with the TV references, Father."

"I try to keep up. God be with you, my child."

I exit the confessional thinking Pop was right. I do feel better. I still don't know what I'm going to do but talking it through helped.

After I finish my penance, I find my mom deep in murmured conversation with the lady in the neighboring pew. My mother introduces her as Florence Rubinski then motions me to lean in close.

"Florence here," she says, "has told me some sad stories about that Galena Lang."

CHAPTER EIGHTEEN

"So you know Galena?" I ask Florence.

"My friend's daughter is one of her best friends," Florence explains.

"They're tight," my mother adds for good measure.

"Galena has had a great deal of tragedy in her life," Florence informs us. "She lost her husband and she lost her brother."

"I knew about her husband," I say. "It was his family who started the mortuary business, right?"

Florence nods. "Her husband was barely fifty years old and one day he had a heart attack and that was it."

"That's how it goes sometimes," my mother says. "My friend's husband Frank, same thing." My mom slaps my arm. "Then just this last year that Galena's brother got killed in a hit and run."

"That was a sad case, too." Florence shakes her head. "He was in Viet Nam and got that PSTD."

"You mean PTSD," I say. "Post-traumatic stress disorder."

"He was homeless." Florence lowers her voice as if this is an especially shameful thing to discuss. "Drinking problem. Galena and her husband even tried to have him live with them but he didn't want to do it."

"Maybe he didn't want to live on top of the funeral home,"

my mother suggests. Then to me: "That's where that Galena lives. I'm not sure I'd like that, either."

"I don't think that was it," Florence says. "He wasn't right in the head. Of course Galena didn't talk about him because she thought it would be bad for business if people knew she had a brother who was in that situation."

"That's how it goes," my mother says. "But you can't hide these things. People find out."

This information is rounding out my picture of Galena but otherwise isn't very helpful. "Florence, do you know if Galena ever ran into trouble with the law?"

My mother and Florence both gasp and a woman a few pews ahead of us spins around to tell us to hush up. "Why would you think that?" Florence whispers.

"I'm just asking." After all, I paid Hubble three hundred smackers to learn that Galena "may" have done something illegal. If I get confirmation, that money might go from wasted to well spent.

"I never heard anything like that," Florence says. "Galena's a little funny with the way she does herself up but I never heard she's a hooligan."

"Let me ask you something else. Do you know of any connection between Galena and Ingrid Svendsen?"

"That rich woman who got herself murdered at the new Giant W?" Florence shakes her head. "Why would Galena know her?"

This isn't getting me very far. "Would you do me a favor and ask your friend's daughter if she knows of a connection between them? Of if she knows whether Galena ever got in trouble with the police?" I have another thought. "And one last thing. Galena may have come into money recently. Please find out if your friend's daughter knows anything about that."

"You can tell me tomorrow at Mass what she said," my mother says to Florence. Then to me: "8 a.m. Mass, like I go to at home. Florence here likes to meet her obligation first thing, too."

"I'll bring those coupons we talked about," Florence promises my mother, who might have met a kindred soul.

Back in the rental car my mother slaps my thigh. "You think you're the only one who can do this investigating business. But *I'm* the one who found Florence Rubinski."

"That's all well and good, Mom, but her information wasn't all that useful."

"Someday you'll give me my due," my mother predicts.

"I hope I don't drop dead first."

I continue west on 4th Street. "You ready for lunch?" It's a rhetorical question because my mom, like me, is always game for a meal. "I told Trixie and Shanelle we'd meet up with them."

"That Maggie won't be joining us. Not that I mind." My mother harrumphs. "She had some so-called important errand to do, not that she would tell anybody what it was. She wouldn't let your father go with her, either."

"That's probably okay with him. I think he wanted to talk to somebody about ice fishing."

"That's the one thing he wants to do while he's here in Winona. Hey, this must be the place."

We spy Trixie and Shanelle heading into Bub's Brewing Company, located in an old-style brick building. From outside it looks deserted but inside it's bustling. We pass through a corridor with framed quotes like Mae West's: "Marriage is a great institution but I'm not ready for an institution." And this pearl from Phyllis Diller: "Never go to bed mad. Stay up and fight."

Trixie hails us from a booth. We walk past mounted televisions airing college football and armchair coaches hollering at the action. "Can you believe Bub's is pronounced boobs?" Trixie chortles when we sit down.

"This place has our name all over it," Shanelle deadpans. "I say we share a few burgers and the Cajun fries."

"Perfect," I agree.

"Let's try the beer, too." My mother points to a poster for

Bub's beer, a brew made here in Winona. I gather she's ready to relax after all her praying.

We are contentedly sipping our brewskis when I point out that Trixie seems in an even better mood than usual. She leans forward confidentially. "I wasn't going to say anything because really we should be talking about Ingrid's murder—"

"We talked to a lot of Ingrid's neighbors this morning," Shanelle interrupts to say. "None of them ever heard of Priscilla Pembroke."

"Yes, we'll tell you about that," Trixie goes on. "But the reason I'm so happy is because I had a very interesting conversation with Mario."

"He has a shoot later but he came to Damsgard looking for you," Shanelle tells me. "Apparently you weren't answering your cell phone."

Not after the call from Jason. After which I needed a break from everyone and everything. Even Mario.

"I invited him to dinner, by the way," Shanelle goes on, which elicits a grunt of approval from my mother.

"Anyway," Trixie goes on, "Mario asked what I planned to do after I got the family settled in Savannah and I told him of course I would look for a job at a bridal salon. And you know what he said? That I should open my own!"

"You should," I say. "You were better at running your old salon than the owner."

"That didn't stop her from firing me," Trixie says.

"Her loss," Shanelle says. "Anyway, tell them the rest of what Mario said. The *really* good part."

"I'm almost afraid to say it but here goes." Trixie takes a deep breath. "Mario said he was very impressed with how I pulled things together for the Teen Princess of the Everglades pageant and so if I was interested in opening my own salon he was interested in becoming an investor!"

"Wow!" I cry. "That is amazing, Trixie! Congratulations!"

We all toast with our chilled beer steins. I am delighted to hear this: it is yet more evidence that in addition to his other charms Mario Suave is one good guy. Trixie goes on. "But here's the hitch. I have to write a business plan, which I've never done before in my life."

"I told her I'd help," Shanelle says. "And Lord knows *I* need something interesting to do."

"I don't like the sound of that," I say.

Shanelle shakes her head. "I know I should be content because everything is fine. Lamar is fine; Devon is fine; I'm fine. The problem is I'm bored. You two know nothing about that," she says to Trixie and me. "You both have exciting things going on."

My mother slaps my thigh. "Like what, in your case?"

"Oh"—my mind cranks—"Shanelle means trying to solve this murder."

I can tell my mom's not buying that answer but the last thing I want to do is raise the dreaded topic of Jason accepting a NASCAR pit-crew job in Charlotte. Fortunately Trixie plunges forward. "You need something new to strive for, Shanelle, now that your pageant days are over."

"Exactly," Shanelle says. "This queen needs a new goal. But what?"

We brainstorm the entire time we're eating but don't come up with anything that floats Shanelle's boat. As we're paying the check I remember what Shanelle said earlier. "So nobody in the neighborhood knows Priscilla? She told us she has all kinds of connections in the area."

"Nobody we talked to ever heard of her," Trixie reports.

"And we must've asked a dozen people," Shanelle adds. "Did you check in with Detective Dembek?"

"I tried. I had to leave her a message." We bundle up against the cold and head outside to find overcast skies and a chill wind that probably blows no good. I turn to my mom. "Will you go back to Damsgard with Trixie and Shanelle? I want to stop by the funeral home." I thought of a pretext for visiting Galena the Goth Mortician and as we all know, there's no time like the present.

"Be back before 4," Trixie says. That's when the candlelight tour begins.

I arrive at Lang Funeral Home just as the hearse screeches to a halt out front. Galena emerges wearing a knee-length black coat that makes me wish I had a Goth side. It's made of twill with faux leather buckle straps to cinch in the waist and stud ornamentation at the shoulders and cuffs. "Do you always drive the hearse?" I ask as I trail Galena to the front door.

"It doesn't get tickets." Her tone is as chilly as the weather. It's clear that like Peter Svendsen, Galena Lang is less than thrilled to see me.

We enter the foyer and I spy a framed hand-embroidered saying I missed last time. *The really frightening thing about middle age is the knowledge that you'll grow out of it – Doris Day.*

"What can I do you for?" Galena whips off her coat to reveal another stylish piece: a knit tunic dress in a black and crimson stripe. "My pending came through so I'm kind of in a rush."

"I was wondering if you could direct me to some of Ingrid Svendsen's friends." I watch Galena closely but she reveals no reaction. "Ingrid's wardrobe is going to her sister but we thought it might be nice to give some of her pieces to her closest friends."

Galena narrows her eyes at me. "How would I know who her friends are?"

Even though I'm fresh from confession, I tell a lie. "I thought maybe you two were friendly, both long-time residents and all."

Galena turns away. "If there are things her sister doesn't want to keep, she can take them to a consignment store."

I boldly follow Galena into her office. "I'm getting the impression Ingrid Svendsen didn't have that big a fan club here in town."

Galena pulls open a file drawer. "I wouldn't know."

You've got to say this for Galena: she's doing a bang-up job of pretending she and Ingrid had nothing to do with each other. Since Ingrid hired a P.I. to dig up dirt on Galena, I doubt that was the case.

I pick up a hat lying on Galena's desk. "This is gorgeous," I declare, and that's no lie. The hat is a concoction of purple feathers, black velvet and white pearls that looks like something from a different era. "It reminds me of those hats aristocrats wear in England to go to royal parties. Is that where you got it?"

Galena snatches the hat from my hand. "Look, I don't have time to bond over millinery. I can't help you and I've got work to do." She shepherds me out of the funeral home and, short of digging in my high-heeled booties, I can't do anything to resist her.

For the second time in mere hours, I find myself pushed outside onto somebody's stoop. Apparently I need to go back to charm school for a refresher course. I've been in Winona only a few days but already I'm pretty darn unpopular.

CHAPTER NINETEEN

I'm one of those women who love the holiday season. I don't go gaga but I do enjoy decking the halls. Sending out cards. Baking cookies. Making homemade gifts. Going around the block with a few neighbors and singing carols. So as I stand in Damsgard's glorious candlelit living room surveying the fabulous Christmas tree and all the other Yuletide décor—the poinsettias, garlands, nutcrackers, Santas, and snowmen—I should be awash in delight. Instead it all falls a little flat for me this year.

I'm plagued by doubt and uncertainty, never good for the mood. Where will I celebrate Christmas next year? Will my family be around me? Change is supposed to be good but, boy, can it be scary, too.

The truth is I dread what the New Year will bring. For sure it will bring an empty nest. Rachel will graduate high school and go off somewhere, probably to parts foreign and unimaginable. My reign as Ms. America will end. Jason will be living in Charlotte. Most likely I will be, too. I'm excited about the international competition in my future, but that brings lots of pressure, too. I'll have to work really hard to get back into competition shape, and into the competition mindset. This will be the first—and no doubt, only—time I represent the U.S. of A. on the international stage and this queen is determined to make her nation proud.

If by some miracle I win, then I'll continue to be a beauty queen, something I know and love. But much more likely, I won't win. And once my reign is over I'll have to relinquish my Ms. America crown. So my title, tiara, and sash days will be over. Who's Happy Pennington if she's not a beauty queen? Talk about a big question to have to answer.

From out of nowhere Trixie appears to rub my back. She's adorable in a sleeveless emerald-green sheath with a lace bodice and satin tulip skirt. We queens never need much of an excuse to get all dressed up so it took us but a nanosecond to decide that the candlelight Christmas tour required festive garb. "You know," Trixie murmurs, "I really do believe things work out for the best."

"How do you always know the exact right thing to say?"

"All you have to do is think about it a little bit more and you'll know what you want to do about moving to Charlotte."

When I got back to Damsgard from the funeral home, I pulled Trixie and Shanelle into my room and told them Jason had accepted the job offer. It felt good to talk about it but I'm as confused as ever.

"Charlotte's really nice, you know," Trixie adds.

"That's what everybody says."

"I'm going to be really sad to move, and it's terrible timing with Jason's new job and all, but I am pretty sure I'm going to love Savannah." She grins. "Look at it this way. If you move to Charlotte, I'll be only two hundred fifty miles away. That's just a car ride."

"I'll be a lot closer to Shanelle, too in Biloxi."

"See?" Trixie smiles and rubs my back again. "But first things first. Let's have a good time with this house tour then keep trying to figure out who murdered poor Ingrid. I think the memorial book was a really good idea."

We set it up on the foyer table next to a photo of Ingrid. I doubt anyone will write anything revealing in it but you never know. "Let's all three of us do a lot of mingling," I say. "See if we can find out something new about Ingrid."

"All four of us will be mingling. Your mom wants in on this, too. You look very cute, by the way." Trixie steps back to admire my dress, which features a navy lace overlay over a white sheath. "I love that scalloped hem. And lace is really trending this season."

Shanelle joins us in a fuchsia fit-and-flare dress with a black floral motif that gives it a screen-printed quality. "Man, this house looks spectacular!"

"All the candles make it so magical, don't they?" I say. Per the instructions we were given by the historical society, we're using electricity only to light the Christmas trees. To replicate a Victorian-era atmosphere, our only other light source is candles. "It's no wonder so many places burned down back in the day, though."

"I think a lot of these old houses were built with shredded paper as insulation, too," Shanelle says. "Can you imagine how fast that would go up?"

"We have to make sure we douse every last candle before we go to bed," Trixie says.

I'm in the kitchen putting the White Christmas Dream Drop cookies my mother baked on serving platters when she calls to me from over by the sink. "Look what I found in the garbage," she crows, and waves a slip of paper in the air.

"Mom, you're too dressed up to be digging in the trash." She's sporting a blue paisley wrap dress, yet another fashion-forward acquisition.

"It was near the top. Look at this," she repeats.

I pause in my task. My mother's find is a small greasy piece of paper filled with Ingrid's signature written over and over again in blue ink. "Well, I agree that's weird, but it doesn't mean anything."

"What are you talking about? Your father has taken out the trash since that woman died. She didn't write this," my mother concludes.

"We don't know that. The fact that it got thrown out recently doesn't mean it was written recently."

My mother throws out her arms. "Who practices writing their own signature?"

"Pretty much no one," I admit. "No one who's an adult, anyway." I haven't practiced a signature since I was seventeen years old and just found out I was pregnant and was anticipating my shotgun wedding by repeatedly scrawling Mrs. Jason Kilborn in my Chem notebook.

My mother flourishes the paper triumphantly. "Only one person would do this and that's that Maggie. You dust that paper for prints, that's what you'll find."

"It's not a crime to practice writing somebody else's signature."

"Not on a piece of scrap paper, no. But you mark my words." My mother folds the paper in half and stuffs it in her bra. "That's not the only place she's writing it."

"You realize you're pretty much accusing Maggie of fraud."

My mother juts her chin. "Fraud, murder, who knows what that floozy is up to?"

The doorbell rings and we hear Trixie answer it with a cry of greeting. "Don't tell Maggie you found that," I instruct my mother, handing her a platter of Dream Drops to transport to the dining room. "Give me a chance to feel her out on it when she and Pop get back." Heaven knows where they are. We were told not to expect them back till late.

Now I hear a real commotion in the foyer. It appears the Christmas tour has officially begun.

The next few hours pass in a pleasant flurry of guiding visitors through Damsgard, probing them for tidbits about Ingrid, and guarding the library so Priscilla doesn't use this opportunity to sneak in to snatch the Erskine above the mantel. Nothing very interesting happens until I meet a fiftyish couple sparring mildly as the female half writes in Ingrid's memorial book.

"It was in 2009 that we did *Love's Labour's Lost*," she says. "We did *Merchant of Venice* in 2008."

"Are you sure?" He gives her a dubious look. "You might be right."

I introduce myself. "Are you talking about the Winona Shakespeare Festival?"

"Actually it's called the Great River Shakespeare Festival." The woman straightens from the memorial book, where I see she's penned quite the tribute to Ingrid. "Mrs. Svendsen was a big sponsor every year. We're so sad what happened to her."

"Did you know her personally?" I ask with hope in my voice.

"Only from afar," the man replies, "although my wife and I have been volunteering from the beginning. We've been ushers and helped with hospitality—"

"That's the best," the woman interrupts. "Then we get to meet the actors."

"Really? Did you by any chance get to know Priscilla Pembroke when she played Hermione in *The Winter's Tale*?"

They both frown. "Priscilla Pembroke?" the man says.

"Never heard that name," the woman declares. "Wasn't it Kim Martin-Cotten who played Hermione?" she asks her husband. "Kim is so wonderful," she tells me. "She's been in so many of our productions."

"You could look it up online," the man says. "You'll find photos from all the productions."

Why didn't I think of that? "Thank you. I will," and I usher them into the dining room, where there's a crowd who've stopped touring to scarf the Dream Drops instead.

Sure enough, I realize a minute later, standing in the foyer to scan the photos from *The Winter's Tale* on my cell phone. There was no Priscilla Pembroke in that play. For all her gushing about Hermione, Priscilla was nowhere near that role. That's just another lie she told. What is up with that woman? She tells lies as often as I apply hand cream.

I'm wondering whether anything Priscilla told me is true when I sense a hulking presence to my left. I glance over to see a bulky older man in a parka and wool cap squinting at the framed 8-by-10 glossy of Ingrid beside the memorial book. It is hard to see it clearly in the candlelight. He looks vaguely familiar but I can't place him. That is, until Trixie sashays into the foyer bearing a platter of Dream Drops. Then his attention shifts from Ingrid's photo to Trixie. He calls out her name.

Well, sort of her name.

"Trudy Barnett!" He bellows the name so loudly I bet he gets the attention of every visitor on Damsgard's first floor. He points a stubby finger at our makeshift memorial to Ingrid. "You let me think Mrs. Svendsen was alive! What the heck kind of trick you trying to pull?"

Uh oh. It's Hubble.

CHAPTER TWENTY

"When I met you at that boat landing," Hubble thunders, "you told me Mrs. Svendsen might need my services again. Since I don't investigate in and around the pearly gates, I don't see how she could!"

"And you told me your name was Trixie!" a gray-haired doyenne accuses. By now the cookie-munching crowd from the dining room has migrated to the foyer and is gearing up to watch this impromptu drama unfold.

Trixie gulps. "Trixie, Trudy, who can keep it straight?"

"We are beauty queens, after all," Shanelle offers. "Not too much upstairs."

"You're smart enough to take up residence here at Damsgard, the nicest place in town," a male voice calls out. "I don't know how you managed to pull that off."

"Yeah! What's going on here?" the Shakespeare man demands.

I step forward and take Hubble's beefy arm. "Just a little misunderstanding," I call out cheerfully. I try to urge the P.I. toward the living room. "Everybody please enjoy the Dream Drops and go on with the tour."

Hubble whirls on me. "You! You're the one with the cold who pretended to be Mrs. Svendsen on the phone!"

A gasp rises from the multitude. And I will admit I sound pretty malevolent from that description. I better take swift action or we three queens might face some Victorian-era justice. "My name is Happy Pennington, I'm the reigning Ms. America, and my friends and I are houseguests of Mrs. Svendsen. We came to town to participate in the Giant W opening ceremony." I speak in as forceful a manner as my congestion will allow. "Mrs. Svendsen's sister Maggie Lindvig is staying here, too. I'm sure many of you remember her from back in the day."

"Maggie Lindvig, yes," the Shakespeare woman says. She lowers her voice. "The one who had the baby out of wedlock."

My mother pipes up. "That's the one."

"Whoever you people are, I don't like being taken for a fool." Hubble picks up Ingrid's photo and waves it in the air. "I didn't know Mrs. Svendsen real good but she was a classy lady and she always treated me right."

"Didn't you say you were doing some investigating for her?" the Shakespeare man wants to know.

"You should investigate these beauty queens!" the doyenne cries. "I think they had something to do with her murder!"

The crowd recoils in horror. Trixie almost drops the platter of Dream Drops.

"They're up to no good, that much I know." Hubble gets right in Trixie's panic-stricken face. "You led me to believe Mrs. Svendsen was your Aunt Ingrid and now I know that's a flat-out lie!"

"Murderers!" the doyenne yowls.

This crowd is turning on us faster than a ballerina can pirouette. I don't know if Hubble plans to punch Trixie in the nose but all of a sudden he spins around to return Ingrid's photo to the foyer table. Unfortunately he's so het up that he knocks the frame into the tall candles we set up next to the memorial book so visitors could see clearly enough to write. As if it's happening in slow motion, I watch the candles tumble. One of them sets the memorial book on fire and the other ignites the wreath encircling the sconce above the foyer table.

"Oh my God!" my mother hollers. "Everybody out! The whole place is going up!"

I wouldn't go that far but the wreath is burning but good and a surprising amount of smoke is billowing toward the ceiling. The smoke alarm begins to shriek.

Nothing clears a crowd like the prospect of being grilled like a New York steak. The tour visitors skedaddle so fast you'd think they were Olympic sprinters. No sooner do they escape out the front door than I am astonished to see my mother aim a fire extinguisher at the blaze. She sprays foam all over it and in seconds it's out. We're left with a charred wreath, a crispy memorial book, a slightly fried wall, and a smoky foyer. But other than that, Damsgard appears unscathed.

For a few seconds we all just stand there panting. Then I move forward to take my mother in my arms. She's trembling, I'm trembling, and I bet Trixie and Shanelle are, too.

Trixie is the first to break the silence. "My Lord, Mrs. P! You look like you've been doing that all your life!"

"I practice every year around the holidays." My mother breaks away from me, sets down the fire extinguisher, and wipes her hands on her pretty paisley dress. "We always get a live tree and put lights on it and you never know what can happen."

I find my voice. "I can't believe you reacted so fast! How did you even know where the fire extinguisher was?"

She blinks at me. "Soon as I saw all the trees in this house, I looked for it. It was in the kitchen, where you'd expect it to be."

I'm giving my mother another grateful hug—and thinking I really shouldn't underestimate her—when a fire truck wails to a halt out front. A trio of firemen race inside to assess the scene. One of them succeeds in shutting off the smoke alarm.

"I'm glad somebody called us but you ladies handled this real well," the senior fireman pronounces. "This situation could've gotten out of control fast."

I point to my mom. "This lady here deserves all the praise!"

My mother bows her head. "Don't say anything about this to your father, Happy. I wouldn't want to show up that Maggie."

We blow out every candle in the house and offer the firemen a Dream Drops reward. They depart soon after their sugary jolt. I call Detective Dembek once again and this time I reach her. We have a brief catch-up on the investigation and agree to talk in more depth in the morning. I return downstairs to sink onto a velvet sofa in the living room. In short order Trixie and my mom join me.

Shanelle brings up the rear bearing a tray of lovely pink drinks in martini glasses. "Poinsettia Mimosas. Boy, do we deserve these. You most of all, Mrs. Przybyszewski."

"Don't mind if I do," she replies.

I find out they're made with sparkling wine, Triple Sec, grenadine, and cranberry juice. I let out a big sigh after the first sip. "Between this and the broken window, we have got to be the worst houseguests in the state of Minnesota."

"Neither of those was our fault," Trixie points out.

"Tell that to Peter Svendsen." I set down my cocktail and drop my head back against the plush cushions. "I am dreading having to tell him about this. I assured him we'd do a great job with the tour but instead we nearly burned down his house."

"Put off telling him till tomorrow," my mother suggests. "It's always better to get bad news first thing in the morning than late at night."

That's a piece of folk wisdom I am ready to embrace.

"Plus," she goes on, "the meat pie's about to come out of the oven."

"*That's* what smells so delicious!" Trixie cries.

"You made cookies *and* a meat pie?" Shanelle says.

"I knew that Mario was coming over for dinner so I wanted to make something extra good." My mother cocks her chin at me. "They say the way to a man's heart is through his stomach. In my opinion other parts work pretty good, too."

"Mrs. P!" Trixie yelps.

"Whatever works," my mother concludes. We're all agreeing that she's quite the pistol when the doorbell rings. I expect to find Mario on the stoop so I'm pretty surprised to see Hubble there instead.

"I want to apologize for starting that fire," he says without preamble. He looks past me at the singed foyer table. "Glad it didn't turn out worse. I'm not happy you people told me a tall tale but I had no business getting everybody so riled up."

I wave him in out of the cold. "I owe you an apology, too. And an explanation."

It does not surprise me that Hubble prefers a beer to a Poinsettia Mimosa. He joins us in the living room, where I detail my sleuthing history and my quest to figure out who shot Ingrid Svendsen. "So that's why we weren't upfront with you. I thought the fact that Ingrid hired you to investigate Galena Lang might have had something to do with her murder."

"Maybe it did. Maybe it didn't."

"And all you know about why Mrs. Svendsen hired you to investigate Galena was that she thought Galena was trouble?"

Hubble pauses to swig some beer. Then, "She didn't say it in so many words but I got the idea Mrs. S wanted something on Galena Lang. Something she could use against her. Tell you what." He pours more beer down his gullet. "How about I keep snooping around Galena Lang? For free this time. I owe it to Mrs. Svendsen and it'll make up partway for the damage I did to her house."

We shake on it. I don't admit it to Hubble but I could use the help. "Would you like to stay for dinner? My mother's meat pie is about to come out of the oven." Made with ground beef and pork, cinnamon, nutmeg, and allspice, it is winter comfort food at its finest.

Hubble declines and heaves himself to his feet. "The boss is waiting for me at home. I'll be in touch."

We've done some cleanup in the foyer and have moved on to setting the mahogany dining table for dinner when Mario shows up wearing chinos and a burgundy crewneck sweater beneath his cashmere overcoat. Naturally the incinerated state of the foyer requires explanation.

He shakes his head when our story is told. "Tomorrow I'll be shooting at a place where a man burned to death but there was no other sign of fire."

"That sounds like a ghost story," Trixie breathes.

"Pour me a drink and I'll tell you about it." Primed with a mimosa and a plate of meat pie, Mario begins. "Heffron Hall is a dorm on the campus of Saint Mary's University. In '89 *USA Today* named it 'Minnesota's Most Legendary Haunted Place.'"

"Here we go again," my mother says.

"Let him tell the story," I say. "Go on, Mario."

"It was back in 1931," Mario continues, speaking in his somber *America's Scariest Ghost Stories* style, "that the body of the Reverend Edward Lynch was found sprawled across his bed. He was burned almost beyond recognition. But nothing around him showed any sign of fire; not the sheets, not the bed."

"I'm not liking the sound of this," Shanelle mutters.

"Not only that," Mario continues, "but the priest's Bible is reported to have been burned, too, except for a single passage that has to do with the Lord returning to earth on the last day to the sound of trumpets."

"Thessalonians," my mom says.

She is positively dazzling today. "I'm guessing there's special significance to that passage," I say.

Mario nods. "There's another priest who died in 1943 who spent the last decades of his life in a mental institution after being found not guilty of murder due to reason of insanity. That second priest shot and nearly killed a beloved bishop while the bishop was saying Mass. The priest was known for screaming that particular passage at Reverend

Lynch and it is his ghost who's said to haunt the third floor of Heffron Hall."

We eat in silence for a while, partly because the meat pie is so delectable and partly because it's hard to chow down while the hair is rising on the back of your neck.

Then Shanelle pipes up. "Maybe Father Lynch died of spontaneous combustion. It's rare but it happens."

"Maybe," Mario says. "The coroner concluded that he was electrocuted when he turned off his reading lamp while also touching a steam radiator. But would a 110-volt current be enough to kill him? *And* burn him beyond recognition?"

"I don't know anything about electrical currents but I don't think so," Trixie opines. "I can't believe you have to shoot there tomorrow. I wouldn't go within a mile of the place."

"I was hoping you'd come with me." Mario issues the invitation to all of us but gives me a wink. "For moral support."

"It'd be really fun to see a shoot for your show," I say, "but I'm not sure I'm up to tangling with ghosts."

"What, you prefer murderers?" my mother bellows. "I can't believe my own daughter thinks something so crazy."

We've cleared the table by the time Pop and Maggie return from their prolonged excursion. Once again we have to explain the singed foyer. I ignore my mom's bogus instruction not to tell my father she was the one to douse the flames. "She had the whole thing extinguished in a matter of seconds. I didn't even have time to react."

Pop gazes at his ex with such admiration I almost feel bad for Maggie.

Almost.

"Well, it's Peter Svendsen's problem now, isn't it?" She whips off her pea coat to reveal a sweater that's so tight and low-cut it might've given even Dolly Parton pause. But not Maggie Lindvig. She brightens. "We had a terrific time today, didn't we, Lou? Lunch, shopping, dinner, a movie, the whole nine yards."

Pop tears his eyes away from my mom, who's pretending not to notice. "We blew off a lot of steam, all right. Probably could've done without the movie."

"What are you talking about? You love staying out late. I'm going upstairs to soak in the tub." Maggie flounces upstairs while my mom smiles into her sleeve. We all know my father likes late nights like he likes visits to the gastroenterologist.

Pop lingers in the foyer sniffing the air like a bloodhound. But it's not the smell of smoke that gets his attention. "That your meat pie, Hazel?" he wants to know.

"Everybody had seconds, but there might be a little left," she allows.

"I already had dinner, but maybe I could find room for seconds, too," he says.

My mother throws a triumphant glance in my direction as she leads my father into the kitchen.

I've got to give her credit. She scored a lot of points today.

And I bet it wasn't Mario's heart she was aiming at with that meat pie of hers.

CHAPTER TWENTY-ONE

Even though it's twelve degrees and pitch dark out, Mario suggests a walk around Windom Park. This queen is all over it.

We walk side by side with our hands in our pockets like schoolkids. I'm bundled in my plum-colored coat and matching bouclé knit cloche with accent bow. My high-heeled booties crunch on the pavement, sprinkled with salt to melt the ice and snow. The streets are deliciously deserted. Our only companion is the moon, almost full, pouring buckets of silver light on our heads.

I feel Mario's eyes on my face. "I bet your dad is a lot more attached to your mom than he lets on," he says.

"Really? You think so?" If that were true, my heart would be as full as the moon.

"I do. Even though he's trying to hide it."

"Don't tell my mom. She wouldn't be able to resist lording it over him." We enjoy a chuckle. "I'm starting to wonder if the age difference with Maggie is getting to Pop, even though it's only a few years. He told me once that one of the things he liked best about her was how energetic she is. But he can have trouble keeping up."

"Like tonight."

"Maggie might be oblivious but my mom sure isn't."

"After all those years of marriage, I'm not surprised."

Mario pauses and I get the feeling he's turned his thoughts from my parents' marriage to mine. "So how are you, Happy? Is everything okay with you? You've seemed preoccupied the whole time you've been here in Winona. And I don't just mean by the murder."

I hesitate, then, "I'm okay."

"I hope I haven't done something to upset you."

"No, it's not that." I fall silent. Then, "I don't think I should talk about it."

This is the problem when you get close to a man who's not your husband. It doesn't feel right to talk about your husband with him. It feels like a betrayal. It's one thing to talk about Jason and my private business with a priest or Pop or even my BFFs. It's another to discuss it with Mario, who's pretty much said flat out that he'd like to be in the more-than-friends category where I'm concerned.

"All right. I won't press it." Mario sighs. I can tell he's disappointed that I've put up this wall between us. "So what's the latest with Rachel?" he wants to know. "She must be up to her eyeballs in college applications by now."

"I wish. You know that overseas program she interviewed for in Miami? She got accepted." Which doesn't surprise me in the least. My daughter is a star.

"You don't think that's good?"

"Don't get me wrong. I'm really proud of her. It's a competitive program and it's very impressive that she got picked. But I'm just so afraid that if she doesn't go to college now she never will. She'll make the same mistake I did, for different reasons."

"She's a wonderful girl, Happy. You and Jason did a tremendous job with her." Mario raises his head to look at the moon. As moonbeams illuminate his face, I notice a line creasing his forehead and a few more fanning out from his eyes. For the first time I imagine what he'll look like as an older man. Then, too, he'll make my heart stop.

I force myself to return to the matter at hand. "You're

saying I shouldn't worry about Rachel. That she'll make good choices."

"Not only that. I've heard you say many times that you try not to push her the way your mom pushed you."

"I think about that all the time. The irony is that when my mom pushed me into pageants, she had my best interests at heart. Just like I do now when I'm pushing Rachel toward college."

"Look at it this way. Your daughter is doing a much better job making choices than mine is. Although I get the idea the setbacks Mariela's had lately are making her take stock a little bit."

Mariela Machado Suave is one lucky teenager if the worst disappointments she suffers are coming in fifth in a beauty pageant and failing to nail a callback for a role on TV. "You'll make sure her head is on straight, Mario. Plus she adores you. What you think really matters to her."

"Some of the time, anyway. By the way, she's totally focused on L.A. for college. And not just because I'm there."

I giggle. "Because Hollywood is there."

"Celebrity awaits. No matter how much I caution her, Mariela is sure of it. It's so annoying how they have minds of their own, isn't it?"

"You'd think we raised them that way."

We share another chuckle. Across the street at a cheerful berry-colored Victorian with yellow accents, the white lights strung through the trees click off, a sign that the sidewalks are officially rolling up. In the distance a train's horn cuts through the night quiet. We're almost back at Damsgard.

"So it's Jason then," Mario says. "That you don't want to talk about."

Since I don't know what to say, my silence serves as an answer.

"Do you know how much I envy him?" Mario says.

"He wouldn't believe that in a million years."

Damsgard is the next house. Its outside lights are off, too.

Only one upstairs window glows in the dark.

"Jason has something I don't," Mario says.

He doesn't have to say what he means. "Mario—"

He stops walking and takes my gloved hands in his. "Don't get me wrong, Happy. I'm very proud of how far I've come. Ten years ago I never would've believed it. But as thrilled as I am with all of that, the career, the houses, the cars, there's something missing. Something that Jason has and I don't."

We gaze at each other. Again Mario speaks. "He has you."

Around us Winona sleeps, overhead stars twinkle, and somehow time finds a way to stop, the way it so often does when Mario and I are alone together. I'm propelled back to Oahu, to those days when Mario Suave seemed light years away from me. Then he was a stunningly handsome man, smart and charming and successful to boot, who moved in a whole different universe than Happy Pennington. Now he's here on an empty winter street, holding my hands, telling me in no uncertain terms that I'm the one he wants.

I find my voice. "I'm not sure you should be saying that, Mario." *And I'm not sure I should be hearing it.*

"It'd still be true even if I didn't say it."

He glances down the street, still holding my hands. Again I see those faint lines on his face. Mario isn't the youngest man. He's seen enough to know disappointment. He's lived enough to know that things don't always work out in the end.

"For what it's worth," he goes on, "I have tried to get you out of my mind." He laughs softly. "I haven't tried too hard, though. The truth is I don't want you gone."

"Well, if we're being completely honest, I don't want you gone, either."

We're all alone, or we might as well be. No one in the century-old houses that surround us is watching. This is the time for the lovers to kiss. If only they could be lovers. If only they didn't have husbands and children and vows they hold dear.

That's what stops me. That's what propels my hand onto Mario's chest, where it's been before when I've found the strength to stop him from bundling me into his arms. Because I know he would. And if I were the teensiest bit less stalwart, I would let him.

Would I ever.

Instead Mario kisses my hand, glove and all. "I can dream, can't I?"

"You shouldn't be dreaming. You should be living your life."

"I'm doing that, too." He lets go of my hands and with a gentle finger traces the curve of my cheek. "If I find someone like you, I'll let you know. But don't hold your breath."

I couldn't anyway. After that conversation, I'm breathless.

Arm in arm we stroll up the path to Damsgard's front door. "So you want to join me for my shoot at Heffron Hall tomorrow?" he asks.

"I'd love to. Even though I'm terrified a ghost will show up."

"Not much chance of that."

"The thing is I really do have to focus on the murder. I think about it constantly but it's been four days since Ingrid died and it's still all a muddle in my head. And I was supposed to fly home tomorrow."

We mount the steps to the porch. "You'll be staying on instead?" he asks.

I'm guessing it's not a casual question. "For a while. I can't stay forever, though. I have to figure this out soon."

"You will. I have confidence in you." He glances up at the porch ceiling. "Still no mistletoe. I really do have to remedy that." He gives me a devilish wink as he turns to go. I can't help laughing. "Hey, it's the perfect excuse!" He trips lightly down the stairs back to the path, waving his arm in the air as he goes.

I watch him walk all the way to his car, because I can't

help it. And when I go inside and upstairs and collapse on my bed, still wearing my coat and cloche, I replay every word of our conversation in my mind. It consumes me as I put on my PJs and wash off my makeup and moisturize as if my life depended on it. And when I stop thinking about Mario I start thinking about Jason. Because later this very day—it's after midnight now—I have to give him my answer about moving to Charlotte.

The next morning I awaken to snow flurries and the smell of something heavenly in the oven. Maybe the aroma succeeds in breaking through my congestion because it carries me back to winter Sunday mornings when I was growing up. I pad downstairs in my jammies, my hair in a messy ponytail, to find my mother putting round baking pans on cooling racks.

She's not alone. Trixie and Shanelle are in the kitchen, too, perched at the island nursing mugs of coffee and watching the action. Like me, they're in their jammies. My mother is so ready to depart for Mass that she's got her trendy funnel-neck coat on.

"Who can stay in bed once they smell this?" Trixie wants to know.

I position myself over the steaming pans and smile at my mom. "You made your maple butter twists."

She slaps my hand, anticipating my next move. "Don't touch. Not until I get the frosting on."

I can't resist slipping a finger beneath the drizzling flow of frosting. Of course Trixie and Shanelle do the same thing. My mother's reprimand is halfhearted. I bet she's imagining what our house would've been like if she'd raised three girls instead of one.

"Do you want me to go with you to Mass, Mom?" I ask.

"You'll make me late. And I promised I'd sit with that Florence Rubinski. Save me one of these."

As my mother departs and I join in the coffee klatch, I hope Florence was able to got in touch with her friend's daughter to scout out information about Galena Lang. But as

Mario would advise, I'm not holding my breath.

"I'll go running with you today," Shanelle says as we indulge in the sweet rolls. "Even though it's snowing. Otherwise I'll have to stick my skinny jeans in the back of the closet and girl, I hate when I have to do that."

Trixie wipes her lips. "I know what you mean. So I'll go running, too."

Pop and Maggie join us in short order. They down two rolls each, Maggie complaining all the while about how many calories she's ingesting. That's another count against her in my book—as far as I'm concerned, if you're going to eat it, enjoy it—though it's no news flash that I'm disinclined to be charitable where she's concerned. After Trixie and Shanelle go upstairs to prep for running, and Maggie races off to the grocery store to buy ingredients for tonight's fruitcake bake-off, I get Pop alone. I show him the crumpled slip of paper on which Ingrid's signature is reproduced a dozen times.

He squints at it then turns away to freshen his coffee. "Where'd you find that?"

I explain though I leave my mom out of it. I don't want anything to impede a potential rapprochement between her and Pop. "Do you know if Maggie wrote this?"

"It's her sister's signature." He turns back around to glare at me. "Why would she be writing it?"

"I can think of a few reasons."

He sets his jaw and says nothing.

"So can you," I go on.

That gets a rise out of him. "And you wonder why I don't like your so-called investigating? It's because you don't have a head for it. This just proves me right."

That stings but I try not to let it upset me. "Pop, Ingrid did not write this and you and I both know it. The only person who would have is Maggie. Do you know why she'd be practicing Ingrid's signature?"

"Maybe she's imagining that she's the sister who lived in this big house. Or that she's the sister who has the Mrs. in front of her name. Did you ever think of that?"

That shuts me up. Then I admit that I didn't.

"Okay, then, young lady," my father goes on, "let me tell you something else. You know what Maggie did the other day? She went back to the Giant W to return that inflatable fruitcake she took. She admitted to them what she did. Now, how easy do you think that was for her to do?"

"I remember when you and Mom made me do the exact same thing. That time when I was about eight and stole the headband from Claire's." To this day I recall the humiliation of confessing my shoplifting to the store manager. That was the last time I ever did that.

"I'm just asking you to have a little compassion here, a little understanding. Maggie's going through a very hard time, whether you believe it or not. And I'm not even talking about what happened to her sister. All her confidence just disappeared when she came back to this town! And it's because of everything that happened to her here. She got pregnant, the boy wouldn't marry her, and so she felt she had to leave. She's never gotten over any of that."

I think of what the Shakespeare woman said during the candlelight tour. The first thing she remembered about Maggie Lindvig was how she "had a baby out of wedlock." That comes darn close to describing somebody else I know. Me.

Pop goes on. "So what I want to know is when are you going to start giving Maggie the benefit of the doubt?"

"I'll try, Pop. But you have to admit that sometimes she does things that make me suspicious of her."

"She could behave like Mother Teresa and you'd be suspicious of her!" He slurps his java and smacks his mug noisily into the sink. "I'm going to go shovel."

"Wouldn't it make more sense to wait till it stops snowing?"

He ignores me. It's safe to say that didn't go well. And darn it all, now Maggie is back in Pop's good graces.

CHAPTER TWENTY-TWO

Shanelle, Trixie, and I run the nearly five-mile loop around Lake Winona. It's a gently sloping path that this morning is only lightly dusted with snow. Bright yellow signs caution us about the DEEP WATER, though to my eye the lake looks safe as can be. I guess even here in Winona appearances can be deceiving.

I'm reminded of that an hour later when I'm online conducting another search on my suspects. This time I discover something astonishing about Priscilla Pembroke. I pull Shanelle into my room, where my laptop is perched atop the bed. "Look at this."

I haven't showered yet but Shanelle is good to go in distressed straight-leg jeans and a sleeveless black peplum top with a cream-colored lace overlay. Her dark eyes scan the screen. "What's this web site called? Official London Theatre?"

"And look who's currently in rehearsals for a play called *Ghosts*."

She squints at the screen. Then, "Whoa! Are you kidding me?"

"Even as we speak an actress named Priscilla Pembroke is rehearsing in London."

"But that's not *our* Priscilla Pembroke. It looks like her but—"

"It's not her. This is not the woman we know as Priscilla Pembroke."

Shanelle sets her hands on her hips. "How many actresses of that name can there be?"

"I bet there's only one." I point at the screen. "This one here. Meaning we don't have a clue who our Priscilla Pembroke really is. We know she lied to us about all sorts of things and now we can add another lie to the list." I pause for effect. "She lied to us about her own name."

Shanelle shakes her head. "Let me get this straight. You think the woman we know as Priscilla, who looks almost exactly like the real Priscilla Pembroke, is using that name as an alias?"

"Yes. For some reason, she's not using her real name. I can't believe I'm just figuring this out now." I hit the side of my head with the palm of my hand. "I searched the name before but I did it kind of fast and this London stuff didn't come up. I did see photos of the real Priscilla Pembroke but she looks so much like ours, and she's an actress, too, that I didn't realize they're two different women."

"So we have no idea who our Priscilla Pembroke is."

"None."

Shanelle shakes her head. "Girl, this case is getting weirder and weirder."

"Tell me something I don't know."

"What are you gonna do?"

"First, call Detective Dembek and tell her about this. We promised we'd compare notes this morning anyway. Then I have to see Peter Svendsen to tell him about the fire. I am absolutely dreading it. Will you come with me?"

"Wouldn't miss it. He's going to try to kick our behinds out of Damsgard again, you know."

"Who could blame him? Not only are we overstaying our welcome, we're destroying his ancestral home."

Since I don't reach the detective and am once again forced to leave a message, I shower and dress. I've just decided to pair my crimson skinny jeans with a sleeveless black silk georgette faux-wrap top when my mother knocks on my bedroom door to deliver her report from Mass. I don't know if she wanted to show up Florence or Maggie or both but she is once again wearing her stylish zebra-print top and black pants.

"So here's what that Florence Rubinski told me." She ticks off the details on her fingers. "Her friend's daughter doesn't think Galena Lang even knew that woman who got shot, what's her name, Ingrid."

I think my mother has a mental block about Ingrid because she's Maggie's sister.

"Number two," she goes on. "She never heard anything about Galena getting in trouble with the law. But"—she raises her finger in the air—"there is an explanation for the sudden money. Veteran's benefits."

I frown. "Who was the veteran?"

"Her brother. You remember, the one who was homeless on the streets after he came back from Viet Nam. Galena was his only living relative so she'd get the benefits."

"I guess she would. And the timing works." I meander over to the mirror to attach my drop earrings—onyx cabochons in highly polished sterling silver.

"You don't look happy," my mother observes.

"I'm a little disappointed. None of this helps me figure out what was going on between Galena and Ingrid. Something was, or Ingrid wouldn't have hired Hubble to investigate Galena."

"Well, that Hubble said he'd keep digging around for free. Maybe he'll come up with something." She shrugs. "I wouldn't bet on it, though. You ask me, he's a few clowns short of a circus."

Shanelle and I are in the foyer putting on our coats when Trixie finds us. "I'm sorry I'm not coming with you but I want to help your mom prepare lunch. She got a good head start, though. Last night she put a strata in the fridge that she made with goat cheese, artichokes, and smoked ham."

I throw out my arms. "I don't even know what a strata is!"

"It's like a casserole," Trixie informs me. "Actually it's kind of like an egg custard, too. And I guess some people think it's like French toast because you put day-old bread on the bottom that the custard soaks into."

I lower my voice. "Last week my mom didn't know what goat cheese was but all of a sudden she's cooking with it. That woman is concocting meals like she wants a slot on *Top Chef*. You know what she's up to."

"Girlfriend's got a plan," Shanelle whispers. "And we best not get in her way because maybe it'll work."

Shanelle and I make our way to the windblown Svendsen manse, where this time Barbara answers the doorbell. The good news is that she's dressed in an adorable outfit: teal-colored ballet flats, slim-cut jeans, and an ivory pointelle sweater with a scoop neck and scalloped hem. The bad news is that in the privacy of her own home she's wearing no makeup and it is glaringly apparent that the poor thing is suffering from chloasma, the skin discoloration that sometimes accompanies pregnancy.

I introduce Shanelle then plunge right in with my confession that something happened at Damsgard and I came by to tell Peter about it.

Barbara sighs heavily as if she can't take another piece of bad news. "All right then." She waves us inside. "He should be back soon but with him you never know."

It sure sounds like Peter being late is a perpetual problem between them.

Shanelle and I settle on two upholstered chairs in the living room. Barbara is about to make a break for it when I pipe up. "Maternity clothes are so much cuter now than they were years ago. I love your sweater. Is it from the Heidi Klum line?"

She brightens. "Jessica Simpson. I love the jeans but I can't wait to get back into my regular ones. Probably by New Year's, right?"

Shanelle and I exchange a look. "Well ..." Shanelle says. I spit out the truth. "It'll take longer than that. But you look really fit and that'll speed things up."

"Breastfeeding helps a lot, too," Shanelle adds. "Plus that's good for the baby."

"Your figure is the last thing you should be worrying about, though," I say. "Once the baby's born just enjoy your little one and try to relax."

Barbara nods, eyeing us. Then, "Did either of you have this?" She gestures to her face.

"I did, a little bit," Shanelle says. "That's from your hormones going crazy. You know what helped me? Tretonin."

Barbara lowers herself onto the couch. "I think my doctor told me about that. That's the Vitamin A that's supposed to speed up cell regeneration, right?"

"You have to be careful you don't get too much Vitamin A, though," Shanelle says, and she launches into an explanation that Barbara interrupts to offer us herbal tea. She disappears into the kitchen.

"Thank you for warming her up," I whisper to Shanelle. That's good for me because as usual I have a secret agenda.

"What do you know about color-corrective concealers?" Barbara wants to know when she returns.

"Girl," Shanelle says, "we are experts. I used a blue-violet shade because my patches were brown. Yours are more on the gray side so you'll want lavender."

"Put it on after moisturizer and sunscreen," I say, "but before foundation."

"And blend," Shanelle says. "That's the mistake most women make."

We've exhausted the topic of pressed-powder versus matte-finish liquid foundation when Barbara glances at her watch, a trendy bangle style in bronze. "I'm sorry to keep you so long. I thought Peter would be back half an hour ago."

Here's my opportunity. I lower my voice and lean confidentially close. "Maybe he's having another problem with the bagman."

"He *told* you about that?" Barbara yelps.

"It just kind of popped out once," I lie.

"It's been one problem after another with that bagman!" she cries. "Everybody gets everything organized just the way they want to do it and then at the last minute the bagman has a bunch of ideas how they should change things. Of course that screws the entire thing up."

"You sound pretty matter of fact about it," I observe.

"I have to be. Doesn't your husband have a habit or two you've had to get used to?"

Not like this, I'm thinking. "So there's a whole group involved?"

Barbara looks taken aback. "Of course! It's not the sort of thing you do alone."

True enough. I suppose it's called "the Mob" for a reason. "Has Peter been involved for a long time?"

"As long as I've known him. He just can't get away from it. He tried a few times but it never lasts."

"I guess once they get your hooks into you," Shanelle murmurs.

"The truth is it's in his blood." Barbara shakes her head. "He gets a real kick out of it."

Shanelle and I exchange a glance. That's kind of sick.

"He's loved it ever since he lived in England," Barbara goes on.

I find that detail surprising and apparently Shanelle does, too. After all, she's seen all three Godfather movies and was a diehard fan of *The Sopranos*. "Not Italy?" she says. "I would've thought Italy. Or maybe Jersey."

"There are certainly groups in Jersey," Barbara agrees. "From what I can tell they're pretty much everywhere."

Even here in homespun Minnesota. I never would've thought that. I'm so naive.

"To be honest with you," Barbara goes on, "it's been a real problem between us. I don't like it at all. I try not to think about it."

If Jason were in the Mob, that would be a problem for me, too. But I don't think turning a blind eye is a good approach.

"By any chance," I say, "was Ingrid Svendsen involved?"

Barbara looks shocked at the question. "No! Women are never involved. Except when they watch."

Now I'm shocked. "Sometimes they *watch*?"

"Some women love to watch. I'm certainly not one of them," Barbara is assuring us when I hear a door open in the adjacent kitchen. Peter Svendsen calls for his wife.

The Minnesota mobster has returned home. Not only is Barbara's confession of her husband's illicit activity now over, the time has come that I must tell him his beloved ancestral home almost burned down on my watch.

CHAPTER TWENTY-THREE

It doesn't go particularly well. Fortunately Barbara is now on our side.

"Peter, let it go!" She stomps her foot in its cute teal-colored ballet flat. "You told me you hated the way Ingrid redecorated the foyer anyway. This gives you a good excuse to re-do it."

"The damage really is minimal," I add.

"There shouldn't be any damage," Peter insists. He tosses his overcoat toward the couch but misses. It puddles messily on the carpet. He stomps over to pick it up, his shoes leaving angry smudges on the carpet. "At least this'll be the end of it. Today's the day the pack of you head home, right?"

Now comes the next hard part. "There are still a few things we need to clear up so I was hoping we could stay a little longer—"

"Of course you can stay," Barbara says before her husband can again erupt. "Everybody in town knows that Ingrid is gone and it's better that the house be occupied."

"*We* could occupy it," Peter says.

"You cannot expect a woman who's about to give birth to move houses," Barbara says. "I'm not going anywhere until the baby is born."

"Maybe it's time we get out of your hair," Shanelle suggests, and as usual her timing is spot-on. We say our goodbyes and make our escape. "Do you think Ingrid's murder might've been a Mob hit?" she asks once we're back in the rental car.

"It's a possibility, wouldn't you think?" In the deepening gloom I ease the car onto the road from the shoulder, where the snow is already piled high. The sky is full of fat gray clouds that echo Peter Svendsen's mood. I'm a little shaky from the encounter with Peter, even though it was relatively mild. Knowing what I know now, from here on I want to avoid making him mad. I am not optimistic that my pepper spray would hold up well against a Mob contract. "Even though Barbara says that women aren't involved in these activities," I go on, "we all know they get whacked sometimes."

It is on that somber note that Shanelle and I return to Damsgard. Thanks to Maggie concocting her fruitcake, the kitchen is a hotbed of activity. While a mess has overtaken every horizontal surface, she does look like she's having a good time. Despite the fact that she's got flour all over her skintight red sweater, her skin is flushed from exertion, and her hair is askew, she's whistling a happy tune.

My perfectly put-together mother—who is standing beside her golden-brown strata placidly brushing her fruitcake with yet more brandy—greets us with a beatific smile. "Glad you're back, girls. Lunch is ready. Happy, go get your father."

I pull her aside. "Mom, shouldn't you be helping Maggie? She looks like she could use a hand."

My mother looks appalled at the suggestion. "*Help* her? This is a competition!"

"She wouldn't let me help her, either," Trixie murmurs. "Even though I told her we sometimes help each other even on pageant night."

It's when we're all around the mahogany dining table inhaling my mother's strata, hot scalloped apples, and homemade biscuits that Maggie pipes up with a story that grabs my attention. "I made a new friend at the grocery store," she says.

"I love making new friends!" Trixie chirps.

"She came up to me in the baking aisle," Maggie goes on, "and said 'Aren't you Maggie Lindvig?' and I said 'Yes, I am,' and she said 'I thought I recognized you,' and at first I was embarrassed because I didn't recognize her but some people you remember more than others."

I glance at my mother, who somehow manages to bite back the comment I know she's dying to let rip. "What was her name?" I inquire.

"Priscilla Pembroke," Maggie says, and I almost choke on my strata.

"Priscilla Pembroke!" Trixie, Shanelle, and I cry in unison.

"That hoodlum who tried to steal the painting of the boats?" my mother says.

"What painting of the boats?" my father wants to know.

"She's not a hoodlum!" Maggie cries. "She's the nicest woman you'd ever want to meet. She remembers me from back in the day here in Winona and told me I haven't changed one bit. She wanted to know how long we'll be staying at Damsgard because she wants to get together with me for lunch."

"That's not why she wants to know how long we'll be staying," I say. "She wants to know when we'll be out of the house so she can try to break in again to make off with the Claude Erskine painting. Did she tell you where *she's* staying?"

"No." Maggie frowns at me. "Why would I ask her that? That's a weird question to ask. And I can't believe you think she's a thief." Maggie spears her strata as if it's a beast she's trying to kill. "I hate to say it but you're suspicious of everybody, Happy. That's your problem."

"Well, in this case I have reason to be suspicious." Then I see Maggie's crestfallen expression and feel bad. I also note my father glaring at me across the table and remember our conversation earlier in which he reminded me how sensitive Maggie is to how she's regarded in Winona. "I'm sorry,

Maggie, I really am. I know she seemed nice to you but it's just that I've had a few run-ins with this so-called Priscilla so I know her better than you do."

"What do you mean, 'so-called Priscilla'?" Maggie demands.

"Let's just say she's not who she says she is." I don't want to get into all the details. "I think she was trying to use you to get information."

I bet "Priscilla" was watching the house and followed Maggie. After all, Maggie and my father are the only current residents of Damsgard who don't know who "Priscilla" is; she knows she can't get any useful information out of my mother, Trixie, Shanelle, or me. So she got us where we're weak.

"Priscilla was not using me!" Maggie cries. "She thinks I'm fascinating, that's the word she used, and she wants to be friends with me. She wanted my cell phone number and everything."

I watch my mother grip her cutlery as again she succeeds in remaining silent. She must really think she has a chance of getting my father back because it's very rare that I see her exhibit this much restraint.

My father turns to Maggie. "I'm with you, Maggie. I'm sure there are lots of people in this town who wish you'd never moved away, including this Priscilla."

Immediately a smile breaks over Maggie's face. "Thank you, Lou."

I watch the two of them exchange warm glances across the table. My mother sees it, too. I can almost see her spirits fall. For the first time it occurs to me that it may not be good for my mom to be in such close proximity to Pop, even if only for a few days. It's dangerous to her wellbeing to believe they might reconcile. Despite what Mario says, I still think their getting back together is a long shot.

"Just so everybody knows," Pop says, "I called the airline this morning. I'm trying to get Maggie and me on a flight that goes out Tuesday night."

"Really?" This revelation stops me from eating. "This is the first I'm hearing about that." From my mother's startled expression, I gather this is the first she's hearing about it, too.

"No reason to stick around," Pop says.

"I've got a meeting tomorrow with the lawyer to wrap things up," Maggie says. "Get a check from her to pay the funeral expenses, that sort of thing. I'll squeeze that in after Lou and I get back from ice fishing," she adds, giving Pop a conspiratorial wink.

That cozy interplay dampens my mother's mood even further. Apart from the food, the rest of lunch is a pretty sullen affair. After we queens rise to clean up, my mother wordlessly disappears into her room and Maggie returns to her fruitcake making, this time with Pop at her side. They're enjoying a joke when my cell phone rings. It's Detective Dembek.

I take the call upstairs in my lovely bedroom, telling the detective everything new that I've learned. On the "so-called Priscilla" front, I now understand why she wanted to break into Damsgard: to steal the Erskine, which turns out to be tremendously valuable. I also suspect, but don't know for sure, that she's lying about her identity.

"She befriended my father's girlfriend to try to get information about when we'll be leaving Damsgard," I add. "I wish I knew where she was staying! It'd be great if you could question her but how can you if we can't find her? I do have her cell phone number. Would that help?"

"I would have to get a warrant to force the carrier to pinpoint her location. It would be hard to justify at this point though I'll certainly keep it in mind."

Thus thwarted, I move on to my information about Peter, which is even juicier. But to my dismay, Detective Dembek dismisses the Mob connection. "I really don't think so, dear. The Mafia does operate in Minnesota; that's true. In fact, the main family is the third most powerful criminal organization in the entire Midwest, after the Chicago and Detroit families. But if Peter Svendsen were involved, we would know about it."

"But how do you explain the whole bagman thing, which his wife confirmed just this morning? And the prison cell on the third floor of Damsgard?"

"I don't know what to tell you about the bagman references but Peter Svendsen has told me he has no knowledge of the prison cell. And I must say I believe him."

"How does he explain the cell then? Wait; don't tell me. He thinks it's more of his stepmother's craziness."

"That pretty much sums it up. Dear, you are discovering some very interesting things. I am finding your information quite useful. Continue to be careful and we'll talk again soon. I'm so glad you're staying in Winona for the time being."

The call ends. The detective was extremely gracious but I know a brushoff when I hear one. To cheer myself up, I call my daughter. "How the heck are you, Rach?"

"Pretty good. For one thing I aced my physics test."

"That's great!" Then I have to bite my tongue.

Of course my rocket scientist of a daughter can tell. "Don't say it, Mom. I don't want to have to get into it again."

I glance out the window, where across Windom Park a young mother is bundling her baby's car seat into the back of a minivan. As draining as caring for an infant can be, I often think raising a teenager is more challenging. When a baby pushes your buttons, it's an accident. Sometimes I think teenagers do it for sport.

"Rach, it's just that when you do so well in school, I hate it even more that you're not going to be putting those smarts to use."

"I will be putting them to use. And they won't disappear. My grades won't, either. After I'm overseas for a year or two—"

"Two?" I shriek.

"—I'll be an even stronger applicant for college. You have to distinguish yourself to get into a good school, Mom, you say that all the time."

I hate when she throws my own words back at me.

"So let's talk about why you really called," she goes on. "Dad's new job. He's totally psyched about it, you know."

"I know."

"He can't stop talking about it."

"I know."

"I'm really psyched for him but I'm already sick of hearing about it and he hasn't even started yet."

"Are you happy he's going to tell Zach yes?"

"He should totally take this opportunity. And so should you."

From the day she could talk, my daughter has been bold about voicing her opinions. "I just don't get how you can be so blasé about us moving away from the place where you've lived your entire life."

"That's because I'll be moving away myself. Look at it this way, Mom. You're going to go crazy missing me. This way you'll have something new to obsess about."

I dread the day my daughter moves away from home. I'll be so proud of her but I'll be a basketcase, too. How ironic that all this will happen in September, the very month I'll have to relinquish my Ms. America crown.

"Besides," Rachel goes on, "if he doesn't like it, he can quit and you can move back to Cleveland."

She makes it sound so easy. "But I'd have quit my job and we'd have sold the house and—"

"You don't have to sell the house. You could put everything in storage and rent it out. Then give yourselves a year to decide if you want to stay in Charlotte. If Dad likes his job and you both like the place, you'll want to."

I hadn't thought of renting out the house. It's a good way to hedge our bets.

"Grandpa will be okay," Rachel goes on. "He's got Maggie. It's Grandma I'm worried about. All this will freak her out. And I don't like to think of her by herself."

"I know what you mean. But she has friends. And now she has a job. Not to mention Bennie Hana."

"He doesn't count."

On that, too, Rachel and I agree. "I have thought of asking her to move with us."

"Only one problem. If she lives with you, Dad will freak."

She's right. Jason and I could land in divorce court if he's forced to reside with my mother. Or I could be solving a murder case that hits very close to home.

"You've got to decide soon, Mom," Rachel reminds me.

"I know." I try to ignore my stomach clenching. "Tell your dad I'll call him tonight."

CHAPTER TWENTY-FOUR

A few minutes later as I'm brushing my teeth—I usually brush after lunch; it's good for the pearly whites—I force myself to stop thinking about my own life and to start thinking about Ingrid Svendsen's.

In every murder case I've solved so far, the victim was involved in something that got him or her into trouble. In some cases, it was in no way the victim's fault. In others, the victims were taking risks that eventually landed them in serious trouble.

I don't have a strong basis for it but I believe Ingrid wasn't living her life entirely on the up and up. Call me crazy but I'm suspicious of someone who has a prison cell on her third floor and who has such a beef with another individual that she hires a P.I. to ferret out dirt about them.

I cannot shake the feeling that something gnarly was going on in Ingrid Svendsen's life. I wish I knew what it was. What the heck could it be?

And where would there be evidence of it?

I've already snooped around the desk in the library. The police pored over her files and computer, I know, and if they turned up anything crooked Detective Dembek hasn't seen fit to share it with me. Shanelle and I did a thorough search of Ingrid's bedroom and the only thing we found that was remotely odd was the receipt from the body shop in

Minneapolis. Where else should I be looking?

As the obvious answer hits me, I want to slap myself upside the head. Sometimes we beauty queens deserve our reputation of being a few fries short of a Happy Meal.

I head downstairs to the secret room. I must be hopelessly bourgeois because while I admire the painting above the mantel, what I really enjoy are the festive Christmas decorations: the tree in the corner all done up in red ornaments and bows and the cheerful Santas straddling the rolling bookshelf ladder. I unlatch the secret room, prop open the door, switch on the standing lamp, and begin my examination. Because if I were Ingrid Svendsen and I had secrets, I'd hide the evidence in my secret room.

Wouldn't you?

The problem is, I soon realize, there's not much in this room. Hence it's tricky to hide anything. There's the fabric-covered shrine, with the candles and gold vases and small animal sculptures and lump of amber, and then there's the bookshelf, loaded with leather-covered volumes. There is an aged oriental carpet but nothing on the walls.

I start with the shrine, scrutinizing each item, and then make sure nothing is hidden beneath the carpet or amid the capacious fabric that crashes to the floor. Sadly, I come up empty. I'm about to move on to the bookshelf when I hear Shanelle call my name. "I'm in the secret room!" I holler.

She joins me and sets her hands on her hips. "What you up to, girl?"

"I don't know. Hoping against hope that I'll find something that'll help me crack the case."

"Well, do it fast, because your mama is raring to get the fruitcake bakeoff started."

"I wonder why." She knows she'll blow Maggie out of the kitchen and can't wait for her moment of triumph. I'm not as convinced as she is, though, that Victory in Baking will win her Pop's heart back. "Remind her we have to wait for Mario to get here. We can't have an even number of judges."

Shanelle sidles closer and lowers her voice. "In my opinion it doesn't much matter how many judges we have."

True enough. Not with the lopsided results we're all expecting. "Let's wait anyway."

"I'll tell the troops." Shanelle departs. I regard the bookshelf. There's *Robinson Crusoe*, which I started the other day, and *Tess of the d'Urbervilles*, into which Trixie dipped. Then I spy a book I've never heard of before. *Peace Within*. I don't know who wrote it because there's no author's name on the spine. The only other book I know of like that is the Holy Bible.

I slide it off the shelf and frown.

Wow. This is weird. This sure looks like a book—it's got a red leather cover with fancy gold lettering—and it even sort of feels like a book, except that it's oddly lightweight. But this is not a book.

I encounter the tiniest bit of resistance lifting the cover and then find myself staring into a small box lined with crimson felt. The box isn't empty, either. It contains papers. And these aren't any old papers, I soon realize. This is a bank statement.

For a moment I stop to catch my breath. Yes, I do believe I've found something interesting at last.

I set aside the faux book and unfold the statement. It has Ingrid's name and address on it and it's from last month. There's only one account listed, a standard savings account. I eye the bottom line and inhale another sustaining breath.

That's a pretty stout balance. $169,326.46. I look at the transaction history. Only one transaction is noted in the entire month: a mongo deposit in the amount of $84,652.31 that is described as VIGILANZ TRAC PAYMENT 03582 3104177433 INGRID SVENDSEN.

Everybody's heard of Vigilanz. It's a major life insurance company. There seems only one conclusion to draw from this: Ingrid was the beneficiary of somebody's life insurance policy. I would guess Erik's. As his widow, there's nothing bizarre about that. But why in the world did she keep this lone bank statement in this fake book in her secret room? When all her other bank statements and important papers were filed in the desk in the library?

It sure looks to me as if she were trying to hide that statement.

I grab my cell and call Detective Dembek. Happily, she answers. I relay what I found, and where.

"That is very strange," she allows. I hear papers rustle and computer keys click. "Tell me again the name of the bank? And please read me the account number." Half a minute later the detective again speaks, this time with something like excitement in her voice. "This is the first we're hearing about that account, Happy. It's especially odd because Ingrid Svendsen did all her banking elsewhere."

"So does that mean you didn't know about the life insurance benefits, either?"

"No, we didn't."

"Wow." I can't help feeling a frisson of pride at my discovery. "So Ingrid had a lot more money that we realized," I add, just as my mom barrels into the secret room with Maggie at her heels.

"I don't want to wait, I want to do the bakeoff now," my mother says before she realizes I'm holding my phone to my ear.

"What do you mean, Ingrid had a lot more money?" Maggie grabs my arm. "Who's that you're talking to on the phone?"

"I'll send an officer right over to pick up that statement," the detective tells me.

"You'll get a warrant to make the bank tell you more about this, right?" I ask. "And the life insurance company, too?"

"Yes," Detective Dembek says as I spin away from Maggie to prevent her from snatching the bank statement from my hand. "But today's Sunday, so the soonest I can get in touch with them is tomorrow. Excellent work," she adds, which is much nicer to hear than the mild brushoff that ended our last conversation.

"I want to know who you were talking to." Maggie points to the bank statement in my hand. "Let me see that. I'm Ingrid's sister and I have more right to that than you do."

I hold it against my chest. "The police are coming by to pick it up." But not before I jot down the account number. I make for the desk in the library, Maggie trailing me as closely as a puppy terrified of losing its mistress. She watches over my shoulder as I jot notes. I hear her suck in an enormous breath.

"A hundred sixty-nine thousand dollars?" she chokes.

My mother arches her brows. "That's a lot of pedicures."

I suppose Maggie does have a right to know about this. I straighten. "Yes. From a life insurance policy, apparently."

"That means I'll get it." Maggie's face lights up so bright she could guide an aircraft in for a landing. "I'm getting that other life insurance policy of Ingrid's but that one is only five thousand dollars. Oh, my word." She clutches her hands to her chest, fully on display thanks to yet another Dolly Parton V neck sweater. "Donovan and I will be set now."

"You won't need Lou's pension," my mother points out.

"Oh, my word. I'm going to call Donovan." Maggie spins out of the library faster than a dervish on steroids.

The doorbell rings twice in rapid succession, the first time to herald an officer from Winona P.D. and a second when Mario arrives. I have to believe the day will come when my heart does not thwack against my rib cage every time I see him. But I'm not there yet.

I wink as I relieve him of his to-die-for overcoat. "Any ghosts today?"

To my surprise he doesn't wink back. Nor do his dimples flash. His expression remains as grave as I've ever seen it. "That's no laughing matter, Happy."

"Are you kidding me?"

He shakes his head. "I'm like Trixie now. I don't want to

set foot anywhere near Heffron Hall ever again. But I have to go back tomorrow." He shudders. He literally shudders. "The entire crew was freaked out shooting there today. There is the oddest vibe at that place. And then—"

"What? What?"

He swallows. "We kept hearing footfalls on the floor above us even though we were absolutely positive nobody was up there. Not only that, when we checked our videotape we saw that we had captured these filmy white, I don't know what they are, *formations* that nobody can explain." He brushes his hair back from his forehead with a jerky motion. "The suits at the network are thrilled. They think I'm brilliant to come here, like I pinpointed the hottest paranormal vortex in the country. But at the rate we're going I'll have to stay till New Year's."

I'll be gone well before that time, whether I solve Ingrid's murder or not. Somehow I'm more optimistic now that I will. I feel I've made a breakthrough.

Even though his story is pretty darn spooky, I give Mario a have-no-fear pep talk as we repair to the kitchen for the fruitcake bakeoff. Trixie and I move aside the poinsettias that festoon the island and set the fruitcakes side by side. Even merely from an appearance point-of-view, my mother's offering seems far superior. For one thing, she baked her fruitcake in a sculpted Bundt pan rather than a boring rectangular dish. For another, hers is a lovely golden color with candied fruit pieces artfully arranged on top. Maggie's is a dark brown lump. It bears an unfortunate resemblance to a half-burnt log.

"I'll cut the slices," Trixie offers.

"Why don't we judges write our votes on slips of paper," Shanelle suggests, "and throw them in a bowl?"

"Good thinking," I say. That way we can keep our votes anonymous, unless, of course, everybody votes the same way. I believe there's an excellent chance of that outcome. "I'll get a bowl," I offer, but even as I bustle about assembling what we need, I can't help but be distracted by the bank statement I just found.

One thing seems odd to me. There's a big deposit in the account from last month and it's just shy of half the balance. Meaning there was probably one other deposit of the same size at some point, and over time interest accrued. I can safely conclude that so far there have been two deposits from the life insurance company.

If these are benefits from a policy Erik Svendsen purchased, isn't it odd that the deposits were made to his widow so recently? He died over three years ago. Then again, I think as we five judges and two contenders gather around the island, maybe it's not so odd after all. Maybe in a case of big disbursements like these the process takes a while.

Our group gathers around the kitchen island. Two people look particularly cheerful: my mother, who senses victory at hand, and Maggie, because my life-insurance discovery has put her on top of the world.

"Everybody has some of each fruitcake on their plate," I say. I regard my two samples, one of which looks yummy and one of which looks considerably less so. "We all ready to taste?"

I start by tasting my mom's, since I'm the type who wants the good news first. It is delectable, in more ways than one. "How much brandy did you put in this?" I ask her.

She looks away. "I don't like to stint when I bake."

To my left, Shanelle coughs. I see she's tried Maggie's first. "I'm going to get some water," she chokes.

"Get some for all of us," Mario requests. He started with Maggie's, too.

I glance at my father. Since he started with my mom's, his expression is rapturous. He's chewing slowly, his eyes closed, as if he were tasting heaven.

Eventually all of us toss our votes in the bowl. We appoint Mario to read them. He clears his throat. "Hazel," he says.

That vote has to be Pop's. He's the only one who would call her that.

"Mrs. P," Mario reads. That vote could be mine. Mario continues, reading the same name again.

"Three votes," Pop says. "That means you win, Hazel."

She bows her head. "What a nice surprise."

"You did a wonderful job, too," he tells Maggie.

She giggles. "Not bad for my first time making it." In the wake of the life-insurance news, I think nothing short of thermonuclear war would dim her good mood.

"I think you did a wonderful job, too," Trixie says. "So you should keep reading the votes, Mario."

I frown at her. At least now it's not clear that the vote is unanimous. She eyes me steadily.

"If you insist," Mario says. Then, "Maggie," he reads with obvious surprise.

I understand what happened even before I see the little heart drawn over the "i" in Maggie. In true Ms. Congeniality fashion, Trixie voted for Maggie so Maggie would get at least one vote.

"Mrs. P," Mario finishes. "Congratulations to both you ladies. Job well done."

We judges give both contenders a round of applause.

"Well," Maggie says, "I didn't have the luxury to work inside the home and learn how to bake. But maybe someday soon I'll be able to." She winks at Pop and races out of the kitchen. "See you all later. I have to make a few phone calls."

"What's that all about?" my father wants to know.

"Your lady friend got some good news," my mother says. "Let's have some more fruitcake and I'll tell you all about it."

I wonder what spin my mom will put on *that* story.

"More fruitcake," Pop says, "don't mind if I do," and I watch my parents take slices of my mother's fruitcake to the living room to enjoy it there. Alone. Together.

I only wish I weren't worried this will all end with a fresh break in my mother's heart. Mine, too, truth be told.

Not long after, Mario bids us good night. He has to spend the evening with his producer sorting through ghostly video.

The rest of us pass a few hours of leftovers and conversation. I am lost in my own thoughts.

And then, late, I call Jason with my decision. Afterward it takes me a while to relax enough to sleep. But eventually I do.

CHAPTER TWENTY-FIVE

The next morning I make for the Blue Heron Coffeehouse, a cozy space adjacent to a small bookstore. I order a latte and a frittata with olives and grab a seat by the window. It's very pleasant on a frigid Monday morning to sit inside toasty and warm, heating your hands on your mug, watching the world go by.

It is in that serene frame of mind that I watch an older man carefully park his pristine cream-colored Mercedes sedan on 2nd Street. He enters the coffeehouse, orders coffee and oatmeal with raisins, and sits down with his electronic tablet.

You know me. I'm not shy. I march over to his table and interrupt his reading. "I couldn't help but notice how beautifully you keep your car. It looks in terrific shape."

He beams. "It's a 1985 380 SE. It's got almost a hundred sixty thousand miles. I won't part with it, though, if that's what you're getting at."

"Actually I was wondering if you know of a good body shop here in town."

"Oh, there's a terrific one. Titus Collision Center."

"Really? So you don't have to leave Winona to find a good body shop?"

He scoffs at that idea. "Titus is so good, people from out of town come *here*."

I thank him for the tip and buy some quiche to go. By the

time I get back to Damsgard, my mom, Trixie, and Shanelle are in the kitchen. I join them for a second cup of coffee and pass around the quiche. "Any sign of Pop and Maggie?"

"Your father got up early to go ice fishing," my mother informs me. "Maggie talks big but she didn't go with him."

"There's only one thing she wants to do today," Shanelle says, "and that's meet with Anita the lawyer about those life insurance benefits you found."

I shake my head. "I think she's a little overconfident about that money."

My mother frowns at me. "You don't think she'll get it?"

"I don't think it's a slam dunk. Remember, Ingrid directed some of her assets to that animal shelter."

My mother harrumphs. I know she believes Maggie's interest in Pop will wane if her financial situation improves.

"You know, Mom, it's Monday morning," I point out. "Isn't Bennie expecting you back at work?"

She scowls at me. "How could I go back to work? You're still sick!"

"I'm not that sick." I've been medicating myself so consistently I can barely even tell I've got a cold anymore.

"You're sick," my mother declares. "I told Bennie my place is with my sick daughter and he'll see me when he sees me."

"Not many people can get away with an indefinite leave when they've only been working for a few months. Are you sure *you're* not being overconfident?"

"Apparently you don't remember what that Bennie said to me. He told me I was indispensable. You may not know what that means, young lady, but I do."

"Maybe he was being facetious."

She raises a warning finger. "Don't you start throwing those big words at me. Now if you don't mind"—she picks up her coffee and one of the slices of quiche—"I'll eat this in peace in the dining room."

We three queens chuckle as my mother flounces out of the

kitchen. "So *that's* why she's still here," Shanelle murmurs. "Because you're sick, Happy."

That only gets us going more.

"Did you see how she and your father sat in the living room and ate her fruitcake last night?" Trixie giggles. "I think they got a little tipsy. They were so cute."

Mario's words come back to me. *I bet your dad is a lot more attached to your mom than he lets on. Even though he's trying to hide it.* Wouldn't that be fantabulous?

"So what investigating are you going to do today?" Trixie wants to know. "And how can we help?"

"We were just talking about how we better help," Shanelle says, "if we're going to justify our continued presence here. Lamar is starting to ask a lot of questions. Not to mention my boss."

"And I'm dying to see Rhett and the kids," Trixie adds, "but I'm happy to put off packing up my house."

"Let me check one thing out," I say, and I lead my fellow queens to the library. It takes me but a moment to locate Ingrid's file on her Mercedes and see that on two occasions she did indeed patronize the Titus Collision Center here in Winona. I explain what I learned at the Blue Heron Coffeehouse.

"You're thinking about that receipt from the body shop in Minneapolis," Shanelle says, "and how weird it is that Ingrid took the trouble to go all the way out there."

I hesitate. Then, "It's probably nothing."

"You know what?" Trixie says. "Since it might be important but it might not be, how about Shanelle and I make a day trip out of it and go talk to them? That'd give us the chance to see Minneapolis. I'd hate to fly back home without looking around some."

"That's so much to ask—"

"We'll do it on one condition," Shanelle says. "That you tell us what you told Jason last night."

That's more than fair. I lower my voice. "You can't tell my mom. I have to pick the right moment to tell her."

Trixie starts jumping up and down and shrieking into her hands. "Oh my Lord! You're moving to Charlotte! You're moving to Charlotte!"

I take a deep breath. "You won't be the only one packing up your house, Trixie."

Shanelle starts shrieking, too. "You will be *so* much closer to Biloxi! I am so excited! I can't believe it!"

This momentous news calls for a jumping up and down group hug. After a while we calm down. "What made you finally decide?" Trixie wants to know.

"I just realized I don't want to be the sort of person who gives in to fear. I don't do that in other parts of my life so why should I do that here? It makes no sense at all. Plus it's ridiculous for a grown woman to be afraid of moving to a new place and building a new life. And I should go all out to support Jason as he chases his dreams. He's done that for me all these years so I should absolutely do that for him."

It's really obvious, when it comes down to it. So obvious that I can't believe it took me so long to get it clear in my mind.

There's another aspect to my decision as well, which I don't share. Jason moving to Charlotte by himself, with me staying in Cleveland by myself, feels like a serious threat to our marriage. Sure, we'd go back and forth constantly, but the fact remains that it would be a real rupture. Already with my Ms. America travel we're not together as much as we used to be and that's putting a strain on us.

Then there's the Mario factor, because in my heart of hearts he is a factor. I am already so drawn to him. Should the distance between Jason and me grow wider, there's a real risk Mario could step further into that gap. Then what? As tantalizing, as tempting as Mario is to me, I am not ready to venture down that path.

"Your mama is not going to like this," Shanelle says.

"Well, it may help that Jason and I are going to take it slow. We're not going to sell the house right away, for example. We'll just rent it out. That was Rachel's idea."

"How does Rachel feel about all this?" Trixie wants to know.

"She thinks we should both go to Charlotte and give it a try. We'll have to figure out the timing because she's still got five months of high school." None of which I want to miss, so that'll have to be sorted out. "But anyway, if it all works out in Charlotte I'll encourage my mom to move there, too."

"Bennie Hana would never allow it," Trixie warns, "your mom is indispensable to him," and we all collapse in giggles again.

"Bennie Hana won't have a dang thing to say about it," Shanelle predicts. "It's your mama who's leading him around by the nose."

It's after Shanelle and Trixie depart for Minneapolis, dropping my mother off on the way to do some Christmas shopping in downtown Winona, that I get a call from Hubble. He says he has something big to tell me and so wants to come right over. I don't get too excited because so far Hubble hasn't produced much. By the time he arrives I've showered and put on my skinny rust-colored cords and charcoal long-sleeved tee, which is super soft and features a flattering ballet neckline.

Hubble passes on coffee and won't be enticed to sit down, either. All he'll do is pace the living room. "I thought I'd find something on Galena Lang," he tells me, "but never anything like this."

"What in the world did you find out?"

"I'm not one hundred percent certain—"

Great. Already here we go with the caveats.

"—but she might be trafficking body parts."

"What?" I shriek. "What are you talking about?"

"Biomedical companies want the parts. Or sometimes they go to R&D. I heard about this happening a few years ago in Jersey. In that case it was a ring of morticians who were paid about a thousand bucks a corpse."

"That is vile! That is disgusting!"

"It's a way to make money. And the funeral directors, sometimes they fake consent forms from next of kin, make it look like the family gave permission."

"It may be lucrative but it's big-time illegal. Immoral, too." The bereaved families would be outraged to learn that a mortician was dismembering their loved ones to make extra money on the side.

"Desecrating human remains is a crime," Hubble says. "People go to prison."

"For a long time, I hope." Then I remember how Hubble started this conversation. "Wait a minute. You said Galena *might* be involved."

"I got it on excellent authority that a D.A.'s office in Wisconsin is investigating whether a certain funeral director in this area is involved in a multistate ring that's doing this trafficking."

"But there's more than one funeral director around here. What reason do you have to believe they're focusing on Galena Lang?"

"I gave my source that name and he confirmed she's being looked into. And with Galena Lang, there's also the fact that suddenly she's come into money."

"There's a plausible explanation for that. I was told she received veteran's benefits after her brother died." I rise from one of the velvet chairs and begin pacing myself. "You know this is a very serious allegation."

"You don't have to tell me that."

"Would the local police be aware that a D.A. in another state was investigating a citizen in their jurisdiction?"

"Maybe. Maybe not."

I'm thinking I really should put Detective Dembek on speed dial when the front door crashes open. I race to the foyer to see my mother burst inside. One look at her face and I know something terrible has happened.

"I just got a call," she pants. "Your father's in the hospital."

CHAPTER TWENTY-SIX

I think my heart stops. I clutch Hubble's beefy arm. "What do you mean Pop's in the hospital? What happened to him?"

My mother is too flustered to answer any questions. "You have to drive me to that hospital. I don't know how to find it. I don't have a car, either. I got somebody to give me a lift back here to the house." She dumps a shopping bag in Damsgard's charred foyer then walks right back outside. "We've got to go now."

"We'll go right away." I pull her back inside the house and grab her in a hug. Her entire body is trembling. "But first I want you to calm down and tell me exactly what happened."

"I don't know what happened! I was in that shop where they have the Christmas decorations put up so nice and I got a call on my phone. It's from the hospital, who tells me that your father fell through the ice when he was doing that fishing."

"He fell through the ice. Oh my God." Visions of Pop flailing desperately in frigid water fill my brain.

"We've got to get to that hospital," my mom repeats.

I have to restrain her to keep her from racing back outside again. "We will. Right away. Do you remember the name of the hospital?"

She does. Hubble offers to drive us. I know he can easily

imagine us getting in a wreck given the state we're both in.

"I don't know how long we'll be there," I tell him, "and I can't ask you to wait so please just write down the address for me so I can put it in the GPS. Better yet, will you put it in the GPS for me?" I hand him the keys to the rental and race to the hall closet for my coat. "Mom, what did they tell you about Pop's condition?"

"They told me he's stable. Hurry up."

The second I hear the word "stable," I feel one iota calmer. Something else occurs to me. "We have to tell Maggie." My mother erupts but I ignore her. "She'll want to come with us."

At least so I would have thought.

"Oh, I can't go to the hospital. I wish I could but I can't." She rights the towel on her head. Apparently she's about to conduct the important business of drying her hair. "You said he's in stable condition?"

"I did, but what are you talking about? Nobody likes hospitals but—"

"Oh, your father will understand," she assures me. "You won't even have to explain. He knows I'm terrified of hospitals."

I'm thinking that what she's really terrified of is missing her appointment with Anita the lawyer to talk about life insurance benefits. Playing Weak Woman is just a way of getting what she wants. But I restrain myself from voicing that suspicion. Instead I race outside, exchange quick goodbyes with Hubble, and rev up the rental.

The hospital is not in Winona so my mother and I have a drive ahead of us. Fortunately the sky is blue and the roads are clear of snow and ice. I have the presence of mind to give Detective Dembek a quick call to ask if she might put a squad car outside Damsgard so "Priscilla" doesn't use this opportunity of the house being empty to try to steal her favorite painting.

"Your father was only in the hospital once in all these years," my mom tells me about ten minutes in. "That time he took a bullet."

It was more of a grazing wound but now is not the time to quibble. "I remember. He's strong as an ox, mom. He'll be fine." Maybe if I say it, and think it, it will be so.

My mother was in a perpetual state of worry during Pop's decades as a cop. Now as an adult, I don't understand how the spouses of law-enforcement personnel handle the daily danger to their loved ones. Props to them.

We're close to the hospital before something else occurs to me. "So were you the first person the hospital called, Mom?"

"I'm number one on your father's speed dial."

She's too upset even to gloat. But I find that a memorable tidbit.

My father is asleep when we get to his hospital room. He's bundled up in blankets and looks just fine but even so it's an unpleasant jolt to see him in that bed, a monitor at his side beeping with all his vital stats. My mother tucks the blankets in tighter, smoothes the hair back from his forehead, listens to his breathing, and then settles in at his bedside. Nothing will pry her away from there, I know.

I pull a young Asian female doctor into Pop's room to give us the 411. It turns out that a fellow fisherman saw Pop fall through the ice, helped pull him out, and got him here. Pop was smart enough to dress in layers and wear a personal flotation device but he shouldn't have been fishing alone.

My heart thumps a few times. "So he was lucky."

The doctor nods. "He certainly was. The other fisherman says your father got most of the way out on his own but he did need some help. And as you may know, people can succumb to hypothermia in just a few minutes."

"The second he recovers from this, I'm going to kill him," my mother says.

Now that we've been assured that my father will be okay, my mother is returning to normalcy. I take a place by his bedside, too, and we watch him snooze. Usually that would not be my activity of choice but right now there is nothing I would rather do.

"He snores pretty darn loud," I remark.

"Always has," my mother replies.

And he twitches. And he mumbles. After one particularly noisy bout a smile spreads across my mother's face. "You hear that?"

"Hear what?" I say.

"Hazel," my father mumbles.

There can be no doubt what he said that time. My mother arches her brows at me. "You notice what name he *didn't* call in his sleep?"

I certainly did. I hope Maggie is having a successful meeting with Anita the lawyer because at the moment she's not doing too well on the Lou Przybyszewski front.

A while later the nurse bustles in to check on him. Her prodding wakes him up.

My mother reaches around the nurse to poke him in the side. "You nearly got yourself killed out there with that ice fishing! Now look at you."

His expression turns sheepish. "I'm sorry to be so much trouble, dragging you both out here."

"I bet you didn't catch anything, neither," my mother goes on.

"How could I?" he cries. "I fell in the lake!"

"Well, we're really relieved you're safe now, Pop." But I can't resist one dig. "I can't believe you went out there alone! You know you're not supposed to do that."

"I had my auger with me! I checked the ice!" He looks away. Then, "Truth is I did something else wrong, too." He turns to my mom. "I ate four slices of your fruitcake before I left the house. I'm not sure I was thinking straight."

"Oh my God!" my mother hollers. "You were soused from my fruitcake! It's me who put you in that hospital bed!"

Pop grabs her hand. "Don't blame yourself, Hazel. I knew I shouldn't have been eating so much but I just can't resist it."

"The second I get back," my mother says, "I'm going to throw the rest of it out."

"Don't do anything hasty," I say. "We'll just put everybody on a one-slice limit."

My father straightens to look around the hospital room. "Hey, where's Maggie?" Then he falls back against the pillows. "Oh, I get it. She's not here."

This is awkward. I clear my throat. "She said you would understand."

"She's scared of hospitals," he says. "Ever since her father died in one."

My mother harrumphs softly, as if to say: *That's no excuse.* I have to say I agree with her.

"I know she has that meeting with the lawyer today, too." Pop sighs. "Hope she gets what she wants out of it."

"Well," my mother says, "whether she does or not, we're here."

Pop reaches for her hand. "Yes, you are. I'm real glad of it, too."

We're having a family hug when my cell phone rings. It's Shanelle. "We found out something pretty weird from the body shop here in Minneapolis," she tells me.

I excuse myself and make for the hospital corridor, leaving my parents in amiable conversation and trying to force my mind back into investigative mode.

Shanelle goes on. "The car Ingrid had work done on wasn't her Mercedes. It was a rental."

"What? She took a rental car to a body shop?"

"The guy I talked to said Ingrid told him she was too embarrassed to tell her husband that she crashed the rental. So she brought it in here to get it repaired before she returned it."

I watch an elderly male patient push his walker slowly down the corridor. "But didn't this happen in the summer? She didn't have a husband then. Erik was long dead."

"I don't know how to explain that."

"Maybe she didn't want to admit that she didn't want her

insurance company to find out that she crashed a car."

"She did tell the guy here that she didn't want to involve her insurance company. By the way, he said she crashed the car but good. He'd hate to see what she ran into."

We fall silent. I know for my part I'm remembering the fender benders in my past.

Then Shanelle pipes up again. "I'll say this. If I ran into something with my rental car and I wanted to keep the whole sorry episode a secret from Lamar *and* the rental-car company *and* my insurance, I would take the vehicle to a body shop. And not the one we usually use, because I know the minute I walked out of there that mechanic would get on the horn to my husband."

"In my case my husband *is* my mechanic. And in those circumstances I could see myself doing exactly what you would do. I don't know why I'd bother, though, because I'd end up confessing anyway. At least to Jason."

"I would, too." Shanelle sighs. "But why would Ingrid Svendsen, a rich widow who lives alone and doesn't have to hide anything from anybody—"

"Well, except for the prison cell on her third floor and hiring a private investigator to dig up dirt about Galena Lang and worshipping the heathen goddess Freyja—"

"Except for all that stuff. Does it really make sense that she'd go to the trouble of taking a rental car to a body shop in Minneapolis or anyplace else just to hide the fact that she had an accident?"

"Even if it cost a lot to fix and her insurance went up, I find it hard to believe she'd care." And I am certain Ingrid would have no fear of standing up to even the most formidable rental-car clerk.

"There's another bizarre thing," Shanelle says. "She paid in cash. And the bill was a few thousand bucks."

Elderly Walker Man finally makes it to the end of the corridor. He painstakingly turns around to do it all again. "Who pays that big a bill in cash?" I ask.

"You know how she explained it? She told the exact same lie about having a husband. She told the guy here that if she paid by credit card, her husband might see the charge on the statement and she couldn't risk that."

We fall silent. Then, "I don't understand how," I say, "but this seems like a big deal to me."

"I agree," Shanelle says. "Ingrid was obviously trying to hide something."

I watch Walker Man make his slow but steady progress. He's kind of like me, methodically advancing step by step. "Now I need to find out what she was trying to hide," I tell Shanelle. "And from whom."

CHAPTER TWENTY-SEVEN

"So Pop landed himself in the hospital," I tell Shanelle by way of introducing a new topic of conversation.

I give her the lowdown on his ice-fishing accident and of course she wants to drive back immediately to join Mom and me at the hospital.

"No, no," I say, "you and Trixie have a nice lunch in the city." I don't need to look at my watch to know it's lunchtime. My stomach is telling me. "I may drive back to Winona soon myself. Pop is out of danger and I know my mom will stay with him so he won't be alone." And I'm fretting about my investigation.

We arrange that Shanelle and Trixie will swing by the hospital on their return trip both to visit Pop and to ferry my mother back to Damsgard. I'm getting the idea the docs will want to keep Pop overnight just to be on the safe side.

An hour later, after my mom and I watch Pop make a manful attempt to eat the hospital food that is put in front of him and we strap on our own feeding bags at the cafeteria, I am once again on the road. No sooner have I pointed the car toward Winona than my cell rings with a call from Jason. I share the major news of the day.

"I'm going to read your father the riot act about going out on the ice by himself," Jason says. "Isn't it too early for ice fishing, anyway? I thought the season was more like in

February."

"I guess it's not too early because there was another fisherman out there. Thank God for that. I hope somebody got his contact information. I want to thank him."

"There must be something in the air today. Kimberly was telling me there was an accident at her climbing gym."

"Who's Kimberly?"

"I told you about her, remember? She was the photographer for the calendar."

That's right. He did mention her before.

"Anyway," Jason goes on, "some woman apparently forgot to clip herself into the safety harness and just let go about fifteen feet up as if she thought she was clipped in. I guess she'll be okay. Kimberly says she was an experienced climber, too."

"So did Kimberly call you?"

"I called her to let her know I'd be back in Charlotte later this week. I hope you're back by then. Zach needs me to do a few things and actually Kimberly wants to take some new shots. Maybe we can do that this week." He chuckles. "She's thinking she could sell a calendar with shots of just me. Can you believe that?"

I'm dubious but I keep that to myself. "So does this Kimberly woman live in Charlotte?"

"She lives in New York but lately she's been spending a lot of time in Charlotte. Her sister's going through some stuff so she's helping out."

"You think if she lived in New York, she'd be in New York."

"Well, you live in Cleveland but how often are you here lately?"

I guess I don't have a leg to stand on.

"I know it's crazy to ask," Jason goes on, "but Mario's not in Minnesota, is he?"

Shoot. I hoped this would never come up. Now that it has, I could lie. But I won't. "Actually, he is here."

Silence. Then, "You are kidding me."

"There's a *huge* amount of paranormal activity here in Winona—"

"Happy, do not try to tell me that's why Mario's there. I can't believe this." He pauses, then, "Everybody in the world would understand if I flew out there and punched that guy in the nose."

"I know."

"I am really glad you're moving to Charlotte with me, Happy, really glad. But I am telling you we are going to have a do a few things differently from now on."

"I know what you're saying."

"Geez, I was thinking you might be jealous of Kimberly. But the only one who should be jealous is me."

"Don't be jealous of Mario, Jason." Heck, *Mario* is jealous of *Jason*. But this is not the time to point that out. I honk at the driver ahead of me who hasn't noticed the red light turned green ten seconds ago. "Should I be jealous of Kimberly?"

"Well, she did tell me I'm the hottest guy she's ever photographed."

"What about the other guys in the calendar? Aren't they hot?" I bet some of them are hot *and* single.

"Well, *I* made the cover."

Kimberly may be an excellent photographer but I don't think I like her much. I decide that just this second.

Jason speaks up again, and this time there's that husky note in his voice that I love so much. "Sweetie, I'm glad we've got this whole moving thing sorted out because I did not want to move down to Charlotte without you."

"Even though you've got Kimberly to keep you company?"

He chuckles softly. It sounds sort of like it does when we're cuddling. You know. After. "Kimberly doesn't keep me company the way you do."

"She better not."

"Maybe you two could have a catfight. You might be able to take her. But she's pretty buff. I don't know. Either way I'd like to watch."

Now I'm chuckling, too. And relieved that Jason sounds like his usual easygoing self. "You are a very naughty boy," I tell him.

"I'll prove just how naughty when you get home."

Ironically, that kind of kills the mood. Because as impatient as I am to see Jason, and Rachel, I don't want to leave Winona until I solve Ingrid's murder. I hope I have my priorities straight. Sometimes I wonder.

We end the call with Jason assuring me that as soon as she gets out of school, he'll tell Rachel about her grandpa being in the hospital. I am unnerved as I drive the rest of the way back to Winona. I find it startling that Jason has forged enough of a friendship with this Kimberly woman that he's calling her to alert her to his whereabouts. And what's this about her spending more time in Charlotte lately? Is it really because she's going all out to support her sister? Or could there be another draw? Like a six-foot-two-inch hunky pit-crew guy? Who, if she hasn't noticed, is wearing a gold band on the ring finger of his left hand?

Then again, Mario tries to slide right past the diamond ornamentation I've been sporting on my left ring finger for the past seventeen years. And sometimes I'm pretty darn close to letting him.

Thanks to Winona's finest, the Erskine still hangs above the mantel in the library when I get back to Damsgard. I brew fresh coffee, allow myself only a nibble of my mother's killer fruitcake, and try Detective Dembek one more time. I called her unsuccessfully from the car to share what Shanelle and Trixie learned at the auto-body shop and also Hubble's speculation about Galena Lang. I didn't leave a detailed voicemail then but I do now. Then I boot up my laptop so I can input my new information about Ingrid and stare at my suspects spreadsheet. I know from experience that if I gaze at it long enough, eventually a synapse or two fires. In this case I don't have to gawk for long at those columns crammed with bits and pieces of information. I realize that even now, six days after Ingrid was murdered, this beauty queen has left a few investigative stones unturned.

So even though it's already pitch dark out and hence my plan scares the bejesus out of me, I force myself up one staircase after another until I reach the third floor. With selfish disregard for Damsgard's electric bill, I switch on every light I pass.

I don't care that it's drenched in fluorescents: the room that holds the prison cell gives me a serious case of the creeps. Let's assume that Peter Svendsen was speaking the truth and this cell did not exist while he was growing up at Damsgard. Did it go in during Erik's marriage to Ingrid? Was it a kinky sexual thing between them? Or did Ingrid have it constructed after Erik was dead for some freakish reason of her own?

In one way this room is a lot like the secret room. There's not much in it so it doesn't make for a good place to hide things. As usual, I'm not looking for anything in particular. I'm simply looking. I ignore my squeamishness and enter the cell itself, examining it inch by excruciating inch. I find nothing of interest. The only thing that's notable about this prison cell is that it exists at all.

I move on to the room next door. It has no furnishings. Dusty cardboard boxes collapsing from age are stacked in one corner, on a dry and uneven hardwood floor. The walls, now chipped and faded, are painted a sort of Shamrock green. I can't even guess when that color was popular.

With the overhead light on I can't say I'm frightened, although it is mildly uncomfortable to be alone on this abandoned floor in this century-old house. You have to wonder what's happened here at Damsgard over all these years. Arguments. Parties. Lovemaking. Births. Betrayals. Secrets. Deaths.

I shake off my morbid mood and lift down the top box

from the stack. Fortunately I'm not scared of spiderwebs, because if I were I'd be paralyzed. I don't hesitate to blow the dust off the box and open it up. One thing I've learned about solving murders: you can't be afraid to pry into people's private business. Either you make their business your business or you're done.

It soon becomes clear that this is a box of mementoes from Erik Svendsen's undergraduate career at the University of Minnesota, class of 1953. He majored in econ, I see, and played football. I can tell from his transcripts that he performed well academically but the Gophers were only middling, at least his senior year: five wins, three losses, and two ties. In another box I find old clothes of Erik's, perhaps items Ingrid couldn't bring herself to donate or throw away.

The third box I delve into is more entertaining. It's full of treasures from those too-short years when Erik's children were growing up. I smile at handmade cards with crooked printing in bright crayon colors, like the kind Rachel drew for Jason and me, in this case Nora and Peter scrawling *World's Best Dad* next to renderings of picnics and baseball games and swimming pools.

I take a break to stretch my legs and turn on all the Christmas lights. Since it's already close to 7 p.m., I should have done it hours ago. I'm surprised Shanelle and Trixie aren't back yet with my mom. Maybe they got caught in commuting traffic. And where's Maggie?

I'm elbow deep in the next box—which contains papers having to do with the family's stained-glass company—when Mario texts asking if he can come over. You will not be surprised that I reply in the affirmative. I'm about to move on to the fifth and final box when he shows up. Of course, he's fresh from shooting while I'm a dusty mess. Apparently I've even got a streak of dirt on my cheek, which Mario carefully wipes off.

I explain my mission. "I'm not going to wash up until I go through the last box in this room. There are probably more in the other room, which is just as well because I haven't found anything yet." I turn to head back up the stairs. "You game to help?"

"Absolutely." He bounds up the stairs behind me. "How's your dad?"

Mario already knows about the ice-fishing fiasco. On my drive back to Winona, I left him a voicemail.

"I am delighted to be able to tell you that Pop's fine." Mario joins me on the floor and we pry open the last box. "It turns out the hospital is keeping him overnight." I found that out from a text from Trixie. "Since he went ice fishing by himself, maybe they've decided he needs his head examined. Oh, look what's in here. Photo albums."

Judging from this, the Svendsens are a lot more organized than the Przybyszewskis. Our family photos aren't carefully organized in albums. They're tossed haphazardly in the credenza in the living room.

I pull the top album out and realize that the next one down is a wedding album. I'm enough of a girly girl that of course it captures my attention. It's reminiscent of my parents': the cover is white pearly embossed vinyl with gold lettering that spells out *Our Wedding* in stylized calligraphy. I open to the information page, where a feminine hand has listed the bride as Lillian Marie Borger and the groom as Erik Noris Svendsen.

"Fun! This is the album from Ingrid's husband's first marriage. I've never seen a picture of his ex-wife." I turn to the first photo page, whose corner is trimmed in gold filigree. There before me is a large black-and-white of a beaming bride and groom. "They look so young, don't they? And Erik Svendsen must have had a favorite type because this Lillian looks a lot like Ingrid." I'm about to make another observation when it stalls on my lips. I peer more intently at the photo.

"What is it?" Mario wants to know.

Now I'm too stunned to speak. I flip through a few more photos.

Yes, it is a fact that I've never before seen a photo of

Erik's first wife. But that doesn't mean I haven't seen an older version of this woman in the flesh.

The only thing is, I know her as Priscilla Pembroke.

CHAPTER TWENTY-EIGHT

I fall back on my heels. "No wonder so-called Priscilla knows Damsgard so well! She lived here for years!"

Mario takes the album out of my hands and scans the photos. "We knew she was lying about who she was but I never guessed this."

"You've never met Peter Svendsen. I have and I still didn't figure this out." There's not much resemblance between mother and son but still I'm embarrassed that I didn't make the connection. This explains why so-called Priscilla bolted the first time I met her, when Peter suddenly showed up at Damsgard. She didn't want him to know she was in town. I rise and start pacing. "I'm trying to remember what Peter told me about his mother. He did say that one day she just up and left—"

"She abandoned her husband and kids? When was that?"

"I don't know. To this day, though, Peter has no photos of his mother hanging in his house because he's so resentful that she walked out." I must say I can't blame him. "He also says he doesn't keep in touch with her."

"He could be lying about that," Mario points out. "The two of them could've murdered Ingrid together. They might both have had motive."

That stops me in place. "You're right."

They both could have wanted Damsgard for themselves.

Or wanted Ingrid out of Damsgard. If so-called Priscilla understands the value of the Erskine, she no doubt understands the value of the entire property. I could easily imagine her not wanting her husband's second wife, whose tenure as Mrs. Erik Svendsen lasted only four years, to play Lady of the Manor, even if she lost that role herself.

A second motive comes to mind. I recall what my mother said about why one woman would kill another. *She hates her because she has something the other one wants. A guy, usually.* That would be Erik Svendsen. True: if I'm to believe Peter, it was his mom who left his dad. Hence so-called Priscilla had already rejected the man in question. But her ego would still suffer when he found a replacement.

Commotion breaks out downstairs. "Hallo!" I hear Trixie yodel.

"They're home." I am excellent at stating the obvious. "We'll be right down!" I call. Then I turn to Mario. "We'll have to take a break for dinner. I wonder if there are more boxes to search through in the other room on this floor."

There aren't. That's okay, I decide. Figuring out the true identity of so-called Priscilla qualifies as a major discovery.

I race downstairs to hear the latest on Pop. Once I am assured that he continues to improve and will be released in the morning, I share the latest 411 with Trixie, Shanelle, and my mom. "I wonder if anything that broad Priscilla told us is true," my mother says.

"What did you find out about her when you googled her real name?" Shanelle wants to know.

When I admit I haven't done that yet, I am shooed upstairs to get my laptop. By the time I return, Shanelle has gotten to work on the cocktail of the evening and Trixie is helping my mother prepare dinner. "Chicken Surprise," Trixie says.

"The real surprise is that your father isn't here to eat it," my mother says. "Mario, don't just stand there. Set the table."

It appears my mother has gotten used to having Mario among us. She's bossing him around as if he were no one special.

I am sitting at the small table in the kitchen nook conducting an online search on Lillian Marie Borger Svendsen when Shanelle hands around tall berry-colored drinks garnished with lime wedges. "I present to you the Jolly Gin Fizz," she says. "Made with gin, ginger ale, lime juice, and pomegranate juice."

"Pomegranate juice!" Trixie chirps. "Healthy."

I raise my glass. "To Pop. May the next ice he encounters be in his glass and not above his head."

"To Pop!" we all cheer.

"By the way, does anybody know where Maggie is?" I inquire.

"She showed up at the hospital," Shanelle reports.

"Despite supposedly being terrified," my mother sniffs.

"What did she say about her meeting with Anita the lawyer?" I ask.

"She didn't want to talk about it," Trixie says.

"Meaning it didn't go well," Shanelle adds.

I return my attention to my computer screen and soon am able to report that Lillian Borger is indeed a Manhattan-based actress. But her résumé isn't nearly as impressive as Priscilla Pembroke's. "She does small-time community theater. And she doesn't get the starring roles, either."

"I understand why she used a fake name when she came to Winona," Trixie says, shredding smoked Gouda so my mother can stuff it into the pockets she's cut into the chicken breasts. "Even if she didn't murder Ingrid, she did want to steal that painting so she wouldn't want anybody to know she was here. But why didn't she just use some random name? Why did she use the name of another actress?"

"Probably because she gets a kick out of being Priscilla Pembroke," Mario says, returning to the kitchen to fetch cutlery. "And they resemble each other enough that Lillian can get away with it."

"She certainly had me fooled," I say. "Okay, here we go.

I just found something that explains why she knows how valuable that Claude Erskine painting is." I click through to another link to read more. "She works at an art gallery."

Shanelle pipes up. She's helping with the cooking, too, coating the stuffed chicken breasts with flour, egg, and bread crumbs. "Maybe she and Peter were in cahoots. They might've had a deal that if they joined forces to get rid of Ingrid, he'd let her live here at Damsgard. Or he'd give her a share of the value."

"I don't think so," Trixie protests as she and my mother begin to sauté the chicken. The aroma is mouth-watering. "Remember what Peter said the day we met him? 'God save me from actresses,' he said. It stuck in my mind because it was so weird. But now I think he was talking about his mother."

"If he said that about his mother, I don't like him," my mother says. "No man should talk that way about the woman who gave him life."

"Remember what else happened that day?" I say. "So-called Priscilla left all of a sudden by escaping out the kitchen door."

"Yes!" Trixie cries. "Without any goodbyes to anybody. At the exact moment Peter showed up."

"It *may* be she didn't want him to see her," Shanelle says, "or it *may* be they were in cahoots. Anyway, one thing is for sure. Peter doesn't have to like his mother to conspire with her to commit murder. Remember that old adage: The enemy of my enemy is my friend."

Half an hour later when we've sat down to dinner—the chicken dish with sides of sautéed spinach and steamed string beans—I bring up something that's puzzling me. "If so-called Priscilla murdered Ingrid—"

"You should start calling her Lillian," Trixie points out.

"True. It's hard to get used to, though. So if Lillian murdered Ingrid, with or without Peter, why would she stick around in Winona after the deed was done? You think she'd want to get out of Dodge."

"She wants that painting," my mother says, "even though it's only got boats on it and no people."

"If she and Peter were in league together," Shanelle says, "she could get the painting after he moved into Damsgard."

"But Peter might want the painting for himself," Mario says. "If he knew what it was worth, he certainly would. Then his mother would have to steal it before he moved into Damsgard."

After dinner, while Mario takes over Pop's shoveling duties and we three queens help my mom clean up the kitchen, Detective Dembek returns my multiple calls. Now I have fresh information to share.

"No wonder Priscilla Pembroke looked familiar to me," the detective says.

"Did you know Lillian Svendsen when she lived here?"

"I knew of her. The Svendsens have always been so prominent in town."

"Is it true what Peter says, that one day she up and left her husband and kids?" That's the sort of gossip that would make the rounds for sure.

"That's how the story went. And it had to be, oh, twenty years ago." She pauses, then, "This is another valuable discovery you've made, Happy. Now I can justify getting a warrant to go after the mobile carrier."

To require them to pinpoint Lillian's location.

"It'll take time," Detective Dembek goes on.

"I had an idea that would be quicker. How about we smoke Lillian out? We have Maggie tell Lillian we're all flying home. Then you have a squad car secretly watch Damsgard. Because I guarantee you Lillian will come back to steal the Erskine."

Detective Dembek agrees that's not a bad strategy. "It's odd to use one suspect to smoke out another but I've seen nothing to tie Maggie Lindvig to her sister's murder."

"I agree." By now I've pretty much abandoned the Killer Sister theory myself.

The detective wants to think on my scheme. I hope she gives it the go-ahead.

I expect Mario to be back inside the house by the time my call is done. Instead I find the best-looking snow remover in the state of Minnesota still out in the cold, staring at a streetlight, his shovel abandoned and fresh snow making mock of all his hard work. I join him on the sidewalk.

"Mariela just called," he tells me. "Boy problems. You remember Theo?"

"Do I ever." He's a teenage Adonis I found scampering around outside Mariela's bedroom in his skivvies.

"There's some new girl he's paying more attention to than Mariela likes."

I know how she feels. Jason's altogether too chummy with Kimberly the Photographer for my taste. "What did you tell her?"

"Well, between you and me I don't know that Theo's such a great catch. But I told her to be the warm, funny, sweet girl I know she is. And if she does that, it won't take Theo long to remember why he likes her."

"That sounds like good advice."

He shakes his head. "That's not the only thing that's bothering her. Her mother asked her the other day what she thinks of *her* new flame."

"So Consuela *is* seeing someone new?"

"Some guy named Manny del Rio. He's a developer. It's gotten hot and heavy fast. Mariela thinks they're pretty serious."

I bet Consuela would move at the speed of light if she found a marriage-worthy man on her horizon. "You seem less than thrilled about it."

Mario looks away. The streetlight shines full on his face. As usual I find him mesmerizing. I could watch him for a shockingly long time and never get bored.

"Consuela's not the type to be alone," he says. "And she's been divorced for a few years now. But she can be impetuous.

She doesn't really know this Manny guy. And I hate that Mariela gets pulled into all her romantic drama."

"It's good that Mariela talks to you about this stuff."

"I just wish I were there more. I don't like these prolonged separations from her. Sure, we text, we talk on the phone, we Skype, but nothing is like being there."

"Nothing is. I agree." I turn away.

He shovels a bit more. Then, "So what are you thinking about?"

I turn back around. "What you said made me think about Rachel." I pause. "And about Jason, too."

He stops shoveling.

I keep talking. "Something happened that makes me worry about being away from Rachel. Jason got offered a job on a pit crew. It's in Charlotte. He's taking it. And I'm going with him."

It all requires some explanation. I didn't expect to get into this but now that I've started I can't seem to stop. Mario stands the shovel in a snow bank and listens. Finally, "I'm happy for you," he says. "If you're happy, I'm happy."

"I am happy." Then I make a confession for the second time this week. "It wasn't the easiest decision in the world to make."

We stare at each other. I know he understands what I mean even though I haven't spelled it out. I don't have that kind of wordless communication with a lot of people but I have it with Mario.

"Any other decision would've been really hard to make, too," he says. "I get that." He retrieves the shovel from the snow bank and in silence we meander up the driveway to the garage.

It's only after he stows the shovel and we're standing there mindlessly watching the garage door close that Mario speaks again. "Maybe you were right, what you said the other night. That I shouldn't be waiting for you."

A car drives by. Out of the corner of my eye I see the

upstairs lights in the house behind Damsgard switch off for the night.

"You shouldn't be waiting for me," I force myself to say. "It's not good for you and really it's not good for me, either."

He shakes his head. "You know, it's funny. Most of the time I just don't think about Jason. I just don't think about him. It's the sort of thing Mariela would do."

I smile even though by now I'm feeling pretty sad. I can see what's coming and I know I shouldn't stop it no matter how much I might want to. "Sorry to remind you."

Mario reaches for my hand. I let him take it. I came outside so abruptly I didn't even bother to put my gloves on. "Let's go sit on the porch," he says.

"Now? It's like twelve degrees out."

"Now."

He leads me down the driveway and up the path he just shoveled, up the stairs, past the railing decorated with white fairy lights that twinkle like earthbound stars. They reflect in his dark eyes. Something tells me I'll never forget those eyes of his. We stand in front of Damsgard's cheerful red door adorned with its gorgeous holiday wreath.

"Hey, what do you know?" Mario points heavenward. "Mistletoe."

He doesn't lurch forward to take me by surprise. He stands absolutely still and watches me, giving me every chance to pull away, make a joke, kill the moment.

That's not what I do, though. This time, for the first time, I move the teensiest bit closer. So it's not just Mario kissing me. It's me kissing Mario. Like I've dreamt of forever. And unlike a lot of those things you dream of, that could never live up to your fevered imaginings, this kiss does. It really does. This kiss is magic.

And then, too soon, it's over.

Mario pulls back but we keep standing nose to nose. "So … I know you'll solve Ingrid's murder," he whispers. "And after that I hope you have a wonderful Christmas. And a really, really great new year."

He won't follow me around the country anymore. I got used to that but I shouldn't have because those days are over. I won't see him again until I don't know when.

For a moment I can't talk. Finally, since I have to say something, I manage to croak out a few words. "I wish the same to you."

"Don't cry, beautiful girl." A rogue tear has escaped, of course. Very gently Mario brushes it from my cheek. "I want you to be happy. I want you always, always to be happy."

He won't get his wish. I know that already.

He raises my hand to his lips, kisses it one last time, and then he's gone.

The moment is over. All those moments that might have been? They never will. I guess I knew this would happen one day. One day the road would fork. And I'd have no choice. I'd have to pick a path.

CHAPTER TWENTY-NINE

It's pretty much impossible to sleep after that. I don't know why I bother trying.

But try I do. I dutifully wash off my makeup—that is, what little makeup I haven't cried off—and moisturize my face and drink the last of my Nyquil and sit in bed reading the romance novel I'm halfway through.

Maybe that's not the right genre for tonight.

A few hours of tossing later, I abandon the effort. I allow my hollow self to get out of bed and confront the depressing specter of five bleak hours until the break of dawn. After which I get to suffer through a really long day during which I must do my utmost to solve a murder that's bedeviled me for a week while simultaneously forcing my rebel thoughts away from a tall, dark, and handsome stranger I never had any business fantasizing about and now really must forget.

I guess I know how I'll be spending the new year.

I lumber downstairs in my pajamas without turning on any lights. I'm perfectly comfortable on Damsgard's first floor in the dark, not to mention that the blackout echoes my mood. I decide that if ever there were a night for eating ice cream straight out of the carton, this is it. Fortunately for this melancholy beauty queen, the refrigerator is stocked with chocolate chip. I curl up on a velvet sofa in the living room, spoon and carton in hand, and try to take joy in the pine scent of the live Christmas tree and the beauty all around me. I can only vaguely see it in the dark but I know it's there.

I should appreciate it while I've got it, I realize. I'll be leaving Damsgard soon whether I solve Ingrid's murder or not. It strikes me that my life is much the same as this gorgeous home cloaked in darkness. There's an awful lot that's good that's packed into it, even if I'm not capable of seeing it right now.

All I can process at the moment is what I've lost. And what is that, really? A fantasy. A fantasy about a man I don't really know; a fantasy about a life I'm not even sure I want.

That doesn't keep me from weeping. After a particularly racking bout, I hear rustling behind me. I spin around to see my mother, wearing her favorite Christmas nightgown, ivory-colored flannel with red trim and an all-over print of Santas and reindeer. Her hair is set in pin curls beneath a net. Most Saturday nights while I was growing up she set it that way so it would look good for Mass on Sunday. She lowers the frying pan in her hand.

"Soon as I heard the crying, I figured it wasn't a hoodlum," she tells me. "Could have been a sad hoodlum, I guess." She sits down next to me and pats my leg. "Mario?"

"How did you know?"

She looks away and sighs. "I couldn't sleep, neither."

"Pop?"

"That Maggie finally showed up at the hospital. Made a big deal of it, too." She turns back to me. "What does that floozy think, that the rest of us love the place? But that's no matter now. Tell me what that Mario did."

"He didn't do anything, Mom." That almost gets me going again but I manage to stave off another crying jag. "It's hard to say what happened. I guess what it comes down to is that even though we weren't a couple, obviously, we sort of broke up." Saying it out loud, it sounds so juvenile.

But my mother simply takes it in with a nod. And soon her light blue eyes look as forlorn as I'm sure mine do. "Why tonight?"

I might as well tell her. I have to soon anyway and we're already both in lousy moods. Plus I feel bad that I told Mario about this before I told her. I suppose that just goes to show how out of kilter I've gotten.

I take a deep breath. "I told Mario that I'm moving with Jason to Charlotte. He got a job with a pit crew."

Her eyes fly open. "Knock me over with a feather! So that husband of yours is finally going to make something of himself?"

"Mom, that's not nice."

"I'll be darned."

"You know, you really shouldn't be so amazed. Jason is a fabulous mechanic and he's extremely athletic and he's really motivated."

"So that's why he spent all those years working as a grease monkey for that Joe? And never wanted to do anything else? Except maybe watch football on the weekend?"

"Well, okay, so now he's got a fire under him. Give him credit for that."

"I'll give him credit if he can keep that job. Then we'll talk."

There's no winning with my mother where Jason is concerned. "So you're not upset that we're moving? Not that I want you to be but I was sure that you would."

"How long have you known about this?"

"A few weeks. Jason just accepted the job today. Well, yesterday."

"Rachel knows?"

"She thinks it's good."

"And your father?"

"He thinks that where my husband goes, I should go. Automatically."

"That's what he would think." She sighs again. "That's what I would think, too, normally."

Meaning if her daughter's husband were any man in the

world but Jason Kilborn, who got her pregnant at age 17. We lapse into silence. I offer my mom the ice cream then rise to get a fresh spoon.

"Yours is good enough for me," she says.

"But I'm sick."

"You're not that sick." She dips the spoon into the carton. "So what does this Charlotte business have to do with Mario?"

I sit back down. I have to think about that. Then, "I think it just brought home to him that Jason and I are a couple. That where he goes, I go. That whatever Mario and I might have had, we can't have."

Because I'm married. And I'm not locked into some hellacious marriage, either. I'm married to a man I love, who loves me, and we have a daughter we both adore. So I should get a grip on myself and recognize that I have better things to do than indulge in schoolgirl fantasies about Latin hunks who host paranormal reality shows.

"That's too bad," my mother says. "I like that Mario."

"I do, too."

"That show of his is stupid but at least he's got a show. Unlike some people."

I throw up my hands. "Mom, you can't get on Jason's case for not being a Hollywood star! He's on the cover of a calendar. He might even get a second calendar. Isn't that good enough for you?"

She shrugs. "A calendar isn't the same as a show."

She's infuriating. But I love her. "So tell me what happened with Pop."

"Nothing. That Maggie showed up at the hospital as if she was the bravest thing anybody's ever seen. And like it didn't matter that she was six, seven hours late. She made a big point of saying that so-called Priscilla called her, too."

"Really? Did she say what they talked about?"

"You think I asked?" My mother shakes her head. "Anyway, your father and I were having a good time until she showed up."

"I'm glad about that. But I'm worried you're getting your hopes up too much where Pop's concerned."

She spoons more ice cream and says nothing.

"You know," I go on, "I'd like you to think about moving with us to Charlotte."

"That's not for me," she says immediately.

"Why not? I hope not because of Pop."

"Never you mind why not," she says, which is how I know for sure that it is because of Pop. "Remember, your old mother has a way of getting what she wants. I got you, didn't I?"

After I don't even know how many miscarriages, my adoption came through. "I'm very glad you did."

"I'll say." She sets down the ice cream so we can have a good hug. On my side at least, more tears are shed. And this time not for love lost but for love I will never lose. "I think you should get on with solving that murder," my mother says when at last we let each other go. "So we can go home already."

"I'm with you. I just don't know how." My angst over Jason, Charlotte, Mario, all of it, hasn't helped my brain cells much. Most people would give them a poor rating in the best of circumstances.

"Sleep on it," she tells me, "so you'll be nice and fresh in the morning."

I don't know about "nice and fresh" but maybe I can manage "slightly rested." I'm back in my room about to set my cell phone's alarm when I notice a voicemail I missed. It's from Detective Dembek and includes two interesting pieces of information.

One is that she wants to go ahead with my "smoke out Lillian" plan. I find that gratifying. The other is that Peter Svendsen professed astonishment when the detective told him that his mother spent the last week in Winona, incognito. He produced a fresh email from his mother in which she asked if she might visit after Barbara delivered the baby. Apparently the tone was of a woman pleading to see her grandchild despite years of estrangement from her son.

Detective Dembek had the same reaction I do: maybe the estrangement continued and maybe it didn't. If those two were in league to murder Ingrid, they could well want to maintain the fiction that they'd had nothing to do with each other for years.

This time when I crawl into bed, I'm able to sleep. I can't clear Mario completely from my mind but at least he's pushed to the back. Front and center in flashing red neon is a major distraction: How to Lure Lillian.

CHAPTER THIRTY

It turns out I don't need my alarm to wake up. Maybe some people can sleep through heartache, but this beauty queen isn't one of them.

I shower, put on my caramel-colored corduroy bootcut jeans and black stretch cotton short-sleeve tee with mock turtleneck, and march downstairs to make coffee and an egg-white and tomato omelet. It's past seven thirty before the sun deigns to rise and by then the whole household is awake.

I make omelets for everybody. I'm in a mode that'll work for me today, I think: I'll be busy at all times. I won't let myself think about anything except solving Ingrid's murder. And whether I solve it or not, I'll fly home tomorrow.

That brings me to the lie I tell Maggie, Shanelle, Trixie, and my mom. "I heard from Peter Svendsen last night," I say after everybody's slurped their coffee and scarfed their eggs and should be able to take the "news." "He wants all of us out of Damsgard first thing this morning."

This declaration is greeted with howls of protest and a few quizzical looks, notably from my mother and Shanelle.

"Mom," I go on, "you and I will have to move into a hotel for our last few nights."

Trixie is philosophical. "Me, too, I guess. Well, we have been here a week, which is a lot longer than I thought we'd be staying. But boy, I hate to leave this beautiful house. And all of you, too!"

We spend a few minutes hugging each other, nothing new for us. I hug Maggie, too, because I don't want her to feel left out.

"That Peter Svendsen just can't wait to get his greedy hands on this place," she says, an accusation that could easily have been lobbed in her direction a few days back.

I grunt in false agreement. "So Maggie," I go on, "I guess you'll have to call Priscilla and let her know that you won't be able to get together after all because we've all got to clear out of Damsgard."

"But her name's not—" Trixie starts to say, until I quiet her with a warning touch.

Maggie doesn't know that so-called Priscilla is actually Lillian Borger Svendsen, the first Mrs. Erik Svendsen. Maggie didn't get back to Damsgard from the hospital until we were all in bed and so she missed our discussion of that eye-opening discovery.

"You're right," she sighs, "I will have to call and tell her. Because if your father weren't in the hospital I might have time to see her, but as it is I've got to get over there right away." Then, with a prideful note in her voice: "She called *me* yesterday, by the way. I was waiting at Anita's office for Anita to get out of court and Priscilla wanted to tell me again how much she hoped we could get together."

I'm curious what Anita the lawyer told Maggie but I don't want to distract her with questions on that touchy subject. "Well," I force myself to say, "what a shame you won't be able to see her." I, on the other hand, expect to get an eyeful of Lillian. Detective Dembek agreed to let me hide out in Damsgard in the likelihood that she does indeed try to break in to steal the Erskine. I have a few things to say to her, not to mention a few things to ask.

Maggie rises to clear her dishes from the table. "Your father was so smart to book our flights for tonight. I guess I'll have to pack for both of us and go to the hospital with the suitcases in the car. And stop off at the funeral home on the way to drop off the check. I better get a move on." She bustles out of the kitchen.

It's only after I hear Maggie's door close upstairs that I lower my voice and confess the truth. "The more I thought about it, the more I realized I just don't trust Maggie to keep to herself that this is a ploy to entrap Lillian."

"She might be better at entrapment than you give her credit for," my mother points out.

"I'm not even going to let Pop know the real story until later," I go on.

"So we don't really have to leave Damsgard today?" Trixie murmurs.

"We have to make a show of leaving," Shanelle says. "Roll our suitcases out to the car and everything."

"Exactly," I say. "After she hears from Maggie, Lillian might well watch the house to see when we've all cleared out."

"But you're going to come back later," my mother says to me, "right? Because you haven't figured out who killed that Ingrid yet."

"Whatever happens today, I'm flying home tomorrow." I feel everyone's eyes on me as I carry my dishes to the sink. "It's time. I tried. Maybe something will click for me today but I'm not holding my breath." I turn around to face a trio of disappointed faces. "It just hasn't come together this time. I guess I can't expect a one hundred percent success rate."

Part of me wonders if I've been ineffective at solving this murder because I know that once the case is closed, I'll have to fly back to Ohio to face the challenging reality of my life. I don't really think that's the case but I might be fooling myself.

Trixie grabs me in another hug. "You really, really tried, Happy, and that's all any of us can do. Remember"—and she backs away to raise an index finger in the air—"it's always better to reach for success and fall short than not to try at all."

That's beauty-queen wisdom if ever I heard it.

"So when is Mario leaving?" Shanelle wants to know.

I hang my head. Somehow I can't make myself answer that question.

Shanelle edges closer. Now she and Trixie are both standing right in front of me. I know my mother is still at the table in the nook, watching. "Happy?" Shanelle rubs my arm. "What aren't you telling us?"

There goes my vow that I would cry no more tears for Mario Suave. I recover quickly, though, and manage to get through an explanation. It doesn't help put a stop to the waterworks that Trixie's hazel eyes grow misty, and Shanelle's dark brown eyes, too.

Trixie sniffles a few times then squares her shoulders. " 'I shall be telling this with a sigh,' " she orates. " 'Somewhere ages and ages hence.' "

Shanelle takes it up. " 'Two roads diverged in a wood, and I, I took the one less traveled by.' "

" 'And that,' " I finish, " 'has made all the difference.' "

We have a moment of respectful silence for Robert Frost, American poet extraordinaire, and his 1920 wonder, *The Road Not Taken*.

"Did we all do poetry for our talent at some point?" Shanelle wants to know.

"I usually did tap," Trixie says, "but once after I twisted my ankle I did poetry."

"Happy never did poetry for her talent," my mother says, joining us and handing me a tissue. "But she had to learn that poem in school."

I blow my nose and square my own shoulders. "You know what, ladies? We can't talk about Mario now. And we shouldn't, anyway. Let's do what we have to do to make it look like we're clearing out of Damsgard. Mom, give me your ticket information so I can call the airline and book the two of us on the same flight home."

"I best call the airline, too," Shanelle says.

"Me, three." Then Trixie's expression grows worried. "I know I shouldn't ask this but do you think Mario might not want to invest in my bridal salon now? I mean, I wouldn't blame him—"

"If you come up with a good business plan, he will absolutely want to invest," I tell Trixie, and I mean it. "He's not the kind of guy who would back out of a promise."

"I agree," Shanelle says. "So here's what we do today, girl," she tells Trixie. "We take ourselves to the public library and sit down our behinds and write up that business plan of yours."

Trixie's face lights up. "Oh, that's a good idea. We talked about it when we were driving around yesterday but didn't actually write anything down."

"Then we all meet back here in the late afternoon," I say, "and enjoy our last night at Damsgard." I take my mother by the arm and lead her to her bedroom. "And here's what you and I will do this morning, Mom."

We spend the next two hours flawlessly executing our plan. After confirming that Maggie did indeed speak to the woman she knows as Priscilla—which is essential to our scheme—I usher her out to her car. Ten minutes later, Shanelle and Trixie drive away as well, in the direction of the highway that would carry them to Minneapolis if that were where they were going. Then my mother and I showily load our suitcases into the rental car and even go so far as to pose for one last selfie in front of Damsgard. I drive us several blocks away to a quiet side street and park.

"You're sure you left that kitchen door open?" my mother says as I exit the rental and she settles herself in the driver's seat.

"Positive. I checked it three times. Now you be careful driving to the hospital. It's starting to snow."

"Me, be careful?" She glowers in my direction. "You, be careful. I won't be the one sitting alone in that house waiting for a murderer to show up."

I have to scamper across two properties to access Damsgard from the rear. I was smart enough to plan my route earlier by conducting a reconnaissance mission through the neighborhood, checking for fences and guard dogs. I let myself in through the side door that opens into the kitchen, re-lock the door, and text Detective Dembek that everyone is out of the house but me. She texts back that two plainclothes officers are keeping watch on Damsgard from an unmarked car.

    I set my phone to silent mode and dash upstairs.

    Our trap is set.

    Now all I have to do is wait.

CHAPTER THIRTY-ONE

I can't wait on the first floor because Lillian might spy me through a window. So I wait in my bedroom, a good distance from the windows. I boot up my laptop and stare at my suspects spreadsheet until my brain hurts. I resist napping and I resist checking my cell phone to see if Mario has called or texted. (He hasn't.) I prepare for Lillian's anticipated arrival by looking up Shakespearean quotes about time and decide that my favorite is: "Pleasure and action make the hours seem short."

Which must mean boredom and inaction make them drag on. I'm getting ample proof of that today.

I'm starting to wonder how much longer I can bear it when I hear the satisfying sound of glass shattering downstairs. I bet it's Lillian announcing her arrival by breaking the new window the hardware store put in on the day of Ingrid's funeral. It sure seems to be the go-to window at Damsgard for those bent on burglary.

I allow myself a few seconds just to enjoy being right. I sure called this one! I have to say I'm not really frightened. If cops weren't watching the house, and if I didn't have my trusty pepper spray near at hand, I certainly would be. After all, Lillian may well be a killer. But as it is, I'm hyped up but not terrified.

I don't move a muscle, though. I am under strict

instructions to keep my distance from our perp. I am not to confront her until I'm sure the cops have her well in hand. And they won't interfere with her activities until she's had time to get the Erskine in her grasp. After all, they might as well add to her list of transgressions.

In short order I hear someone shuffling around on the first floor. It's hard not to get nervous. Even though it doesn't make sense for Lillian to come upstairs, especially given what she's here for, I half expect her to appear at the threshold to my room, as if somehow her criminal radar will sense my presence. Or natural curiosity could propel her to mount the staircase, to tour the rooms of the home where she raised her children and conducted her married life.

I wonder what her plan is. That painting is pretty big. She can't be planning to just meander up the street with it in the full light of day, can she? Then slide it into her rental car like it's the sort of thing a person does every day?

I'm plotting how I myself would steal the Erskine given those constraints when I hear a commotion downstairs. Heavy footfalls pound across the hardwood floor. A man bellows: *Stop! Hold it right there!* A woman shrieks: *No! No!* A man orders: *Put down the painting!*

That's my cue. I race from my bedroom down to the first floor, past the dining room that's once again boasting a shattered front window, to the library. And what do I see but two male officers squaring off against Lillian. As I would expect, she's clutching the Erskine. Per usual she's dolled up in her nipped-waist gunmetal gray parka with the shearling trim, her blond hair perfectly coiffed and her makeup tastefully applied. If you forget that she's brandishing stolen property, you can easily imagine her as the doyenne of Damsgard.

"You!" she stammers when she sees me. "You drove away!"

"So I did. But now I'm back."

"I can see that." Her haughtiness seems to be returning so I guess she's recovered from her initial shock. She stares at me with blue eyes as cold as the December air now coursing through Damsgard.

"Put down the painting, ma'am," one officer says. "Then step away from it."

"This is ridiculous," she sniffs. "What an obvious set-up. This travesty will never hold up in a court of law." She sets down the oil as ordered and brushes her hands as if her biggest problem were dust. The officer who spoke steps forward to move the Erskine further away from her; the other snaps handcuffs on her wrists and recites her Miranda rights.

When he's done, I pipe up. "I'm not surprised to see you again today"—I pause for a moment—"Lillian."

Her head swivels in my direction. She juts her chin in a show of defiance. "It took you long enough to figure out who I am. Admit it. I'm a better actor than you gave me credit for."

"Maybe. But I'm on to you now. And that means you might end up getting charged with something a lot more serious than burglary."

"What are you talking about?" She sounds disdainful but the days when I might have bought her act are over.

"The way you've been behaving—lying about your whereabouts, assuming a false identity—I expect Detective Dembek will find enough on you to make a murder charge stick."

She's wearing a fairly thick foundation but I can still see her face pale. "That's preposterous! Why would I care if Ingrid Svendsen lived or died?"

I cock my chin at the Erskine. "You came close to being a million dollars richer because she's dead."

"I have more right to that painting than anyone," Lillian hisses. "I was the one who wanted to buy it in the first place. Erik could study for a thousand years and never recognize a masterpiece." She looks away. "And I don't just mean a piece of art, either."

"So he didn't give you your due? Is that why you walked out on him and your children?"

"My children were adults by the time I left. They could get along just fine on their own. And if Erik had ever understood what the stage meant to me, if he'd ever once supported my talent, maybe I wouldn't have had to go."

She makes a theatrical show of raising her eyes to the ceiling. I bet she'd be throwing out her arms if her hands weren't cuffed.

" 'If you try to be anyone but yourself,' " she cries, " 'you will fail. If you are not true to your own heart, you will fail. Then again, there's no success like failure.' "

"That doesn't sound like Shakespeare," I point out.

She turns a withering gaze on me. "It's not, you fool. It's Bob Dylan."

"Whoever it is," one officer says, "it's about time we wrap things up here."

"Just one minute more," I say. Then, "You must've gotten to know Ingrid at some point, Lillian. After all, you knew about the Freyja shrine in the secret room."

The cops glance at each other as if to say: *This I've got to hear*.

"I told you before, I have friends in Winona," Lillian says. "Ingrid wasn't smart enough to do a good job of hiding her goddess worship. In fact, she might have been stupid enough to be proud of it. Fancied herself a warrior goddess or some such thing."

"Okay, that'll do it," one officer says. "You going to be all right?" he asks me. "Know how to get that window repaired?"

I assure him that I can handle it from here. The officers begin to lead Lillian away. I bet she won't step inside Damsgard again for a long, long time.

"Erik and Ingrid deserved each other," Lillian adds as she exits stage left. "What neither of them deserved was this house."

Somehow it always comes back to Damsgard. I stand in the frigid foyer and call the hardware store that was kind enough to repair the broken window the first time around to request their services yet again. As soon as possible, I plead. Until then I'll be walking around the house wearing my plum-colored overcoat. In fact I'll be wearing my bouclé knit cloche and gloves, too.

I'm pensive as I put a bowl of soup on to warm. I'm still no closer to knowing who killed Ingrid. Lillian might have done the nefarious deed but I doubt it. Her feelings about Ingrid just don't seem powerful enough to compel her to commit homicide. What Lillian is passionate about is the Erskine. She wants it either for itself or for the money it could bring her.

True, the scenario might change if Lillian is in cahoots with Peter. But in that case, why would she have to steal the Erskine? Wouldn't it be her payoff for participating in the murder? Her son gets the house and she gets the painting?

As I stir the soup I realize there's another hugely valuable thing Lillian might gain if she helped Peter murder Ingrid: an improved relationship with her son. And at the very time that he and his wife bring her grandchild into the world. It would be a huge irony if it were homicide that ushered in a new era of filial warmth. But it's possible.

The soup is just what the doctor ordered: warm and filling. After I've dispatched it, along with a handful of crackers, I go up to my room to brush my teeth and freshen my lipstick. Then I plop down on the bed and send Shanelle and Trixie an update via text. My mother I call. There's no point texting with her. She's too grudging a participant. The only response any of us have ever gotten out of her is: *Ok.*

She answers from the hospital corridor since she's been shooed out of Pop's room so the nurse could conduct a final pre-release checkup. After I relay the day's events, she wants to know if she can tell Pop what really went down at Damsgard.

"I don't see what harm it could do now," I tell her.

"He and that Maggie are going to want to come back, too,"

she says. "Your father couldn't get two seats on the flight home tonight so they're going back tomorrow. I wanted to say, hey, just leave that Maggie behind."

I chuckle and shiver at the same time. "Good work keeping that suggestion to yourself, Mom." Even though I'm on the second floor wearing my coat, cloche, and gloves, I am absolutely freezing. What with the broken window, it must be as cold inside Damsgard as outside. I should probably get a fire going in the living room fireplace and huddle next to it.

"So are you happy that Lillian showed up today?" my mother wants to know. "It's what you thought she would do. So you were right about that."

"I am pleased I figured that out. At least that."

We both fall silent. I know she can tell I'm bummed that I haven't solved Ingrid's murder.

She pipes up. "Remind me again where you found that bank statement that showed the insurance payments?"

"In the secret room, remember? In the book that wasn't really a book."

"That's right. So was that the only book that wasn't really a book?"

"I think so." I frown. "I mean, that's the only one I saw." Of course, I stopped looking after I found the one.

"Maybe you should go check in there again," my mother suggests.

She doesn't need to say it twice.

I race downstairs, access the secret room, and switch on the standing lamp. It takes me a little while but eventually I do spy another "book" that's a virtual twin of the faux book I found the other day. The only difference is this one is bigger. It has the exact same red-leather cover and fancy gold lettering. This one is titled *Higher Power*, and like *Peace Within* there's no author's name on the spine.

For a second I hold it against my chest. If there is any sort of clue inside this "book," my mother will never, ever let me forget that searching these shelves a second time was her idea.

That's just fine, I decide. If anything here helps me crack this case, I'll survive never being able to live this down.

I open up the faux book. And just like its smaller twin, it's got papers inside.

Documents, as a matter of fact: a certificate of marriage and a certificate of death.

CHAPTER THIRTY-TWO

The marriage certificate is from Hennepin County, Minnesota, wherever that is, and it was issued three years ago. I am astonished to see that the bride was none other than Ingrid Jane Lindvig Harris Svendsen. She married a man I never heard of, a man I had no idea existed, whose name is Joseph Michael Fuchs.

Even though there are no chairs in the secret room, I have to sit down. So I drop onto the oriental carpet and stare at the documents in my lap. I cannot believe this. Ingrid married again, less than a year after Erik Svendsen died, to some man named Joseph Fuchs.

How in the world did I investigate this woman's murder for an entire week and not know that she married again after Erik Svendsen?

Then again, I'm not sure that Detective Dembek is aware of this. She never breathed a word about it. Maggie didn't say boo about Ingrid having a third husband, either.

Matter of fact, I'm only assuming that Joseph Fuchs is Ingrid's third husband. There could be other Husbands of Ingrid I don't know about, who preceded Erik Svendsen. I tell you: so often it's the women who seem the most proper who have the most scandalous lives.

I rise to my feet and start pacing. I wonder if Ingrid kept this marriage to Joseph Fuchs under wraps for some reason.

For one thing, she didn't take his name. She took the Harris name and obviously the Svendsen name, too, but not Fuchs. Of course that might be explained by the fact that here in Winona the name Svendsen carries a certain prestige. Knowing Ingrid, I would imagine that mattered to her.

Could this Joseph Fuchs have been an embarrassment somehow? Or maybe Ingrid was lonely and found that embarrassing. She didn't want to admit she sought the companionship a spouse would provide.

I turn to the death certificate, issued in Winona County this past August, just months ago. The deceased is Joseph Fuchs, the mystery husband, who died at age sixty.

Well, I do understand why there was no mention of Joseph in Ingrid's will. He was already deceased.

I wonder what he died of. I consult the death certificate again. The cause of death is sort of surprising: "blunt force trauma." What does that mean, exactly?

I throw off my coat, cloche, and gloves. It's amazing. Even though freezing air continues to course through the house, I'm not cold anymore. Right now I don't even care if the hardware-store guy doesn't make it here till tomorrow. I guess there's nothing like startling new information to get your blood pumping.

I walk out of the secret room into the library and gaze at the Erskine, still propped against the antique desk where the cops left it. It's starting to get dark out, I realize. The days are so short this time of year.

I look around me at the stunning library. In this house, I can never get over how one room is more gorgeous than the next. I do know that Ingrid lived here at Damsgard from the day she married Erik Svendsen, so Joseph must've lived here, too. I suppose they could've had a long-distance marriage, exactly what I contemplated for Jason and me, or one of those marriages you read about where husband and wife live in two separate properties in the same town because they both value their privacy so much. But it seems unlikely.

Boy, wouldn't that have irked Peter Svendsen? It's one thing to have your father's widow reside in your family's ancestral home. But if she's moved on to the extent of marrying another man, wouldn't it get on your last nerve to have both of them installed in the home you covet? That might've given Peter even more motive to want Ingrid dead.

Then again, I realize, maybe this explains why Ingrid kept the marriage to Joseph Fuchs on the QT, if she did. Maybe there was language in Erik Svendsen's will that if Ingrid remarried, she'd have to cede Damsgard to Peter. That would make sense.

I have to call Detective Dembek about this. I race up to my room, where I left my cell phone, and am about to place the call when I hear something unexpected. I stop everything and listen.

Yes, I just heard it again. Overhead. Creaking floorboards.

Slowly I turn my gaze toward the ceiling. I shouldn't be hearing that. I'm alone in this house. The others haven't come back yet. I would have heard them if they had. And Lillian couldn't have snuck in again because she's in police custody. There simply cannot be anybody walking around on the third floor.

Oops, I hear it again. Somebody is definitely walking around on the third floor.

Or ... some*thing* is.

Mario's description of his shoot at Heffron Hall comes back to me. *We kept hearing footfalls on the floor above us even though we were absolutely positive nobody was up there. Not only that, when we checked our videotape we saw that we had captured these filmy white, I don't know what they are,* formations *that nobody can explain* ...

Remembering that gets my heart pounding. I cannot believe this! Winona must truly be the hottest paranormal vortex in the country. Not only is Heffron Hall haunted, and that house on Cummings Street, and the Historical Society, but

Damsgard, too.

Well, what did I tell Mario? That he had to conquer his fears.

It's easier to give that advice than to take it. But I guess I have to go up to that third floor to see what's what. I'll take my phone with me on the chance that I can capture yet more "filmy white formations" for Mario's show. I'll also take my pepper spray. It worked on a crocodile. Let's see how it works on a spirit.

Thus armed, I exit my bedroom and creep up the staircase to the third floor. Around me Damsgard is deathly quiet. And, it must be said, it's cold as a tomb. My nerve nearly abandons me halfway but I force myself to climb the final flight of stairs.

It's pretty dark up here given the gloomy weather and time of day. And, I'll admit, I have a vague sense that I'm not alone. I'm aware of a presence, somehow. Not that I see anything. Not that I even hear anything anymore.

No fear, Ms. America ...

I force myself through the two normal rooms, which are as I left them, the second with boxes strewn everywhere. I take a deep breath and move closer to the room with the prison cell. This one always creeps me out the most. The door is partway open. I peer inside. The room looks the same as ever, if darker: deserted and bizarre, the door to the cell wide open.

It's only after I push the door slightly more open and step inside the room that I feel a surge of relief. There's nothing here to frighten me. No ghouls of any description. And I should be used to that dang cell by now, weird as it is.

None of that means I want to hang out. I spin around to leave. I don't know what I heard but it must've been—

"Galena." I more croak the name than say it.

She's standing against the wall behind the door I just walked past, obviously trying to hide. Slowly she emerges from the shadows wearing that black Goth overcoat I so admired. She looks like a grownup urchin, with that ivory skin of hers and those big charcoal-shadowed eyes.

"What are you doing here?" I ask. I don't add: *standing in the dark. Hiding behind a door.*

"I could ask you the same question. When Maggie came to the funeral home this morning, she told me that Peter Svendsen ordered all of you to clear out."

I stare at her. If one thing is perfectly clear, it's that Galena Lang has zero business sneaking around Damsgard's third floor. It's the sort of thing Lillian would do.

"So that's what you did," I murmur. "You snuck in through the broken window."

She doesn't bother to deny it. She takes a step forward. I see her glance at my right hand, where I'm clutching my cell phone and pepper spray. I take a step back. A sort of chess game has begun.

It's so funny how the brain works. At least, how my brain works. I can stare at my suspects spreadsheet for hours and make no sense of anything. Or, all the little bits of information I've collected can organize themselves into a coherent whole and suddenly I can make perfect sense of everything.

That's what's happening now.

And it's really too bad it's happening now because survival instinct takes over. I lurch for the door. Galena grabs my arm. We get into a tussle. It's immediately clear that she's fairly strong. I guess you can build muscle in the mortician business. She swipes at my hand and my cell phone and pepper spray go flying. I spin around to go after my spray and she pushes me, hard. Into the cell I lurch, landing hard on my hands and knees. I get up fast but even still I'm too slow. Galena slams the cell door shut and pulls out the big metal key. She stumbles backward but rights herself, panting but holding the key in her hand.

I'm panting, too, but I'm panting inside the cell. With no key in my hand. Big difference.

CHAPTER THIRTY-THREE

"Maggie mentioned this room," Galena tells me. "I had to see it."

I nod. I can understand that. "You had to see where Ingrid kept your brother."

"I thought nobody would be here. She told me you'd all be gone."

"No such luck." That's when my legs give out. I drop onto the cot. I bet nobody's been on it since Galena's brother Joe. Who's dead, thanks to Ingrid. And now I know that Ingrid is dead thanks to Galena. "What are you going to do?" I ask her.

"I don't know. I panicked, okay? I thought nobody would be here," she repeats.

I can hear her clearly but I can't see her all that well. She's across the room with her back against the opposite wall. By now it's dark outside. No moonlight is streaming in through the lone window. And no lights are on inside the house on this floor.

Okay, I order myself, *don't* you *panic*. Sure, I'm alone with a killer. But I won't be for long. Everyone will be back soon—Shanelle, Trixie, my parents, Maggie. Of course I don't want them tangling with Galena any more than I want to tangle with her myself. But there's strength in numbers. And I don't think Galena is armed.

As stealthily as possible I reach forward to pick up my pepper spray. I stash it in my waistband. The stream can't reach Galena across the room but it may come in handy at some point. I just wish I knew where my cell phone landed. That I don't see.

I clear my throat. "So your maiden name is Fuchs."

"Lang is my married name."

Galena married into the Lang family mortuary business, as I recall. And then took it over when her husband died. She did better than her brother Joe, the sibling with the simple name, who served in Vietnam and came back to the States a broken man.

"Did anybody else know that Ingrid and your brother were married?" I ask.

"Nobody knew. She didn't want anybody to know."

That's what I guessed, though I didn't understand why. Now I do. Ingrid Svendsen wouldn't want anybody to know she married a man who was both alcoholic and homeless. But she had her reasons. She wanted to buy life insurance in his name, kill him in a hit and run, and enjoy the financial windfall. It was a malevolent way to make up for the money Erik Svendsen did not leave her.

Galena pipes up. "There were times I lost track of Joe but I always figured he was in a shelter or trying out a different locale or something. I'd keep an eye on his hangouts and if I found him I'd give him a few bucks. Help him buy some food. Or a bottle." She pauses, then, "I should've known something was up. Suddenly he always had a bottle."

No doubt Ingrid fed Joe's addiction to keep him docile. "Some of those times you couldn't find him, he was probably here." Where I'm sitting right now. I wonder how often Ingrid locked him up here. I wonder if he was frightened. We'll never know. "Did he tell you about Ingrid?"

"You mean, did he ever tell me he married some rich woman? He sure did. Then in the next breath he'd tell me he had a dragon on his shoulder. Maybe if I'd believed him, he'd be alive today. But no!" Her voice takes on a hysterical note. She throws out her arm in a gesture reminiscent of Lillian. "It wasn't until after he was dead that I found out about all this. When I got the idea to call the VA to ask about survivor benefits and they told me his wife already called. His wife!"

"That's how you found out about Ingrid."

"Nobody said the name Ingrid Svendsen. I had to figure that out on my own. But it's real easy online. You pay a fee and you can find out anything about anybody. And I knew Joe's social so it was a piece of cake."

I can picture the scene once Galena knew her brother had become Mr. Ingrid Svendsen. "I bet you marched right over here to Damsgard."

"You bet your skinny ass I did. And all Ingrid Svendsen wanted to know was how much it would take to shut me up."

So that was the source of Galena's sudden money. Not veteran's benefits but payoffs extorted from her brother's killer. Then something else clicks in my mind. "Ingrid wasn't going to keep paying you off forever."

Galena is silent for a while. Then, "She finally told me the jig was up."

After she hired Hubble. I bet Ingrid told Galena she hired a P.I. and he'd find something nasty on her if he looked long enough. Except for the fact that it got her killed, Ingrid's bluff worked. Because Galena knew there was something to be found.

I shiver. This probably means those trafficking allegations are true. Galena may have had no compunction blackmailing Ingrid because she was already flouting the law, in a truly vile way.

It's getting pretty late. I'm surprised nobody's come back to Damsgard yet. But talking seems to keep Galena calm. So I'll talk.

"There's something else I don't understand," I say. "Didn't the cops figure out your brother was married when they investigated his death?"

"Are you kidding me?" Galena hollers.

I guess that was the wrong question. Galena's not so calm anymore.

"You must be a moron," she yells, "if you think they investigate when a homeless drunk dies in a hit and run! Sure, the coroner did an autopsy. And he finds out Joe had alcohol in his system. Big surprise. So what do the cops do? Wipe their hands and release the body to me. Case closed."

I'm sure she's right that Winona P.D. didn't call body shops in Minneapolis to find out if any cars had been brought in with damage consistent with a hit and run. "So there were no witnesses? No surveillance video?"

"He was hit in an alley," she spits. "Left for dead. Nobody saw a thing, exactly how Ingrid Svendsen planned it."

Now I remember what Lillian said about why Ingrid might've gotten into heathen worship. Seems to me she took the concepts of warriorship and bold action way too far.

"Do you know," Galena hisses, "how hard it was for me to prepare that woman for burial? If it were up to me, I would've just stuck her in the ground. She couldn't rot fast enough for me."

I try to clear that image from my mind. "You know, Galena"—I make my voice as gentle and reassuring as possible—"a jury would understand why you did what you did. I'm not saying they'd think it was okay but they would understand why you'd want Ingrid to pay for what she did to your brother. What she did was—"

Galena steps closer to the cell. "What do you care about any of this? And how do you know so much about it?"

"It's true I barely knew Ingrid but I was a guest in her house. I wanted to know what happened to her."

"Well, now I bet you wish you didn't." She's sounding more hostile. She starts looking around as if she might find a weapon close at hand. I get hopeful because I know she won't find anything. Then she stands still. "You had a fire downstairs."

I get a hollow feeling in my gut.

"You could have another one," she goes on.

I can't let myself imagine that or I'll freak. I stay silent.

She steps even closer to the bars. I move my hand slowly toward my pepper spray but don't budge from the cot.

"Galena"—my voice comes out kind of strangled—"a jury would understand why you'd want to avenge your brother's death. But there's no way they'd let you get away with doing something to me."

"They wouldn't let me get away with any of it." Her voice is flat. "I already know that. I'd be a goner one way or the other."

"That's not true. They might—"

"Shut up!" She's close enough now that I can see her fairly well. I let my hand close over the pepper spray and slowly stand up. I'm so scared that it's a struggle to stay steady in my stiletto booties.

I think she's got the key in her right hand. If she gets close enough to the bars, maybe if I can spray her and grab the key before she has a chance to react. But she's got to get closer. I can't reach her where she is now.

"How'd that fire start?" she wants to know.

I move closer to the bars. "Galena, don't do it. Let's talk it out. Don't—"

"It doesn't matter how it started." Now she sounds businesslike, in control. And finished with conversation. "I can start another one." She moves toward the door.

"Galena, no!" I shriek. "Don't do it! Please! Believe me, it'll make your situation a whole lot worse! Galena! Please!"

But she's gone. She's out the door. She's down the stairs. She's gone. And she's taken the key to the cell with her.

"Oh no. Oh no." Now I'm a whimpering fool. I force myself to remain semi-calm. I force myself not to think how quickly Damsgard would burn, Damsgard which might have shredded paper for insulation, Damsgard which has a Christmas tree in every room, Damsgard which might as well be a torch.

Think! Think!

My cell phone. Where's my cell phone?

I wish there were some light in this room! There's nothing. How can I find my phone with no light? Where the heck is it?

I hear Galena doing something downstairs. I refuse to listen. It does me no good to listen.

I get down on my hands and knees and scour the floor of the cell as fast as I can. Eventually I have to conclude that my phone is not in the cell, as much as I wish it were.

So, okay, I have to look outside the cell. It might be close to the bars. In fact, it can't be too far from the bars. It went flying toward the bars when Galena pushed me.

I'm crawling along the bars peering into the darkness when I see it. I actually see it. There it is.

I sit back on my haunches and gulp some air. Okay. This is good. I can call for help.

That is, if I can reach my cell.

I reach for it. I can't quite get it.

Come on, come on ...

I reach, I reach, I reach ... but I can't quite get it. I'm forcing my arm as far as it'll go, my shoulder is screaming, but I can't reach it. It's so close! But it's out of reach.

Then—*oh no, oh no*—I think I smell smoke. I'm not absolutely positive but I think I do. Did Galena start a fire? She might have. She really might have.

What can I use to reach the phone?

Of course. What any beauty queen would use. Her stiletto bootie.

I yank off one of my booties, hold it by the front, and try to get the heel behind the phone. I can inch the phone forward that way.

It's coming. I moved it closer that time. Careful, careful ...

The smoke alarm starts to wail at the very instant I grab

my cell phone. I pull it into the cell with me. I'm almost crying from relief.

But not too much relief because now I'm positive that I smell smoke. And I'm still locked in this cell.

I punch in 911. I'm hyperventilating so it's hard to talk. "Yes! My house is on fire!" I give the address, very carefully. I hear commotion downstairs but I can't think about that. "Yes! Quickly! I'm locked on the third floor, in a cell. Yes! You heard me right! I'm in a prison cell, with actual bars, and there's a door but the key is gone. So the firefighters have to be able to get me out of this cell or I'll burn up."

I don't think I've ever sounded so loony in my life. But the dispatcher keeps talking to me in an amazingly calm manner, which is a huge help since I am hysterical. And getting more hysterical by the second because now when I look up I think I see smoke wisping into the room.

I'm still on the phone with the dispatcher when I hear even more of a ruckus downstairs. "Help! Help!" I cry.

"Keep her down, Lou! Keep her down!"

Oh my God. I can't believe it. That's my mother's voice.

"I'm working on that fire!" she bellows. "Maggie, get your behind over here and help me!"

I hear a siren in the distance. It better be on a fire truck and it better be headed this way.

"My parents are downstairs," I tell the dispatcher. "They're trying to put out the fire. And I think they have the woman who set the fire. Galena Lang, from the funeral home."

That elicits some surprise from the dispatcher.

"She killed Ingrid Svendsen," I add. "You have to get the cops here, too, or the firefighters will have to arrest her."

By now the dispatcher has probably put in a side call to the mental ward. But she pretends she believes me.

"Keep her down, Lou!" I hear my mother yell again. "I don't give a hoot that she's in the snow!" Then I hear clomping on the stairs. "Happy! Happy! I'm coming!"

"Mom! Up here! On the third floor! The room with the

cell! I'm locked in!"

"I'm coming!" she bellows.

More clomping. Then the hallway light switches on. My mom has made it to the third floor. A second later I see her in the doorway, silhouetted against the light, panting and wheezing and holding a fire extinguisher in each hand.

Who would've thunk it? My mother is a two-fisted gunslinger, wielding fire extinguishers instead of pistols.

"Here I am, Happy!" she cries. "So what's up with all the stairs in this place?"

I don't think I've ever seen a more wonderful sight in my life. I burst into tears.

CHAPTER THIRTY-FOUR

What do you do when it's your last night in Minnesota and it's a week before Christmas and you want to celebrate that you've just solved a murder? Why, you take a sleigh ride, of course.

The whole gang is piled into a sleek black sleigh, complete with three red leather bench seats and jingle bells, drawn by a team of stately Belgian Draft Horses. When I say "the whole gang," I'm including Detective Dembek but omitting Mario. That's the way it is now; that's the way it must be.

Although I will tell you, dear reader, I did see Mario before we left Damsgard for the evening's festivities, when he appeared at the front door. And both the fact that he showed up, and the look in those dark soulful eyes of his, made me think he's having as much trouble forgetting me as I am forgetting him …

"This is so much fun!" Trixie trills from the seat in front of me. She's riding next to Shanelle while Pop's up front with Maggie, chatting with the driver. I'm in the rear with my mom on one side and Detective Dembek on the other. Even though it's well into the evening and subfreezing, we're all toasty in coats, hats, scarves, and gloves, and bundled under beautifully woven lap robes in rich red hues. I don't know where in the countryside we are but it's a perfect winter wonderland: fresh snow under the sleigh's steel runners and deep forest all around. I love hearing the sleigh bells jingle and the horses' hooves clip clop. If this doesn't get me in the Christmas spirit, nothing will.

I pipe up, my breath puffing in the frigid night air. "Detective Dembek, you're really not going to tell us what surprise you've got lined up at the lodge?" I know that I'll be more than satisfied with the hot apple cider and s'mores that I'm told await us.

"Call me Rita," she says for the third time.

I'm having trouble with that.

"And all I'll tell you," she goes on, "is that it involves a bagman."

"I think I've solved *that* mystery," Shanelle turns around to say, "but I'll keep it to myself so I don't spoil the surprise."

Rita leans forward to speak across me to my mom. "I hear you deserve almost as much praise as your daughter does for figuring out who murdered Ingrid Svendsen."

"I did some quick thinking a few times," my mother allows. "But my big contribution was putting out those fires."

"No kidding," I say. "After she put out that blaze in the foyer during the candlelight tour, she raced out the next day and not only got the fire extinguisher recharged but bought a second one."

"Just in case," my mother says. "And boy, did I need it today. At least that Galena started the curtains on fire instead of the Christmas tree."

I wonder why. Maybe on some level Galena didn't want to fry me to a crisp. Even so, it makes me really sad that Damsgard's gorgeous living room is seriously burned. It's only because of my parents' excellent timing that the damage isn't far worse. And that I'm here to enjoy this sleigh ride. As it is, the fire department is probably tempted to park a truck outside Damsgard until they're a hundred percent sure we've all left town.

"Mr. P deserves a big pat on the back, too," Trixie says. "I don't know what it means to hogtie someone but I guess that's what he did to Galena."

I am so proud of my parents for coming through in the clutch. I gather Maggie wasn't feigning helplessness this time; it sounds like she was too terrified to be of any help. I hope Pop keeps that in mind as he weighs his future romantic options.

"All of you made it very easy for me and for the department," Rita says. "I'm going to look into citizen commendations. You deserve them, in my opinion."

"Peter Svendsen might not agree with you," I murmur.

"You'd be surprised," Rita replies. "He's certainly not happy about everything that happened at Damsgard but he understands justice must be served. And we all know that often comes at a price."

"Well, he can renovate Damsgard any way he wants to now," Shanelle points out.

"I hope he makes some big changes to that third floor," my mother adds.

"How soon do you think Galena will go on trial?" Trixie wants to know.

"On the murder charge, I would guess in a few months," Rita says. "In terms of the trafficking allegations, I can't tell you. That investigation is ongoing."

The detective already told me she's confident that prosecutors will build a strong murder case against Galena. Though she's only begun to search the funeral home, she's already found two pieces of circumstantial evidence tying Galena to the crime. One is the notepaper used to instruct the teenage Giant W worker to keep the lights down after the speeches—in exchange for a twenty. The other is a shredded copy of the schedule for the Giant W's opening ceremony, with Kevin the teenager's home address scribbled on the side.

"Don't take this the wrong way," I say to Rita, "but I have to ask if Galena was right when she said the police did very little investigation of her brother's death."

"I've already checked that file. And I remember the case,

because it was only last summer. All the patrol officers knew Joe Fuchs, just like they know all the longtime homeless. Unfortunately, in that situation it is very easy to be the victim of violence."

I don't doubt that for a second.

"But officers did investigate," she goes on. "No vehicle turned up with the kind of damage we were looking for. We did make one mistake, though, and that was to conclude that the hit and run was a random tragedy. We knew that the vehicle that hit Joe Fuchs was maroon," she adds, "and by the way that is the color of the car Ingrid Svendsen rented, and had repaired, in Minneapolis."

I shake my head. Detective Dembek will be delving into Ingrid's activities, too, as well as Galena's. Though it hasn't been confirmed yet, she believes as I do that the life insurance payments from Vigilanz will prove to be from a policy Ingrid took out in Joseph Fuchs's name, listing herself as the beneficiary. Unfortunately for Maggie, since those monies were obtained via criminal means, they will be returned to Vigilanz.

But for now I'm going to push all that to the back of my mind. Our sleigh pulls up to a lodge that calls to mind a Swiss chalet. One driver leaps out to tend to the horses while the other leads us to a fire pit that provides all the warmth we need. We sit in a circle and soon a mug of hot apple cider is pressed into my gloved hands. I look around at the glowing faces of my parents, Rita Dembek, Trixie, Shanelle, and Maggie. I even feel fondly toward her tonight, though I still hope she doesn't find an engagement ring from Pop under her Christmas tree. The only thing that could make tonight better were if Rachel were here, and Jason, too.

I'll try not to think about who else I miss.

"Shall we make some s'mores?" Trixie wants to know.

There's only one right answer to that question.

We toast marshmallows and layer them over chocolate and graham crackers and it's pretty much the best campfire I've ever been around. I'm about to indulge in my third when Rita claps her hands.

"Ready for your surprise?" she calls.

We whoop and holler, and who comes out of nowhere but Peter Svendsen and five other men, all dressed in pretty wild outfits: white shirts and breeches, clogs, leather strips around the knees that have bells dangling from them, red suspenders, and straw hats decorated with berries. They're also carrying large sticks and handkerchiefs.

Peter steps forward and executes an elaborate bow. "Most often we do this on May Day but in your honor we will perform for you on this December night. May I introduce our squire"—one man steps forward—"our foreman"—another takes a bow—"and our bagman!" A third man steps to the front, laughing heartily.

"We," Peter goes on, "are Morris Dancers," and they launch into a complicated jig that involves hopping, stomping, waving of handkerchiefs, and banging of sticks. The music is country simple, produced by something called a melodeon, which I learn is a type of accordion.

"It's an English folk tradition," Peter tells me afterward, when he and his fellow dancers have joined us around the fire pit. "I got into it when I was in school over there." He chuckles. "Barbara's not too keen on it but I should tell her it's better than being in the Mob."

I feel like an idiot. "Detective Dembek told you about that."

"I can see why you were suspicious of me. Obviously I've never been Ingrid's biggest fan."

"Well, now more than ever, I understand why." I hesitate, then, "I'm so sorry about all the damage to Damsgard. And I'm really sorry about your mother, too. It can't be easy for you that she's been arrested."

He shakes his head. "Damsgard I can fix. My mother, I don't know. She's got a lot of explaining to do. Maybe she'll wise up after paying her debt to society."

Here's hoping.

I accept a warm-up of my apple cider and wander away from the group to look at the moon and stars. They're all out now, shining bright; the clouds have passed.

I hope that happens soon in my own life.

Earlier this evening after the danger had passed, Mario showed up at Damsgard. By then Galena was in custody and the fire trucks were gone. Even the smoke had cleared, and the front window had been patched over with plywood, courtesy of the firefighters.

"It's old habit," Mario told me.

We were standing on the porch. I was trying to ignore the mistletoe dangling over our heads and he was looking as handsome as ever, if maybe a little subdued. Sad, even, and I don't think I was imagining it.

"I keep an eye on you," he said. "I just can't help myself. I always get a little worried when your investigations heat up."

I forgave him. He has a professional interest, too, I told myself, since he's secretly on the F.B.I.'s payroll. "So you heard about my 911 call?"

"I did hear about it, and I came right over. By the time I arrived here at Damsgard, though, everything was under control."

So he came by Damsgard twice today. I found a certain satisfaction in that, and it was as hard to ignore as the mistletoe.

"How are you doing?" he wanted to know.

I had the funniest feeling he wasn't just asking about the aftermath of being locked in the cell. "I'm not great. But I'm okay."

"You are great, Happy. I'll dispute you on that as long as you'll let me."

Then we had one of those moments, one of those stare at each other moments, that might've gone on a short time, it might've gone on a long time, I'll never know. All I know is I don't like when they end.

But end it did. "I'll see you around," he said. "You've got my word on that."

My reverie is interrupted when Trixie rubs my arm. Shanelle is standing right beside her. "You okay, Happy?" Trixie wants to know.

"We're here," Shanelle adds. "We'll always be here, girl."

"That's good." To my credit, I sniffle only the tiniest bit. "I'm pretty sure I'm going to need you."

"Just remember what I always say," Trixie murmurs.

"Here we go again," Shanelle mutters.

"Things work out the way they're supposed to," Trixie finishes. "I really do believe that."

I glance back at the fire pit, where my father, mother, and Maggie are all sitting in a companionable row. Now there's a tableau I never would have expected. I guess it just goes to show that you never know what'll happen next.

You just have to wait and see.

Diana loves to hear from readers! Email her at www.dianadempsey.com and sign up for her mailing list while you're there to hear first about her new releases. Also join her on Facebook at www.facebook.com/DianaDempseyBooks and follow her on Twitter at www.twitter.com/diana_dempsey.

ACKNOWLEDGMENTS

When I had the pleasure of visiting Winona, I was fortunate enough to interview a few key people who helped tremendously with my research. Many thanks especially to Pat Mutter, director of the Winona Convention and Visitors Bureau, and to Walt Bennick, society archivist and author of *Winona: Images of America*. I'm also grateful to Mike Potvin, who gave me a behind-the-scenes tour of Bloedow's Bakery (yum!), and to Karen and Craig Groth at the lovely Windom Park Bed and Breakfast.

My stay in Minneapolis was great fun thanks to former Harvard roommate and longtime WCCO reporter and anchor Esme Murphy, and friend and fantastic Regency romance author Candice Hern. I can't wait for her next book!

I love my Ms America covers and that is because the incomparable Rhonda Freshwater of Freshwater Design creates them. Bill Fuller was his usual helpful self, providing guidance on the manuscript, and my husband Jed deserves props as always. No one (but me) sees the book in a rougher state. The beauty-queen mysteries would not be what they are without his wisdom and insight.

Diana Dempsey traded in an Emmy-winning career in TV news to write fast, fun romantic fiction. Her debut novel, *Falling Star*, was nominated for a RITA award for Best First Book by the members of Romance Writers of America. Other of her novels have been Top Picks of *Romantic Times* or selections of the Doubleday Book Club.

In her dozen years in television news, the former Diana Koricke played every on-air role from network correspondent to local news anchor. She reported for NBC News from New York, Tokyo, and Burbank, and substitute anchored such broadcasts as *Sunrise*, *Today*, and *NBC Nightly News*. In addition, she was a morning anchor for KTTV 11 Fox News in Los Angeles. She started her broadcast career with the Financial News Network.

Born and raised in Buffalo, New York—Go, Bills!—Diana is a graduate of Harvard University and the winner of a Rotary International Foundation Scholarship. She enjoyed stints overseas in Belgium, the U.K., and Japan, and now resides in Los Angeles with her husband and a West Highland White Terrier, not necessarily in that order.

Fruitcake

(From JoyOfBaking.com)

"This Fruit Cake recipe is adapted from Nigel Slater's *The Kitchen Diaries* and it is by far the best one I have ever made. It is jammed with raisins, currants, dried cranberries, dried figs and prunes, dried apricots, and candied fruit and peel (candied fruit is preserved fruit that has been dipped several times in a concentrated sugar syrup). Nuts are also included as is ground almonds. Do try to make your fruitcake about three to four weeks before Christmas so you can brush it with alcohol several times and allow the flavors to mingle and age. This cake can be frozen so it might be a good idea to make two and then you can freeze one for later in the year.

"Each person has their own list of 'must have' foods for Christmas. For me, it is this Fruit Cake; that wonderful combination of nuts and dried fruits with barely enough cake batter to hold it all together. If you have ever made a British Fruit Cake you know that what really sets this cake apart is how we repeatedly feed the cake, over time, with alcohol (usually brandy, sometimes rum). This gives the Fruit Cake a subtle brandy flavor and a moist texture, plus it also allows the cake to be stored for ages and ages. Of course, the step of repeatedly brushing alcohol on the cake means we have to make it well in advance of Christmas. But is that so bad? With all the hustle and bustle of the Christmas season, doing our baking several weeks in advance can only be a good thing."

(Diana here): I have not yet made this fruitcake but I plan to this holiday season. In anticipation, I bought a new springform pan and have ordered candied fruit from The Great American Spice Company. I may not "steep" it to the extent Happy's mother does, but I will use her approach, as described above. Merry Christmas!

Ingredients:

1 cup (227 grams) unsalted butter
1/2 cup (110 grams) light brown sugar
1/2 cup (110 grams) dark brown sugar
3 large eggs
3 tablespoons brandy, plus extra for brushing the cake
Juice and zest of one orange
Zest of one lemon
3/4 cup (65 grams) ground almonds
1 cup (100 grams) hazelnuts, walnuts, pecans, or almonds, chopped
1 1/2 pounds (680 grams) of an assortment of dried and candied fruits
3/4 pound (340 grams) of an assortment of raisins, sultana, dried cranberries and/or cherries
2 cups (260 grams) all-purpose flour
1 teaspoon baking powder
1/4 teaspoon salt

Preparation:

1. Butter, or spray with nonstick vegetable spray, an 8-inch (20 cm) springform pan. Line the bottom of the pan with buttered parchment paper. Also, line the sides of the pan with a strip of buttered parchment paper that extends about 2 inches above the pan.

2. Preheat oven to 325° F (160° C).

3. In the bowl of your electric mixer, or with a hand mixer, beat the butter and sugars until light and fluffy. Add the eggs one at a time, beating well after each addition. Add the brandy, juice and zest of the orange, and zest of the lemon. Then fold in the ground almonds, chopped nuts, and all the dried and candied fruits.

4. In a separate bowl, whisk together the flour, salt, and baking powder. Fold this into the cake batter.

5. Scrape the batter into the prepared pan and, if desired, decorate the top of the cake with blanched almonds. Place the pan on a baking sheet. Bake for 1 hour. Reduce the temperature to 300° F (150° C) and continue to bake the cake for another 90 minutes or until a long skewer inserted into the center of the cake comes out with just a few moist crumbs. Remove the cake from the oven and place on a wire rack to cool completely.

6. Using a skewer, poke holes in the top of the cake and brush with a little brandy. Wrap the cake thoroughly in plastic wrap and aluminum foil and place in a cake tin or plastic bag. Brush the cake periodically (once or twice a week) with brandy until Christmas. The cake will keep several weeks or it can be frozen.

White Christmas Dream Drops

(Diana here): We can thank Dustin and Erin Beutin of Tustin, California, for this recipe, which won *Sunset* magazine's Grand Prize for Holiday Cookies.

They are good! I recommend you take to heart the 1-tablespoon portion size when you spoon the meringue onto the cookie sheets. I made mine a little big but I can correct that mistake next time. And there will be a next time … ;-)

Note from *Sunset*: "Unlike traditional meringues, which are crisp all the way through, these are still chewy on the inside, like mini pavlovas—but with white chocolate chips and plenty of peppermint. For an elegant touch, dip the edges in melted dark chocolate."

Ingredients:

2 egg whites, room temperature
1/8 teaspoon cream of tartar
1/2 teaspoon vanilla
1/8 teaspoon salt
3/4 cup sugar
1 cup white chocolate chips
1/3 cup + 1 1/2 tablespoon coarsely crushed peppermint candies

Preparation:

1. Preheat oven to 250°. Beat egg whites and cream of tartar in a deep bowl with a mixer, using whisk attachment if you have one, just until soft peaks form. Add vanilla and salt. With motor running and mixer on high speed, add 1 tablespoon sugar and beat 10 to 15 seconds, then repeat until all the sugar has been added. Scrape inside of bowl and beat another 15

seconds. At this point, meringue should form straight peaks when beaters are lifted. Fold in chocolate chips and 1/3 cup crushed peppermint with a flexible spatula.

2. Line two baking sheets with parchment paper, using meringue at corners as glue. Using a soup spoon, drop meringue in rounded 1 tablespoon portions slightly apart onto sheets, scraping off with another spoon. Sprinkle with remaining crushed peppermint.

3. Bake 30 to 35 minutes, until meringues feel dry and set, but are still pale. Reverse pan position at halfway point. When done, turn off oven, open door, and let cookies stand 10 minutes. Let cool on pans.

Yield: 32 cookies. Time: 1 ¼ hour. Can make 2 days ahead. Store airtight.

CHASING VENUS

Known for page-turning romantic novels that keep you reading late into the night, Diana Dempsey delivers a suspenseful tale about a man and a woman who must shed the past to embrace the future ...

Annette Rowell's latest novel is leapfrogging up the bestseller lists, and with every surge in sales she's becoming more of a household name. The literary success she's struggled so hard for would be a dream come true were it not for the killer preying on bestselling authors.

Reid Gardner hosts a syndicated crime show dedicated to capturing dangerous fugitives. The former LAPD cop knows only too well how violence can shatter lives. No victim arouses his ardor more than the pretty author who's become the target of a psychopath. Yet falling in love with her could cost him not only the reputation he's spent years building, but the one killer who's eluded him for years ...

PROLOGUE

Death was not on the guest list, but it appeared all the same.

Maggie Boswell, reigning queen of mystery fiction, sat at the signing table as if she were royalty on a throne. Around her, in teetering piles, was her latest bestseller. Grabbing at the books were members of the literary elite—authors, editors, agents. It was a huge irony that Maggie had invited them into her home for this book party. Most of them she disliked. Now all of them she distrusted.

For any one of them might try to kill her.

Someone handed her a book. She scribbled the inscription, struggling to rise above her fear. In the shifting terror of her worst imaginings, even her beloved home unnerved her. Its enormity was no longer a joy, but a threat. It had too many corners, too many shadows. And outside its stucco walls the night was moonless, and the silver-gray Pacific beyond the terraced garden unnaturally still.

A breeze from the open French doors behind her wafted over the back of her neck, chilling her skin like a spectral caress. She shivered, turned to look. Yet there was nothing there, nothing but the unrelieved blackness of her garden.

"Ms. Boswell?"

She spun at the woman's voice, and pursed her lips. A

pretender to her throne, in the form of a brunette wisp with—in Maggie's opinion—dubious talent.

The woman held a book toward her and smiled. "I'm Annette Rowell. I'm a huge admirer of your work."

Maggie took the book but didn't care to smile back. "Are you?"

"I've really been looking forward to this one."

Read it and weep. "Shall I sign the book to you?"

"Please."

Maggie scrawled *To Annette* and then her signature in expansive script. She slapped the hardcover shut and held out the volume.

"You may remember that I have a mystery series of my own," the woman said.

Maggie was well aware of it. "Is that so?"

Again the woman smiled. "Thank you so much for including me tonight."

Maggie wondered how this upstart had made it onto the guest list. She averted her head in silent dismissal and the woman moved along.

The books kept coming, endlessly. Greet, open, sign, hand back, smile, over and over again. At one point, Maggie jolted upright. She'd felt something, sudden and swift, in the nape of her neck. A piercing, like a bee sting, or a needle making an entry into flesh. Deeply and with purpose. Then, just as quickly, gone.

She frowned, twisted to look behind her out the French doors. Again, nothing. Just the yards of flagstone terrace and the lawn sweeping to the sea. With some trepidation she touched the back of her neck, then stared aghast at the unmistakable crimson smear on her finger.

My God. A thought came, a terrifying idea she immediately banished. *It can't be.*

Someone held another book toward her. Mechanically she signed it, her mind whirling. As she returned the volume to its owner, she grimaced again.

An unnatural tingling sensation had begun in her body. Maggie stilled, gave it her full attention. Yet the feeling didn't disappear, but grew, strengthened.

She shivered. Coldness writhed within her. The hideous thought returned, taunted her. *Just like in my second book.* No. She wouldn't believe it. It couldn't be so easy, that what she feared most would simply come to pass. Just like that. All the while the iciness intensified, knifing through her body. A harbinger of doom.

This cannot be happening.

Yet, she knew, it could.

The people around her seemed to grow distant, as if a veil had dropped between her and the living world. She saw their faces, she heard their voices, but she was alone among them in a way she never had been before. She tried to move her mouth to speak but her lips failed to respond.

So fast. It really is so fast.

She was almost admiring of the poison's power. Just as she had written about it, so it was.

"Darling?" Her husband bent over her. Voices echoed, concerned faces loomed. Someone held up something thin and shiny and silver. Maggie didn't need to see it clearly to know what it was. A dart, tipped with poison.

Terror gripped her then, spun in her mind like a grotesque dervish. Her imagination, always vivid, conjured an image of her last breath. Not so far off now, she knew. And, oh, how she would gasp, strain, seek air she could never more find ...

Panic ballooned in the gorgeous living room, an acid cloud only she could see. People were jostling now, bumping into one another, seeking escape. A lone scream rent the air. She tried to turn her head to see who had made the shrill sound but wasn't able. Already that was beyond her rapidly dwindling capabilities.

So fast, so fast ...

Her body slumped to the table. She was powerless to keep her head from slamming onto the book she had been preparing to sign.

My last book. It's over. I'm dead.

Another scream, not her own, for she could no longer draw breath. She knew. She had tried. Nothing came.

Death made its exit, leaving its grim calling card behind.

CHAPTER ONE

Annie Rowell snagged a deep breath of air, her heart pumping, her feet in their worn running shoes pounding the graveled shoulder of the two-lane road. It was dusk, and at this hour few cars passed through these low grassy hills outside the California coastal town of Bodega Bay. Here, a mile inland, she couldn't hear the surf, but still the chill air carried a tang of salt. Overhead a raven cawed, its shriek splitting the heavens.

The route was her usual one and required no concentration. Her mind was free to wander, and it did, to her favorite daydream.

New Yorkers shouldered past her as she stared into the windows of the glitzy bookstore. Snow drifted from the sky, dusting her brunette hair and melting on the long lashes rimming her green eyes, shiny with tears of joy. A businessman, walking fast, bumped into her, muttered under his breath.

She remained motionless. Mesmerized. Nothing could tear her from this sight, one she'd dreamed of for years. Her novel—hers!—stacked in a giant pyramid in the window. In the middle where the bestsellers go.

A shopper inside lifted a book from the pyramid and headed for the registers. More like that and Annie would rise even higher on the bestsellers list. She could just imagine Philip and that new wife of his frowning at each other over their New York Times, *unable to fathom that Annette Rowell's name was printed there, and in such an illustrious position.*

Maybe I shouldn't have divorced her, *Philip would think, eyeing wife number two with the disappointment he'd previously reserved for Annie.* But who would have thought she'd ever amount to anything?

The fantasy generated the usual smile but this time it didn't last long. Annie was abruptly jarred back to reality.

She picked up her pace—just a bit, not enough to be obvious, then raised her chin a notch and resisted the urge to glance over her shoulder.

How long had that car been behind her?

Why wasn't it driving past?

It was late April and the longer days allowed her to get sloppy about when she set off on her run. In January she had to get going by 3:30 or it'd be dark by the time the circuit led her back home. Darkness and jogging solo were a bad combo for any woman. Let alone one who might have a target on her back.

But she'd gotten caught up revising chapter seventeen, and five o'clock slipped by, then six, six thirty ... And there was no way she'd skip the run. She was all discipline these days—in her writing, her workouts, her meals, everything. But it meant that here she was, still out, with the shadows too long for comfort.

The slow-moving car sped up. She could tell from the rev of its engine. Then it appeared alongside her and slowed again to roll at exactly her rate of speed. From inside the vehicle, through the open passenger window, she could feel the driver's eyes on her. Just ... watching.

She kept her gaze straight ahead, her heart thumping an anxious rhythm that had little to do with exertion.

What should she do? *Be bold*, she decided. *Look at the driver.*

She swung her head to the left and got an eyeful of a beat-up maroon sedan. Behind the wheel ... a man. Not an elderly man, either, which might have explained the molasses-in-January pace. Of indeterminate age, and dark-haired. Wearing sunglasses even though the sun had nearly set.

But that was all she could make out, because a second later the car accelerated and shot ahead. At first Annie couldn't understand why, until she realized that another vehicle was coming up from behind. She caught a snippet of animated conversation through open windows as an SUV sped past.

The roar of both engines died away and silence again descended, broken only by the repetitive beat of Annie's footfalls on the gravel.

The SUV scared him off. That's good, right?

Sure, but who was he? And why did he have to get scared off in the first place?

Don't think. Just run. Get home.

For several minutes she made good progress. But the peace was short-lived. Soon she heard a vehicle behind her.

She glanced over her shoulder.

Despite the gloaming, a car was approaching without its headlights on. Was it the maroon sedan? She couldn't tell. Had the guy turned around and doubled back?

Her breath caught in her throat. Should she confront him? No, that would only egg him on. Turn around? But it made no sense to close the distance between them. Speed up? At the bend just ahead she could cross the road and sprint over the smallish hill to the left. It would make for more difficult running but it would also be impossible for him to follow her.

Unless he abandoned his vehicle.

She didn't care to consider that possibility. Nor did she have time to think. She was nearly at the bend now, the softly mounded hill tempting her as an escape route.

Do it. Another few paces. Now.

She made a sharp left turn and knifed across the road, then scrambled up the grassy incline as fast as her aching muscles and pounding heart would allow. It was no easy trick, winded as she was. *Don't let him follow me don't let him follow me ...*

Behind her she heard tires on gravel. Had he pulled off the road? She was only a little ways up the hill, which was steeper than it had appeared. Her breath was coming hard and fast into a dry open mouth that was sucking in as much oxygen as possible. Her lungs were on fire; her brain repeated the silent mantra. *Don't let him follow me ...*

She wished for the fearlessness she'd enjoyed as a girl. In those days she was scared of nothing and no one. Since then, two decades of life had intervened. Philip had intervened, wreaking havoc with the confidence that used to fill her.

Behind her a car door opened. She heard the *beep-beep-beep* of the ignition when the key is left in, then voices, and static, like radio on a bad frequency. A flashlight beam lit up the grass ahead of her.

"Miss!" a man's voice shouted. "Stop!"

She paused—she was almost on all fours, she'd been scrambling so hard—and glanced behind her.

It was a cop, late forties or so, with a thick build, a wide lined face, and a flashlight in his hand. He was standing in front of a black-and-white with both doors open. "Are you all right?"

Now she understood the static sound: it was the police radio. She let herself drop onto the grassy bank, cool against her skin, and watched the cop make his laborious way up the incline. When he got closer, she could see that his badge read HELMS. "Are you all right?" he repeated.

She nodded, for a second couldn't find her voice. Then, "I'm fine."

He motioned at the hill. "Why'd you come up here?"

"I thought I was being followed." She relayed the story. Behind Helms, down the hill, his fellow deputy exited the cruiser. He was white, too, roughly the same age, height, and build as his partner but with a gut that sagged over his belt.

Helms offered her a hand and hoisted her to her feet. He motioned toward the road. "Let's talk down there."

She followed without protest. Once at the base of the hill

she could read Helms's partner's badge: PINCUS.

Helms slid a notebook from his back pocket. "Did you see the license plate?"

"No." How embarrassing she hadn't even thought to look. But the car had sped off so fast she might not have been able to read it even if she had.

He eyed her. "You realize that was us behind you just now."

"Yes, but there was that guy alongside me. Did you see him?"

"In a maroon sedan, you told me."

"Yes. At least the first guy was. I'm not sure about the second. I couldn't see that well because it got so dark." Helms didn't say anything and she got the idea he didn't believe her. "I'm not making this up," she added.

Helms regarded her a second longer then flipped his notebook open and jotted a few lines. Then he returned it to his pocket. "I have a piece of advice for you, Ms. Rowell."

"I know. I shouldn't be out running at this ... " She paused. "You know my name?"

"You're that mystery writer from out of town who rents the old Marsden place."

Pincus spoke for the first time. "You live there alone."

He didn't need to remind her. Nor did she care to remember how that came to be—how Philip left her once he finished the medical training she'd helped pay for, how he'd traded her in for a woman doctor "soul mate," how she'd moved to this remote town to get the lower rent she could afford on her tiny advances.

She looked at Helms and a frightening idea took root in her mind. "Is there a reason you're keeping an eye on me?"

His gaze skittered away. Then, "We've been asked to be on the alert where you're concerned."

"Because of the murders of those writers," Pincus added.

Helms shot Pincus a look that said *Zip it*. Then he turned his eyes again toward Annie. "It's a routine alert given to law-enforcement agencies that have known mystery writers in their jurisdiction."

It might be routine to him. It wasn't to her.

"We'll drive you home," Helms went on. He opened the cruiser's rear door and stood beside it. "And my advice is you shouldn't be out alone at this hour. You need to be more careful."

Truer words were never spoken. She got inside the cruiser and settled on its cracked black Naugahyde.

On a rational level she knew she wasn't a likely target. True, three big-name mystery writers had been murdered. One after the next, in the space of a few months. First Seamus O'Neill, then Elizabeth Wimble, and a week ago Maggie Boswell. All of them literary superstars.

That didn't describe her. She was a little-known name with a small to middling readership. But it was growing. Each of her four mysteries had done better than the one before. And with the latest release, the series was really building.

What if it does really well? What if I do become a bestseller? For the first time it seemed possible. Her publisher was really pushing her. And she knew that *Devil's Cradle*, which had just come out, was her best work. After Philip told her he wanted a divorce, she'd poured her heart and soul into her writing and the effort showed. How ironic it would be if the success she'd struggled so hard for was a double-edged sword.

She gazed out the cruiser's window as hills and trees flew past, hulking shadows in the dark. Mystery writers getting killed was terrifying. It wasn't theoretical, like writing mysteries. There she had no problem spreading bodies around like peat moss.

These people she knew. They were flesh and blood. She'd met them, talked to them. Just days ago she'd gone down the coast to Santa Barbara to attend the book party where Maggie Boswell was killed.

Meaning, she knew, that the murderer had been there as

well. He'd probably had a few drinks, told a few jokes. He might have been within inches of her. Maybe he'd brushed up against her. Maybe he was standing outside when she left the party, watching her go. The same man who shot Seamus O'Neill and plunged the crochet hook into Elizabeth Wimble's throat.

She slid on the seat as Helms made the left turn that led past the churchyard cemetery, its weatherbeaten headstones decades old. She'd been renting in Bodega Bay for almost a year and she completely understood why Alfred Hitchcock picked it as the site for *The Birds*. It was perfect. The windswept terrain and unforgiving rocky cliffs, the fog rolling in from the cold surging Pacific ...

Ahead she could see her house. With none of the lights on, it didn't look welcoming. It was a rambling, rundown yellow Victorian with cockeyed front steps. Several of its black shutters were one storm away from falling to pieces. It needed a paint job and a security system and since it was a rental it wouldn't get either.

Helms stopped the cruiser and Pincus got out to open her door. She thanked them and hightailed it indoors, aware of two pairs of eyes on her back.

Inside the house, she double-locked the door, hooked the chain, then went around and switched on every lamp she owned. When the old house was lit up like a Christmas tree, she headed for the kitchen and pulled a Gatorade from the fridge. Then she sat down at the small pine table tucked into the corner beneath the curtained kitchen window.

You have to stop thinking about the murders. You're not getting enough writing done.

It was so difficult to focus. And tomorrow she had to attend Maggie Boswell's funeral, which would bring it all back full-force. But Michael had asked her to go with him and she couldn't refuse, not after everything he'd done for her over the years.

Nobody's coming after you. Keep your eye on the ball.

Write.
    Her next deadline wasn't far off. And she had to meet it, with a fabulous manuscript. The best way to build her name was to get those books out thick and fast, keep her readership captivated. This was her chance to break through. She couldn't let it slip away because she turned into a basketcase.
    That's just what Philip would expect you to do.
    No greater motivation existed. "That's it." She levered herself up from the chair, tossed a frozen burrito in the microwave for dinner, and marched upstairs to the spare bedroom she used as a study. She'd shower later. For now she'd work. She clicked on the file for chapter seventeen and settled in.
    There was only one murder mystery she would let herself dwell on. The one in her own imagination.

*

    Reid Gardner sat by a bank of phones in *Crimewatch*'s Hollywood studios. Past 2 a.m., it was chilly and deserted, with most of the overhead lights off and the rest dimmed. In the newsroom behind him, the cleaning lady clattered, emptying trash cans, occasionally running the vacuum, humming a tune he couldn't name.
    Still he waited, even four hours after the show had gone off the air; still he hoped for one more call to come in on the viewer hotline. He loved when that happened. It meant they were getting a tip from someone who'd seen the show, a tip that might end up putting a fugitive behind bars. That night, like every other night for the past five years, there was one scumbag in particular Reid wanted to take down.
    An incoming call button flared red. Phone headset on, fresh tipsheet on the computer screen, Reid jabbed the button. "*Crimewatch* hotline."
    "Yeah, I got somethin' to say." The caller was male, youngish. Per usual.
    "Go for it."

"That Espinoza dude on your show tonight?"

Damn. Not Reid's personal Most Wanted. Still, of the ten they'd profiled on the broadcast, an important grab. "You know where he is?"

"Not right now. But I seen him." Cocky. Per usual.

"You're sure it was him?"

Silence. Not a good sign. Then, "Yeah, I'm sure."

Right. This call was rapidly moving south on the priority list. "Where?"

"Outside Omaha, dump of a town called Murdock."

Reid shook his head but moved his fingers dutifully over the computer keyboard. Unlikely. The last place they'd been able to confirm Espinoza's whereabouts was South Florida. "That off interstate eighty?"

The guy chuckled. "Hey, pretty good, man. Nobody ever knows jackshit about Murdock. You got a big ol' map there or somethin'?"

"No." Except for the one in Reid's head. Bagging fugitives wasn't a desk job.

The guy on the line paused. Then, "Who is this, anyway?"

No point lying. "Reid Gardner."

"No shit!" He pronounced it shee-it. "You the host and you answer the friggin' phones? In the middle of the night? Not for me, man. If I was you, I'd be livin' large."

"Not my style." He noted that Sheila Banerjee had come into the newsroom. The scent of patchouli was the first clue. The fact that they were the only two staffers left in the building was the other. "Anyway, give me what you got on Espinoza."

That didn't take long. In the meanwhile Sheila hiked a slim hip onto the table beside Reid's phone and swung her right leg lightly back and forth, keeping her sandal on with a graceful arch of her toes. The soft fabric of her skirt swished rhythmically, lulling Reid into remembering just how tired he was.

He finished the call and peeled off his headset, then leaned back in the rolling chair and pinched the skin between his eyes.

"Finally ready to call it a night?" Sheila's voice was soft, her Delhi accent more pronounced in the wee hours.

He raised his head to regard her. "You didn't have to stay."

She said nothing, just met his gaze. And really, there was nothing to say. It wasn't just loyalty to her producer job that kept Sheila Banerjee at her desk well past midnight, and they both knew it.

She looked away. "There was one tip tonight that might be worth something."

He knew which one. "I saw it."

She read his skepticism and arched her brows. "You don't think it's any good?"

He shrugged. "They all look good until they look bad." *Until they lead to the same dead end.* Abruptly he rose, sending his chair rocketing backwards. "I want to look at the story one more time. I'm not sure I worded everything right."

"We went over it so many—"

"I know." He was already in the control booth, the lights of the high-tech electronic equipment blinking red and white in the chilly, darkened room. He pulled the show archive off the shelf, then popped the tape in a deck and scanned for the segment on Larry "Eight Ball" Bigelow.

The man he hunted above all others. The man who'd changed his life. The man who'd ended Donna's.

Sheila was beside him. "There."

Reid slowed the tape, paused it as a photo of his nemesis filled the small screen. It wasn't a great shot but it was the only one they had. There was Bigelow, his skinny body in a white muscle shirt and worn jeans, bending over a pool table with a cue in hand. Though it was hard to see here, Reid knew Bigelow had a tatt on his right bicep, a black 8 ball featuring the capital letter B instead of the numeral 8. He seemed intent on measuring a shot, so much so that his mouth hung open, revealing a missing tooth or two. Straggly blond hair half hid his unshaven face. And though his eyes weren't visible, Reid had his own mental picture of their ice-cold blue depths. He knew the devil lurked within them. The devil himself.

For years we've tracked him. Reid's recorded voice boomed in the silent booth. *We've gotten close a few times, thanks to the tips you've given us. Those of you who are longtime viewers know this one's personal for me.*

There were a few details about Donna's murder. Bigelow's vital stats appeared on the screen: age, height, weight. A red line crisscrossed a map of the country, showing his known travels to Reno, Cheyenne, Duluth, and back again. The map cut to Reid in a nighttime standup, wearing his signature jeans and leather jacket, in front of a graffiti-spattered wall. His blond hair was cropped short; the bump on his nose from that brawl in college more than any makeup artist could shade away. He looked like the cop he used to be. Only the uniform was different, and the LAPD badge was long gone.

No one is safe with this punk on the streets. Reid was embarrassed by the intensity of his voice. To his own ear, it bordered on desperation. *He's a killer. I want him to pay. Help me bring him to justice ...*

Sheila stopped the tape. Reid closed his eyes, listening to the word *justice* bounce off the control-room walls like a ball he could never quite catch. "You worded it just fine," she said.

He couldn't speak. He'd never used that kind of phrasing before, on the air: *This one's personal ... I want ... Help me ...*

"I know," she said, as if he'd actually spoken. "But our viewers will understand. And they'll help if they can."

He didn't look at her as he ejected the tape and returned it to the archive shelf. "You think we'll ever get him?"

It took her a while to answer. Finally, "Yes, I do."

"We don't always, you know." He turned to face her. He didn't say, *We didn't get yours.*

Like Reid, like many of the staff, Sheila was a crime victim. Maybe it was no surprise that so many victims were drawn to working on the show. Sometimes it felt like more of a calling than a job. Sure, they could make TV like the best in the business. They understood the bells and whistles and quick cuts and handheld-style video that gave cop-type shows their raw edge. But they knew something else, too, something you didn't learn in TV and film school.

Sheila's expression remained stoic. She never mentioned the rape anymore. It'd been years since she made Reid give up the search, stop airing the scumbag's profile.

Reid couldn't understand that but he knew that every victim made his or her own choice about how to get on with the rest of their life. That's what it was, too. There was Before it happened, and After. Before you intersected with evil, when you didn't think it could happen to you, and after, when you knew it could.

Together they abandoned the booth, shut down the studio for the night, and rode the elevator to the subterranean parking garage. Reid accompanied Sheila to her car as a courtesy. The building was secure as a fortress. Given the hate their work generated in the scum-of-the-earth population, it had to be.

Sheila settled herself in her white Jetta and rolled down the window. She seemed to hesitate, then, "Do you want to come over to my place for a nightcap? It might help you relax."

He couldn't let himself go down that road again. It would be no more fair to Sheila now than it had been then. "Not tonight." He kept his tone light.

She nodded. He got the idea his refusal came as no surprise. "Tomorrow do you want to meet here or at the airport?" she asked.

"At the airport." The flight left at 9 a.m. It'd be another short night.

"The funeral is at noon. You have the background file I gave you?"

He nodded. He had it; he just hadn't read it. He couldn't focus on the segment about the writer murders until the Bigelow profile aired. He was too hyped about whether a good tip might come in.

It was naïve, he knew, the triumph of hope over

experience. It'd aired how many times without a tip leading to a capture? Six. That made this seven.

Lucky seven.

He let his hope rise as he walked to his own car.

*

Before dawn broke over the Potrero Hills neighborhood of San Francisco, FBI Special Agent in Charge Lionel Simpson got a phone call. He reached a brawny arm toward his bedside table, kept his voice low so as not to wake his wife. "Simpson."

"It's Higuchi." Simpson's assistant in the local field office. "Sorry to call at this hour but I thought you'd want to know."

"Whatcha got?"

"The prints ID'ed from the blowgun that shot the dart in the Maggie Boswell case."

Simpson sat up a little straighter. "And?"

"We got a few matches. One in particular."

Beside Simpson, his wife hiked the patchwork quilt higher on her shoulders and snuggled deeper into her pillow. He lowered his voice. "Whose?"

"One set belongs to Annette Rowell."

Made in the USA
San Bernardino, CA
05 August 2014